WITCHLINGS

WITCHLINGS

CLARIBEL A. ORTEGA

SCHOLASTIC PRESS

NEW YORK

Library of Congress Cataloging-in-Publication Data available

ISBN 978-1-338-74552-8

10 9 8 7 6 5 4 3 2 1   22 23 24 25 26

Printed in Italy   183

First edition, February 2022

Book design by Christopher Stengel

TO ANYONE WHO HAS EVER
FELT THEY DIDN'T BELONG.
THIS ONE'S FOR YOU.

TABLE OF CONTENTS

In the darkness of the woods
Listen, listen well—
Every little noise you hear
Might be the thing that dwells:
Crunching leaves, a subtle breeze
Or a monster as it breathes.
Now! The monster's hunting you—
It is too late,
We've let him loose.
Lock the windows, shut the lights,
Wrap your little ones up tight.
Hang the rue and heed the bells,
Beware, beware
The Thing that dwells.

—*"The Ballad of the Nightbeast," from* The Twelve
    Towns Book of Folksong

CHAPTER ONE
ANYTHING BUT A SPARE

IT WAS THE NIGHT of the Black Moon Ceremony, and the very last thing Seven Salazar wanted was to be a Spare witch. Now that she was twelve, she'd be placed in her coven, but like every ceremony before, tonight three witches would be left over: *Spares*. Nobody ever wanted to be a Spare. Seven had done everything she could think of: studied for her C.A.T. exams, attended every witching social event she could fit on her calendar. She'd even joined the toad racing team and gotten stuck with the slowest, crankiest toad of the lot. At least his name, Edgar Allan Toad, *sort of* made up for it. But only sort of.

It wasn't like Seven *had* to do all those things either. Everyone in her year got to participate in the Black Moon Ceremony, of course, but it was a long-standing belief among Witchlings that the harder you studied and worked, the more likely you were to get into one of the *cool* covens.

Seven tied her combat boots and slipped on her oversized purple hoodie before securing her pointy hat on her curly hair with some pins. They'd give her a giant black ceremonial robe when she got to the town square, but it was thin and the night was cold. She didn't want to freeze her buns off. She shot a quick text to her best friend, Poppy, telling her how excited she was for tonight.

"Duh," Poppy wrote back. "And me too! Can't wait to be coven sisters!"

Seven smiled at the message as she walked into the kitchen, where her mother, Fox, was putting the celebration cake in the fridge to cool.

"Sev, you've got your amulet, right?" Fox wiped her slender fingers on her apron and let down her curly red hair.

"It's only the whole point of tonight, Mom," Seven said, holding up the amulet that hung around her neck. Later that night, it would light up with the same color as the other witches in her coven. *Please, please let it turn purple.* The color of House Hyacinth, the coven Seven and Poppy had dreamed of being placed into for, oh, just about all their lives.

"Remember, things will work out okay, no matter what happens tonight," Fox said.

"Easy for you to say," grumbled Seven, looking at the bright aquamarine pendant that hung from the necklace Fox always wore. The blue stone signified House of Stars, one of the most popular covens.

Seven would have a much better chance of achieving her biggest dream, becoming a witching-world-famous journalist, if she was in one of the powerful covens, like her mom. It was pretty much the opposite of being a Spare. Because being a Spare meant your destiny and magic didn't match up with anyone else's. Being a Spare meant you didn't belong. And Seven wanted desperately to belong.

As Fox moved around the kitchen, the moonlight hit her pendant and seemed to adorn everything around her with shimmering stars. Seven used to wonder if her mother had gotten her name because of her red hair, which she always thought looked lovely with her deep brown skin and freckled face. Seven looked more like her dad, tawny-brown skin and dark curls. But now she knew it was more likely that her mother had been named Fox because of how cunning she was. In their world, the Twelve Towns, a child's name was a prophecy, passed down from a grandmother or the Town Gran, their leader. Seven had no idea what her name meant, not yet anyway. But like any name given in Ravenskill, one day its meaning would be discovered. It was just a matter of time.

Seven began tapping drumbeats on the closest object, trying to match the beat of her fluttering heart.

"You're still nervous about being a Spare?" Seven's father,

Talis, asked, strolling into the room. He was carrying her baby brother, Braucherei, who everyone affectionately called Beefy, because of both his roundness and his unusual strength. He was also unusually tall for his age, already three toadstools long, when Seven had only been two when she was a baby. Beefy pulled on his father's ear, and Talis cringed; the baby's grip could be painful. Seven rubbed her scalp, war flashbacks of Beefy pulling on her curly hair coming back to her.

"I'm not just nervous, Dad. I'm *freaking out*. What if I didn't do enough, or what if the magic gets fudged somehow, or"—Seven dropped her voice to an ominous whisper—"I get placed with Valley?"

Valley Pepperhorn was the literal *worst*. Valley had been bullying Seven for as long as she could remember. Putting weird things in her rucksack, hiding Edgar Allan Toad before a race, or giving dirty looks to Seven and Poppy. She was mean, scary, and came from one of the families on the Hill. They were the wealthiest witches in town and thought they ran everything. Well, they sort of *did* run everything, actually. The only witches they couldn't go up against were the Town Gran and Uncle.

"The chances of that happening are not high, but even if it does, any witch can be a friend if you just give them a chance," her mother said.

Seven held back a snort. Seven was almost positive Valley was a cuco or, at the very least, part gremlin. Her parents didn't see the way Valley snapped at their professors and didn't seem to care about her schoolwork or how she was always on her own doing sneaky, probably terrible, things. Sometimes, when Seven thought about it, when she thought what her life would be like without Poppy and without her family, she felt almost sad for Valley, who had no friends and the scariest parents ever. But then Valley would do another awful thing and Seven wouldn't feel so bad for her anymore.

None of it would matter after tonight anyway, Seven reminded herself, because once she and Poppy were placed in House Hyacinth, she wouldn't have to deal with Valley ever again.

In all the past Ravenskillian Black Moon Ceremonies she'd researched in preparation, not one showed an example of best friends sorted into different covens. Tiordan Whisperbrew, the famous, coolest reporter of all time and Seven's idol, was sorted into House Hyacinth right alongside their best friend and now owner of the *Squawking Crow* newspaper, Inkpen Killian. They were a dynamic duo, and Seven looked forward to her and Poppy following in their footsteps.

"Come on, then. It's almost midnight, and the Gran will hex us if we're late." Talis grunted as he placed Beefy in his stroller. The baby swung his legs and cooed happily as he was strapped in. When he was done, Talis kneeled down in front of Seven.

"A hug for good luck?" he asked, and Seven smiled as her

dad pulled her into a warm embrace. Talis, short for Talisman, had always been lucky. Seven pinched his cheeks before a test for an extra boost. A brilliant blue pendant hung from his neck, the same color as her mother's. It's how her parents had met, after all: They'd been placed in the same coven as kids.

"No matter what happens tonight, we're all proud of you," said Talis.

Seven scrunched her face at him. "Even Beefy?"

Talis laughed. "Especially Beefy. He has no idea what's going on, but he's still proud of you too. Let's go."

The town square was just across the cemetery, under a bridge and past the Bruised Apple Bookshop, which had been recently taken over by a new family in town. A shadow dashed across the night, and Seven jumped, clutching her mother's arm.

"It was only a rabbit," Fox said softly.

Seven laughed nervously. "I knew that."

She did not know that.

There had been sightings lately. Sightings of a monstruo called the Nightbeast, a giant wolf that ate Witchlings. Or at least that was the rumor at Seven's school. Her teachers had assured them those were all rumors, but she had noticed the older witches around town had begun enchanting their garden gates with stay-away spells, hanging rue from their trellises and above their doors, and panicking on the Ravenskill message boards. All signs that a creature lurked near.

Seven had walked this way to town a thousand times, many times on her own. Tonight, she was grateful to have her family with her on the cold, dark path. Even if it *had* only been a rabbit.

The Salazars arrived just as the other families were gathering around the cascading fountain at the center of town. Lanterns hung from trees around the square in groups of five to symbolize the incoming covens. The light cast a warm orange glow on everything it touched and left a few corners cloaked in shadow.

Poppy and her mother were there—they waved at Seven as she took her place in the circle around the fountain, and Seven felt a surge of happiness. Her oldest friend ran over to her, and it seemed everyone's eyes followed her. Poppy had always been the more popular of the two of them: cheerful and optimistic to Seven's anxious determination. But they had always gotten along.

"Seven, I didn't sleep at all, not one wink," Poppy said breathlessly.

"Me either. I feel like my eyeballs are gonna explode," Seven said.

Poppy laughed.

"Cake at my place after," said Seven.

"Pineapple?" Poppy raised an eyebrow.

"Of course," Seven said, and smiled. Pineapple-jam cake was her favorite, and her family's recipe was famous.

The crowd began to shuffle uneasily. It was almost time. "No matter what," Poppy said hurriedly, "we stay friends. No matter what coven we're in, deal?" She held her pinkie out for their best-friend swear.

"Deal." Seven linked her pinkie with Poppy's, and they swayed their arms to and fro three times. The pair of Witchlings devolved into laughter, the excitement of the ceremony too much to contain.

They hugged, and Poppy ran back to her parents.

The Town Uncle, second-in-command to the Gran, walked around handing each Witchling a long black robe. He was the most powerful witch in Ravenskill after the Gran. Town Grans got their powers from the Stars, while Town Uncles got their powers from nature, and could even speak to animals. The Uncle was charged not only with being the Gran's right hand in everything she did, but also in being the liaison for and caretaker of all the animals of Ravenskill—an immensely important job indeed. He wore the customary special-occasion robe of the Uncle, adorned with trees and various animals enchanted to scuttle about the fabric, and, of course, the bluebird brooch he received when he became Uncle.

"Here you go, Seven Salazar, correct?" the Uncle asked when he reached Seven.

"Yep." Seven took the folded black robe as the Uncle crouched down to coo at Beefy.

"Oh my, look at his fat little feet!" the Uncle said sweetly. Just then, Beefy grabbed the Uncle's furry green hat and began to chew on it.

"So sorry," said Seven, pulling the hat, not without a struggle, from Beefy's grip and handing it back to the Uncle. The Uncle just laughed and moved on to the next Witchling. Talis and Fox retreated to the outer circles with Beefy in tow, giving Seven an encouraging smile and snapping pictures as they joined the other parents.

The ceremony was about to begin.

Seven slipped into her robe, taking deep breaths and softly chanting, *"Not a Spare, not a Spare, not a Spare,"* as if it were a lifesaving spell.

"Sorry!" Someone bumped into Seven from behind and nearly knocked her into the fountain, which was now lit up with a deep green glow.

"Careful," Seven said, straightening up to face the girl who'd bumped her. It was someone she'd never seen before. "The Gran is watching us."

The Gran had arrived and was standing on a floating platform at the center of the fountain, water splashing just below her feet. Though it was dark and foggy, she seemed to eye each of them carefully, and Seven swore she could see inside her brain. Like most everyone else, the Gran was dressed in all black, but the fabric of the Gran's long black coat was enchanted to look like the night sky. She was famous for her coat which held magical objects and changed color like the sky. The most brilliant of the visions was the stars and moon spinning around each other in a glittering sky, an ode to the Gran's real name, Knox—an ancient word that meant *night*. From under her pointy hat fell a cascade of gray braids that she always had done in the colder months, her tight curls loose and flowing whenever it was warm out.

"I'm Thorn," said the girl next to Seven.

Seven gave her the side-eye, taking in her straight, short black hair and bangs, her round, pale face and flush red lips. She was much shorter than Seven, petite in every way. Even her feet were small; her shoes looked like they were less than half a toadstool long. Despite the darkness, she could see her eyes were a deep, dark blue. There were tiny pins, like the kind seamstresses use to hold fabric in place, stuck to her hat. It was interesting her name was Thorn since she sort of looked like a rose and was also being a real pain in the buns.

"You must be the new girl," Seven said.

Thorn nodded so quickly, her witch's hat almost flew off.

"I'm pretty nervous," said Thorn.

Seven sighed. "Seven Salazar, hi. I think we might be starting soon."

"Right, right," Thorn said, and locked her lips up, throwing away the key.

A few moments passed in silence.

"Nice to meet you, by the way. Which coven are you hoping to be placed in?" whispered Thorn, almost immediately forgetting her locked mouth.

Mercifully, the Gran raised her arms then and the crowd went silent, saving Seven from having to fib and say whatever she got would be a blessing. From the moment they began their magical training, they were told, and told again and again, that their coven was their destiny, and that being ungrateful for fate's gifts would curse them with bad luck. Or even worse than bad luck: If you truly didn't accept your given house, then you couldn't be sealed with your coven during the ceremony. They'd *stay* Witchlings. But that hadn't happened in many years.

"Tonight marks the two hundred and fifth Black Moon Ceremony in the town of Ravenskill," the Gran began to say.

Everyone clapped politely. Across from Seven's line of vision stood Valley's parents. They wore expensive-looking coats with sharp lines and leather gloves. They stood rigid, looking in Valley's direction intently. After each one of the Gran's proclamations, while everyone else cheered loudly, they barely clapped, as if this was the most boring event in the world. Valley looked miserable, but then again, she always did. She stood opposite Seven in the circle of Witchlings, scowling, her hair tucked behind her ears and her hat sitting haphazardly on her head.

"I am so, so, so nervous," whispered Thorn again.

Seven had to force herself not to move away. Instead,

through clenched teeth, she warned, "Stop talking, or I'm going to hex you to be my toad's wife."

That shut her up, at least for now.

"And now," exclaimed the Gran, "for the reason we're all gathered here tonight. The forming of the covens."

Where before there was a low murmur of noise throughout the square, now everything was deadly quiet.

"Witchlings, prepare your amulets!"

With a collective ruffle of fabric, the twenty-eight Witchlings pulled out their crystal amulets, which hung from black cords around their necks, and held them in front of their faces.

"Now, intone the spell with me."

All at once, voices rose, reciting the Black Moon Song they'd known all their lives but were not allowed to sing aloud till this night. Seven's heart fluttered as she began:

A coven is five
In death and in life,
To believe
To protect
Never doubt
Or neglect.
Bound with our magic
Before the Black Moon
Bound by a circle

For no circle
Spells doom.

As the final words left their lips, purple smoke snaked from their mouths to dance in the center of the circle, right above the Gran's head. Then, with a flick of her wand, she sent the smoke careening back and straight into the amulets, which began to whir and vibrate. Seven's amulet spun wildly, and she closed her eyes, begging one final time for the thing she'd begged for whenever she thought of this night: *Please let it turn purple.* All around her, covens began to form. Five amulets turned the bright aqua color of her parents' coven.

"House of Stars," said the Gran. "Brilliant, beautiful, generous to all."

The Witchlings squealed and ran off together, holding hands in their own circle. They would be a new wing, a five-witch coven, part of the larger Grand House of Stars now.

Another group got a deep black the color of obsidian for Moth House.

"Mysterious, morbid, dependable friends," intoned the Gran to enormous cheers from the crowd, including a group of parents who looked like they had died last week. Moth House was the creepiest coven. Their black lipstick and pale makeup *was* pretty cool, Seven could admit. Seven was a bit surprised that Valley hadn't been sorted into Moth House, but it was probably the dependable friend part.

Witchlings embraced and joined their new covens happily, and all the while, Seven waited, eyeing Poppy anxiously. Next, the Witchlings for the emerald-colored Frog House (focused, frugal, truthful to the last) were placed. And now there were only two covens left to form before the Spares. There would be three Spares tonight, Seven knew. Valley being a Spare would make sense, since she was always falling behind in all her classes and had zero friends. There were a few kids from her class, ones who never fit in, who Seven could see being sorted into the Spare coven.

A girl named Starlight whooped when her amulet began to glow purple. *This is it*, thought Seven. House Hyacinth. *Her* house.

Next came a boy named Cane, which Seven knew was short for Hurricane. Seven and Poppy looked at each other, and Seven had to hold back a giggle, excited for their amulets to go purple.

A girl she recognized from her class, one who always ignored her and whose name she couldn't remember, was chosen—and then her best friend was too.

Seven's heart gave an awful lurch as the two friends looked at each other with delight. There was only one spot left. She glanced down at her own dull amulet, then over at *her* best friend: Poppy's amulet was a vibrant purple.

Poppy's face dropped as she looked at Seven, all their plans of being coven sisters unraveling. She quickly corrected herself, giving Seven a light smile and turning away to join her new coven. Seven knew that Poppy couldn't betray her assignment. Even one misgiving about what coven you were placed in could spell disaster—could prevent your coven from closing.

That didn't make it hurt any less.

"House Hyacinth!" said the Gran. "Valiant, virtuous, powerful in all things!"

House Hyacinth got the loudest cheers yet, and the awful truth truly sank in.

No, no, no! This couldn't be happening! Seven was supposed to be with Poppy; that's how they'd always planned it: Best friends were supposed to be placed together. So why weren't they? *Okay, Seven, just breathe.* At least there was another coven left. Seven would be in the Goose House coven. Seven focused, taking deep calming breaths and trying not to fidget, as a beautiful pearl color filled one amulet, then another.

A fourth Witchling entered the Goose coven, and there was only one more amulet to go. Seven held her breath . . . but when the last amulet lit up a shimmering white, it wasn't hers.

"Goose House!" said the Gran. "Clever, chaotic . . . mostly good!"

The happy squeals of the other covens turned to whispers and sighs of relief, Seven thought with a cringe. They were all happy—happy not to be her. Shame washed over Seven, and she was glad for the cover of night so no one would see how bright pink her face turned when she was embarrassed.

Seven's amulet filled with the muddy red color of the Spare coven, and she shut her eyes tight, wishing that she could just disappear. Her stomach felt sour, like she'd eaten something rotten, but at least she was keeping her tears at bay. Seven's eyes flew open as she realized she was too caught up in her own panic to notice who was left with her, who shared the shame of being left for last. She followed the red glow from her amulet to the one right next to her, to Thorn. Panicked, she scanned the circle until she spotted the umistakable red glow coming from . . . Valley. Valley Pepperhorn's amulet shone a bright red, and a happy sneer crossed her face.

Not Valley, anyone but Valley. Even her toad would be better than that, but this was her awful reality.

Just three misfit witches, a red glow all around them, and the unmistakable truth that Seven was a Spare.

CHAPTER TWO
FOREVER WITCHLINGS

"THIS IS SO EXCITING!" Thorn said as the three witches gathered in their circle to complete the ceremony.

"It's not exciting. We're the Spares. Everyone is laughing at us," Seven said hotly.

All the soon-to-be-formed covens were assembling into circles around the square, waiting for the Gran to seal their fates. Technically, they were still Witchlings until their circle was sealed, cementing them as a true coven. Everyone's coven had to be sealed by a magical contract, to contain the magic and the witches in their own circles. It was meant to keep anyone from adding more coven members or becoming too powerful. Though Seven couldn't help but think that as a Spare, being powerful wasn't something she'd have to worry about.

Valley just stood there, looking smug. Why would she be smug about *this*?

Exasperated, Seven grabbed the hands of the two Witchlings beside her. She felt a chill as her fingers closed around Valley's cold, clammy hand. Of course she felt like a cold-blooded vampire. It would be a shock if Valley Pepperhorn even had a heart.

Seven couldn't keep herself from shaking her head, even as she saw the other covens around them start to close. "You're both bonkers. Why are you okay with this? Being a Spare is . . . it's . . . the worst thing that could ever happen!" Seven said. She dropped the other Witchlings' hands. "Maybe neither of you understands this, but being a Spare means we will be the town outcasts our whole lives." Seven ticked each point off on her fingers. "No advanced magic. No flying. We'll probably be stuck working for one of the terrible families on . . ."

Seven looked at Valley before finishing her thought: one of the terrible families on the Hill. Valley just shrugged, still looking bafflingly smug, and Seven wanted to scream.

"It's still not the *worst* thing. And we're not supposed to question our coven or be ungrateful. If you don't remember that, our circle won't close," Thorn warned. "Besides, I've never had *two* friends *at the same time*," Thorn said, almost under her breath. "I know being a Spare is not the best, but no coven means we'd be Forever Witchlings."

Panic rose up in Seven's throat. She knew Thorn was right and that she had to adjust her attitude unless she wanted to stay a Forever Witchling: witches who never formed a coven. Witches who lost their magic completely.

Seven took in a deep breath, then let one out. She could *not* let that happen, but fear prickled her skin. It was bad enough she was stuck with a coven of Spares, but being a Forever Witchling was the most awful thing that could happen to anyone in the Twelve Towns. No magic meant all her years of practice and hard work learning spells would go out the window. She'd have no chance at her dream job as a reporter for their town newspaper, the *Squawking Crow*. That required level-five magic, advanced incantations and spells that Spares rarely achieved but Forever Witchlings never ever could. She'd be even worse off than she was today, stripped of all magical powers, without all her current abilities, and never able to learn anything new. Seven thought being a Spare was her worst nightmare, but she had never even considered being a Forever Witchling. That would be infinitely worse.

"You're right, I'm sorry," Seven said. "I was just really looking forward to my coven."

"Well, we're it," said Valley, speaking for the first time.

Seven and Thorn both stared at the odd girl. She didn't look like any of the other kids from the Hill, with their pastel-colored clothing, neat hair, and bright smiles. No, Valley was quite the opposite. For one thing, she was tall, way taller than either Seven or Thorn, and probably all the other kids in their class too. It wasn't unusual for witches to wear black; in fact, it was Seven's favorite color, but Valley never ever wore anything different. It was always black top, jeans, boots, and sweater. She wore dark eyeliner all the time, her nails were always painted black, and sometimes she even wore black lipstick like the Moth House witches. Seven's mom would never let her wear lipstick and especially not black. The only colorful thing was Valley's rusty-colored pink hair. It was the color of a dried-up rose, and Seven thought it was really pretty. She always wished her parents would let her use Enchant-Dyed.

The Gran cleared her throat, and they all fell silent. She raised her wand and began to intone the sealing spell. This was it: Once the spell was cast and Seven's circle closed, they'd be bound for life. What a bummer.

From Witchling to Witch
Let the circles be sealed
Let the covens be closed
And true friendship revealed.

Seven felt a surge of magic, warm and strong, pulse through her body as the amulets shone brightly and began to spin. She tried her best not to look at the other covens, but it was hard not to watch as black, aqua, green, white, and—she felt sick—purple light formed a beautiful circle around each of the covens and then exploded in a burst of color, signaling the completion of the ceremony. Seven waited for the circle above the Spare coven to do the same, but as the seconds and then minutes passed, nothing happened. The cheers of the other covens faded, and silence grew around them until it was a bloated monster waiting to pop. Panic swelled in Seven's chest, and she had to keep her eyes on her amulet, focusing on nothing else, to keep from crying.

Concerned whispers and then snickers began as finally the Gran raised her wand, ready to signal the end of the ceremony. She couldn't signal that this was over, not yet, oh, please not yet. The moment the Gran's wand flourished three times in the air, the ceremony would be over, and if Seven's circle didn't close, they would remain Witchlings forever. Seven would lose her magic.

"I'm gonna be sick," Seven said.

Valley was silent, and Thorn worried the hem of her over-sized black-and-red-polka-dotted dress shirt. The Gran waved her wand once, twice, and—

"Wait!" Seven yelled out, and gasps resounded from the crowd. No one *ever* interrupted the Gran.

"Are you bonkers?" Valley asked through clenched teeth.

Despite her fear, Seven almost smirked. So Valley *did* care about something. She was scared of the Gran. The old woman raised an eyebrow at Seven but kept her wand up, mid-flick. She seemed to be inspecting her, and Seven worried the Gran could see every doubt and fear in her mind. Slowly, slowly, she lowered her wand.

"Seven Salazar," came the Gran's voice, loud and echoing in the crisp fall night. "Step forward."

Seven found her parents in the crowd, and they nodded at her encouragingly but there was worry in their eyes. Beefy made the face he always made when he was pooping. Gross. Seven stepped forward, and Valley grabbed her arm, the cold from her hand going right through Seven's hoodie.

"What are you doing, Salazar? You trying to get us banished from town?" Her voice was low, rushed, desperate.

"Chill. I know what I'm doing."

Seven did *not* know what she was doing.

She stepped closer to the center of the square and looked up at the Gran. She looked even more intimidating up close, like a sea of black fabric and twinkling stars. Like a goddess. Seven's eyes teared up just looking at her.

"Gran." Seven projected her voice as much as she could. Tried to make herself sound confident despite the nervous energy coursing through her. She wanted to run all the way home and hide under her covers forever. Or maybe the ground would just open up right now and swallow her whole. It would be quite convenient.

But she wouldn't run, and nothing would save her right now. She had to do this herself.

"Gran," she repeated, making a circle with her hand and

holding it to her chest in the sign for respect. The Gran pressed the tips of her fingers to her mouth, then gestured at Seven: a blessing. She could speak.

"I'm sorry for the interruption, but I'd like to invoke the Clause of the Impossible Task."

The crowd around them gasped, but Seven continued, undaunted.

"As we've learned, any witch is entitled to invoke this clause in order to save themselves and their coven from permanent Witchlingdom. I know it's not done often, and I know the task we'll receive is impossible, but I am willing to take that chance."

The Gran raised her other eyebrow, so both eyebrows were now high on her face, and she looked equal parts amused and surprised.

"Oh," said Thorn from somewhere behind Seven. Valley just grunted.

The Clause of the Impossible Task was not to be used lightly. It provided a chance for Forever Witchlings to close their circles by completing an impossible task. Impossible because only one coven of the eight who'd invoked the clause in the history of the Twelve Towns had solved it. But Seven had to try. Once they were proclaimed Forever Witchlings, they'd never have the chance to become full-fledged witches again. This was their only shot.

"You said, '*I* am willing to take that chance,' Seven, but in a coven there is only *we*. Is your coven okay with this?" the Gran asked.

Seven turned around, her face pleading, her heart racing. Valley was scowling angrily, her arms crossed. Thorn had her hands clasped and was biting her bottom lip but nodding enthusiastically.

"It's better than being a Forever Witchling," Thorn said. "I say let's do it."

Seven beamed, then turned to Valley expectantly. Valley shrugged one shoulder. "Fine. We're already the literal worst. Might as well try."

Seven gave Valley a reluctant smile and turned back to the Gran. "My coven is on board, Gran."

"Very well. You have my blessing. I will consult with the Oracle, and your task will present itself in the next few hours."

Seven gulped. She had hardly gotten used to the idea of being a Spare; now she'd have to deal with whatever the impossible task would be. Would they have to construct a sea-worthy ship and find the elusive Boggy Crone River creature? Find invisible plants? Defeat a warlock in a magical duel? It could be anything!

"I will then deliver your impossible task in accordance with Twelve Towns Laws. Until then, you remain Witchlings." The Gran gestured for the Spares to come forward, and as they stood there lined up, she made a giant X over their heads, magic to seal the contract until the impossible task began.

And then they would only have three weeks. Three weeks to solve a mystery, three weeks to complete the task, three weeks to fix this or they'd lose their magic and be Witchlings forever.

Seven looked at Valley and Thorn. She wasn't sure how she was supposed to solve the task with her bully and someone she didn't even know. What Seven did know was that she had never given up on anything before—that she was smart, she was capable, and, no matter what was thrown her way, Seven was ready.

CHAPTER THREE
THE IMPOSSIBLE TASK

AS IT TURNED OUT, Seven was not ready.

Moments after the Gran ended the ceremony, the Oracle swept through the square, their long holographic cape billowing in the night breeze, their crystal ball suspended in the air beside them. They spoke to the Gran for only a minute, maybe two, as curious Ravenskillians watched. The Gran looked taken aback by something the Oracle had said, and seemed to say, "Are you sure?" but Seven couldn't be positive. Whatever it was, the look on the Gran's face did not bode well.

Seven's body tensed. Surely, the Oracle couldn't have seen their task already. But the colors inside the crystal ball were swirling. Red, mixed with swirls of gray.

Seven wanted to run to her parents, but she didn't want to look like a baby. She wouldn't give the other witches in her class or the adults who were snickering and looking sorry for her the satisfaction. She'd rather eat her witch's hat.

"Spares," the Gran called out. "I have received your task from the Oracle. Thank you, Sybell," the Gran said. The Oracle nodded and retreated in the Spares' direction. Seven had never seen them this close up. Their high cheekbones shimmered with silver fae dust, a magic enhancer, and their long purple hair flowed in shiny waves. As they got closer, Seven noticed how sharp the edges of their face were, almost like they were carved from a shiny rock.

"Good luck," Sybell whispered as they passed the Witchlings. In their crystal ball, Seven swore she could see two glowing red eyes. Valley too seemed to notice, and the two Witchlings shared a brief glance before quickly turning back to the Gran in unison.

The night buzzed with the whispers of their neighbors gossiping around them. The entire thing was embarrassing and infuriating, but the worst part was Poppy, who was standing with her super-special and shiny coven, smiling and laughing. As if Seven wasn't about to be served her fate. She couldn't even look in Seven's direction. A traitor *and* a coward.

Seven scowled but didn't take her eyes off the fountain. The gossipy Ravenskillians were like a swarm of bugs: annoying and gross, and she wouldn't give them the satisfaction of looking defeated. She put on her meanest, most fearsome look, and kept her chin up in the air.

Thorn had kept her eyes glued to the ground like she was

looking for a missing rat's tail until Valley reached across Seven and flicked Thorn on the chin.

Thorn looked at her, startled, eyes wide as Valley gestured to Seven. "You make your face like hers. Like you're about to hex someone. They want to see you upset. Don't let these butt-toads win."

Thorn wiped at her tear-streaked face quickly and smiled softly at Valley. Seven had to work hard to hide her shock. Valley was being *nice*?

"Ravenskillians!" the Gran said. "After only moments of scrying, the task has presented itself, and the Oracle and I have come to a unanimous conclusion. For the ninth time in history, three Witchlings have invoked the impossible task and will learn what challenge they face."

Seven's insides felt all jumbled, and she felt like everything around her was spinning. *Get ahold of yourself, Salazar,* she thought. The last thing she needed was to barf in front of the whole town.

The Gran clapped her hands together, and a sound like thunder fell over them as the crowd cheered. "We will convene in twenty-one days, to grant you full-fledged Witch status, or for your punishment, which, according to the Oracle . . ." The Gran seemed to pause now, and looked out over the crowd. Seven followed her gaze to the Oracle, who was standing at the edge of the square. They nodded, a grave look on their face. The Gran nodded in response and continued.

"Your punishment, if you fail, will be toadification. Should you survive, that is." The Gran's voice sounded as heavy as Seven's heart felt. Toads. If they could not solve the task, they would be turned into *toads*. She couldn't believe that just hours earlier this night was going to be a happy one. Now it was pretty much the worst one she'd ever had.

Thorn's parents hugged each other as they sobbed. Valley's mother wiped a tear carefully with a black handkerchief, and her father looked like he always did: uninterested. Fox and Talis were standing close, Talis's arm around Fox's shoulder as she held a sleeping Beefy. They looked at Seven the way they always did when she said she couldn't do something. With a look of determination and strength. And love. But they looked as pale as ghosts. "And now . . . for the task." The Gran's voice echoed through the night.

Now everyone was silent; it seemed like the entire town was holding their breaths, waiting to hear what the Gran would say. Thorn looked the color of spring moss, and Valley looked worried. Seven pretended to be brave but wasn't feeling much better herself.

"Valley Pepperhorn, Seven Salazar, Thorn Laroux, your impossible task . . ."

The three Witchlings leaned forward as one. If Seven had been sitting in a chair, she would've fallen out of it by now.

"Is to fell a Nightbeast!"

CHAPTER FOUR

ROLLER-COASTER RIDE TO DESPAIR TOWN

YOU KNOW THINGS are very bad when not even cake can fix the situation. Seven took a bite of her mother's famous pineapple-jam cake and scowled. Nothing could taste or smell or be good ever again, because not only was she a Spare, not only did she have to defeat the legendary wolf-like Nightbeast, but she was still a Witchling too. Pathetic.

Seven looked to her mom, then her dad: To the outside eye, they wouldn't seem to be upset, but Seven knew they were. Fox wouldn't stop touching her amulet, and Talis wouldn't stop making bad jokes, which was what they always did when they were panicking but didn't want Seven to know. She couldn't blame them for being freaked out, really, but her parents still insisted they were proud.

"You don't like the cake?" Fox asked with a hint of surprise.

"I like it, but I'm kind of on a roller-coaster ride to despair town, Mami."

"We know you're disappointed, Seven. Maybe right now it seems like the end of the world, but I'm sure the Gran had a good reason for sorting you the way she did."

"I guess," Seven grumbled, noticing that her mother had not mentioned the Nightbeast. Probably because she figured Seven was toast. She had no idea how she was going to solve an impossible task, especially not with Valley and Thorn.

"I can't believe I'm a Spare," said Seven for about the two hundredth time that night. "What did I do wrong?"

"You tried your very best, we know that." Her father squeezed Seven's hand reassuringly. "But what do we always tell you?"

"Hard work doesn't guarantee success, only no regrets," Seven said automatically, reciting one of her parents' favorite Ravenskillian sayings.

"Exactly. We can't control the outcome of things, but we can try our hardest and be proud of that. That's what you did, Seven," Talis said.

Seven looked over at the tank on the other side of their open living area, where Edgar Allan Toad liked to have his meals. She could try her very hardest and still end up sharing a tank with her toad. He looked back at her, narrowing his eyes, his black mustache twitching, as if to say, "Don't even *think* about making me race." Seven sighed and took another bite of cake.

"We know how hard you worked to make House Hyacinth, and I hope you know we're not trying to make light of this. It's just that your father and I, we believe in you so much, Seven. We know you can do anything you put your mind to," Fox said.

"If that's true, then why didn't I make any of the good covens?" Seven asked. Her heart tugged as she thought of the one thing she'd been trying to avoid thinking about all night: Poppy. Was she with her coven members now? Celebrating at her house or maybe at the House of Seven Ice Cream Scoops? Seven had tried to congratulate her in person, but Poppy had run off before she got a chance to and, when she'd sent her a message on the way home, Poppy hadn't written back. She still hadn't. She had completely ditched her, forgotten their plans. Seven didn't want to read into it, even though her best friend always wrote back immediately. She was probably just busy with her new coven. Her new coven, which didn't include Seven. The thought made something in her stomach flip, and not in an excited way. In more of an *everything is awful and stinks* way. Seven glanced out the kitchen window, still hoping that Poppy would show up. That it had all been a huge mistake.

"Which coven you got placed into was out of your hands. Doesn't mean you didn't achieve what you set out to," Fox said.

Seven quirked an eyebrow.

"Why do you think the crowd gasped when you invoked the impossible task? It's because most of them hadn't seen it done in their lifetimes. And you knew about it, knew how it worked. It's impressive. You know your stuff, and you know your stuff because you worked hard for it. If it weren't for that, you wouldn't have gotten this second chance."

"What about Valley?" asked Seven, still unsure they'd be able to work together.

"Valley might surprise you, and if there are problems, you can come to us. Valley is on your team now. Remember, Seven, you are proving that you three are ready to be bonded as a coven. Maybe you're not ready right this minute, but that will come if you trust one another."

Talis picked up where Fox left off. "Our job is to make sure you don't lose hope. We'll be here."

"Every step," said Fox.

Seven cracked a small smile before cleaning up the dishes, putting the leftover cake away, and going to her room for the night. Seven had the attic bedroom; it had a skylight and tall ceilings, and she'd begged her parents to let her move up there when she was ten. Almost every surface had a tiny potted plant on it, some fragrant, some poisonous, and some Seven used for potion ingredients. Seven's potions collection included everything from las veras, which made you tell the truth, to kiliki taka ti, which made you dance really well. And it was all thanks to her trusty plants. Seven loved botánica, the study of plants and plantlike monstruos; it was her favorite after writing class, and she was incredibly good at it. Except of course for the opal-haworthia plant, which Seven had been trying for years to grow just for its invisibility properties, but no dice. The tall walls were covered in posters of famous conjurers, sorcerers; fan art of her favorite book series, the Witches of Heartbreak Cove; her favorite bands, Kill Le Goose and The Love Spells; and, of course, her favorite newspaper articles. Soon there'd be an article about her, about being a Spare, about invoking the impossible task. Seven watered the tiny sprout that was her opal-haworthia plant and sighed.

"Still nothing, huh, little guy?" she asked the plant.

At least she'd finally be in the paper, she thought as she flopped onto her pillow-strewn bed. She checked her portaphone to see if Poppy had answered: nope. She texted her congrats again and waited a few more seconds before giving up.

"Escóndete," she said with a half-hearted flick of her wrist, and the phone hid itself away in her drawer.

Seven stared up at the ceiling, looking at the royal-blue night sky through the skylight, and she let her tears fall. She had failed herself, her family. No matter what they said to try to make her feel better, she knew that what happened this evening was an embarrassment for them. A stain on her family legacy. Not to mention, she'd probably get eaten by a giant wolf monster. Valley would probably help the Nightbeast do it.

Seven had wasted so much time worrying and being anxious about being a Spare. But she shouldn't have, because her greatest fear was always going to come true, wasn't it? What's meant to be will always be; she'd learned that long ago. Worry doesn't change life, or your destiny. And worry wouldn't change the bloodred color that now glittered from Seven's amulet.

But one thing she wouldn't do was give up. She was Seven Nightshade Salazar, and there hadn't been a challenge she'd backed down from yet. As she watched witches fly past her home in the glittery sky, fireworks going off in the distance over the Boggy Crone River, she knew what she had to do: defeat the Nightbeast and save her coven. And somehow, someway, she'd have to stop being repulsed by Valley. She was stuck with her after all. Witchling or not, the one thing that wouldn't change was Valley and Thorn.

CHAPTER FIVE
WAY TOO EARLY FOR MONSTRUO HUNTING

ON SEVEN'S INSISTENCE, the Witchlings met very early the next morning at the edge of Blue Mountain Forest. It bordered the south side of Ravenskill, and was just a few minutes from town. The sky was a royal purple and dotted with fading stars, the light of day just beginning to break through. Seven had a clipboard with her notes and a checklist of ideas. She paced back and forth, tapping her pen on the clipboard as if she were her father's manager at the magical disaster insurance agency doling out instructions instead of a Witchling with no froggin' idea what she was doing.

"So what's your plan?" Valley was leaning against a giant oak, eating a bright pink faeapple.

"Those rot your teeth," Seven said.

"Okay, *Mom*." Valley took a big bite of the apple and smiled.

Thorn was standing practically across the street, her arms wrapped tight around her own body, her face red as if she had been crying.

"I . . . Will . . . the Nightbeast be in those woods?" Thorn peered into the forest.

"Flingo. I was doing some research last night on the Ravenskill message boards. Most of the Nightbeast sightings happened in the forests, so I figured we could start here. Face it head-on—"

Valley let out a loud laugh. "You can't just walk into a forest and find a Nightbeast."

Seven scowled at her. "Okay, monster expert, then what do you suggest we do?"

Valley shrugged and took another bite of her faeapple.

"That's what I thought," Seven said.

Valley was the kid in the group project who did no work and then wanted all the credit. She never tried at anything. Schoolwork, sports; everything Valley did she put almost no effort into. Except when it came to bullying Seven. Seven had promised her parents she would give Valley a chance, but she wasn't going to get eaten by a monstruo because of her. No way.

"We should look for tracks first. They should be a bit bigger than regular wolf tracks," Seven said.

Valley snorted, but Seven tried her very best to ignore her.

"I don't know if I can go in there," Thorn said, beginning to cry.

Seven's eyes opened wide, and she ran over to Thorn. "I know the Nightbeast is scary, and it is pretty dangerous, but between us, I've learned some level-four spells already, so this should be a piece of cake."

Project confidence, Seven repeated to herself silently.

"If a Nightbeast comes at you, just play dead. They like playing with live food, so dead prey isn't as attractive," Valley said.

"Oh my goats," Thorn said, panicking.

"Way to go," Seven said. "Stick by me. Level-four spells, remember." Seven winked.

Valley sighed. "Thorn, you'll be fine, but not because of what Seven is saying. There are no Nightbeasts in Blue Mountain Forest. At least not yet," Valley said.

Seven narrowed her eyes at Valley. "How would you know?"

"You're not the only one who can do research, and I've done way more than a night's worth. I'll admit, I don't know that much about Nightbeasts yet, but I do know a thing or two about hunting monstruos." Valley slung her rucksack off her back and let it fall to the ground before crouching down and opening it. She took out a clear bag filled with water and what looked like see-through fish.

"Jelly bean fish?" Seven made a face as she stepped back. They smelled like death.

Jelly bean fish were pretty enough to look at—they were clear, and their insides looked like hundreds of colorful jelly beans—but if you bit into one, they tasted like spoiled meat and they screamed like banshees to boot.

Valley nodded. "These are old but Nightbeasts won't care. They love these things. I got them when the Nightbeast rumors started to see if I could lure it into a makeshift cage I made, but . . ."

"What happened?" Thorn asked.

"Nothing. My dad tore the cage down and made me stop." Valley stuffed the jelly bean fish back into her rucksack, and her face went red. "Anyway, the cage probably would've been too small."

"Nightbeasts are really big . . ." Thorn said softly.

"Can we use the jelly bean fish in some other way?" asked Seven.

Valley cocked her head. "Maybe we could try to lure the monstruo to a specific place. But we'll have to do it in the Cursed Forest."

"The—" Thorn began.

"It's the only forest around here with caves, and I'm pretty sure the Nightbeast is currently hibernating. Otherwise, it would be roaming around freely and eating witches." Valley smirked.

Seven couldn't be sure if Valley was making it up or if she was being serious. There were many times when she'd tricked

Seven or another one of their classmates into believing something that wasn't true for a prank. Seven knew better than to let her guard down around Valley. No matter what her parents thought.

"We can put the jelly bean fish up in a couple of trees. Hopefully the scent will lure the Nightbeast out. Then we'll come back and see if the Nightbeast left any tracks or markings," said Valley.

"How will we know if it's the Nightbeast and not just a dog?" Seven asked.

"Bigger poops," said Valley. "Gigantic."

Seven made a grossed-out face.

"Plus, they have coarser, thicker hair than normal dogs, and their hair usually gets stuck on the trees they pass," Valley said. "We should probably get to the Cursed Forest. There's no use trying to lure them here."

Seven sighed. "Fine, monster expert, lead the way."

Valley shook her head. "For the record, jumping right into trying to find the Nightbeast before doing any sort of research is bogus. But have it your way. Let's go."

They walked north through town, past the Hall of Elders and Birdsall Tavern, then headed east and to the path parallel to the Cursed Forest. Half an hour later, they stood by what Valley claimed was one of the least dangerous entrances to the Cursed Forest, on a road between the library and Seven's house. Seven kept well away from the opening of the forest near a bench on the other side of the road though, just in case. Thorn stood so close behind Seven, she kept knocking into her rucksack, but Seven didn't have the heart to tell her to get away. She was scared, sure, but of the three of them, Thorn seemed to be having the most trouble with this.

"Throwing them is too dangerous. Don't want the jelly bean fish to start screaming and give us away. So I'll go a little ways in, climb the trees, and place them myself," Valley said, taking a climbing stake from her rucksack. She grabbed two of the jelly bean fish from the bag in her bare hands and looked back at Seven and Thorn.

"Aren't you coming?"

"I'm good right here," Seven said.

Thorn nodded. "Me too."

"Suit yourself." Valley shrugged and walked into the Cursed Forest like it was no big deal.

After a few moments of silently debating the merits of letting Valley go into the Cursed Forest alone, Seven's guilt won out.

"Ugh, we shouldn't let her go in there alone. Come on," Seven said, and they slowly walked, side by side, into the Cursed Forest. A foul stench draped itself through the air, and a heaviness, a deep sadness, fell over Seven. The Strangling Figs shook and seemed to sigh deeply, as if saying, "It's your funeral," before moving aside and letting them in. Seven wasn't sure if it was her imagination, or her fear, or both, but the world seemed to get colder and darker all at once. Without a word, they ran to where Valley was. She glanced at them, an amused look on her face.

"Better get used to this." Valley took out a small plastic pod filled with water in the shape of an egg and put both the fish in there. She then put the pod in her cloak pocket, and they watched in silence as Valley began to climb an enormous tree that seemed as if it had been struck by lightning recently.

"She looks so cool," Thorn said.

Seven scoffed, but Thorn was right. Valley looked like Seraphina Nightingale from her favorite book series, the Witches of Heartbreak Cove, or something. Seven would rather eat her own hat than admit that though.

Valley nestled the pod on a particularly thick branch, then scrambled down, jumping the last few toadstools to the ground. "Gotta move quick. One strong wind and the Night-beast will smell the snacks and be on us like slugs on concrete," Valley said. She ran back out of the forest, the other two following her closely.

"I can climb too," said Seven once they were back out of the forest. She wasn't entirely sure where the words were coming from; she had never climbed before in her life. Valley seemed to figure as much and leveled her with a look that meant "Yeah, right."

"It doesn't look that hard," Seven said. "I'm sure I can figure it out."

"Or you could fall and break your back," Valley said.

"If you can do it, so can I," Seven said.

"Don't be a butt-toad. There's no reason to go back in there now," Valley said. "We should go to the library and get some books on the Nightbeast instead. It'll be a better use of our time."

Seven didn't want to admit Valley was right. She also didn't recognize this calm, nicer version of her bully. She didn't get to suddenly get a fresh start after everything she'd done to Seven. Not without a serious, and Seven was talking mega, apology.

"The Gran didn't put you in charge," Seven said.

"She didn't put you in charge either!" Valley countered.

"It was implied," Seven said.

"You know what, fine. Climb the tree, but if you fall—and you will—then we do things my way tomorrow. Deal?"

Seven wanted to scream. Valley had no idea if Seven would fall. Sure, she'd never climbed a tree in the Cursed Forest before, but how hard could it be? She stuck her hand out before she could talk herself out of it.

"Deal." They shook on it.

Valley pulled her hand away and crossed her arms in front of her chest, a smug smile on her face. "Well, leader of the Spares, go for it." Valley pulled a jelly bean fish from her bag, put it in another egg-shaped pod, and tossed it to Seven.

Seven put it into her cloak pocket and walked into the forest alone. *Why are you doing this, Seven?* a little voice in her head said. She was trying to prove Valley wrong, and she was being an absolute goose. They were never going to solve the impossible task this way, but it was too late to turn back now. Seven found another enormous tree, looked up, and gulped. It loomed over her like a giant, angry teacher after she failed a potions test. The shadows chittered and hissed around her, a chill making goose bumps prickle her skin. Seven shimmied her shoulders, pretending she was shaking off her fears, found purchase on a knob, and began to work her way up. Without Valley's stakes, and without any idea what she was doing, Seven began to sweat and tremble with fear. It was one thing to be standing right at the edge of the forest with someone close by; it was a whole other to be touching an actual tree from the Cursed Forest. It was slimy, and cold, and felt all wrong. Skeletal birds with glowing red eyes blinked at her from the branches above; animals or . . . *something* made weird noises in the darkness around her. She hadn't gotten very high, maybe ten toadstools or so, when she felt herself losing her grip. No, not losing her grip . . . the tree was pushing her off!

As if hands were inside the trunk, a force began to rattle Seven and literally push her off the branches.

"It's trying to get me off!" Seven screamed.

"Come down, now!" Valley responded. She and Thorn were suddenly at the base of the tree, looking up with matching worried expressions.

"No!" Seven found another small knob and started to climb up again. She was going to place another pod if it killed her.

"You're being ridiculous! Just come down before you get hurt!" Valley yelled.

"Yeah, Seven. Please!" Thorn said.

The tree was really shaking now, and she was struggling to hold on. Even climbing down would be hard at this point. Seven started to descend, but before she could take another step, the tree gave one big push with a *whoosh* sound and Seven went flying.

"Ahhhh!" Seven flew through the woods and out into the road like the Cursed Forest had literally spit her out. She was seeing stars, but mostly she was mortified. If the road could roll her up like a burrito and take her all the way home, that would be fantastic. She heard the sound of footsteps running toward her, and Valley and Thorn stood over her, worried looks on their faces.

"You okay?" Thorn asked.

"I'm great," Seven said. "I feel amazing."

Valley and Thorn cringed, and that's when Seven realized they weren't alone. Laughter erupted close by, and despite the dizziness and overwhelming need to barf, Seven sat up fast.

A group of House Hyacinth witches pointed and laughed at Seven as Thorn and Valley helped her up. She tried to pretend like she wasn't embarrassed, but it was pretty hard since she had just eaten it in front of everyone.

"Did they see . . . ?" Seven asked.

"Everything? Yep," Valley said.

"Rats, rats, rats." Seven rubbed the back of her head and silently cursed her awful luck and that good-for-nothing hexed tree.

"We should go home and make sure you weren't really hurt," said Thorn.

"I'm fine," Seven said, but that was a big fat lie.

Seven couldn't help but look over at the House Hyacinth witches standing in a cluster and laughing at her. And who she saw there knocked the wind right out of her lungs. Among the laughing witches was Poppy. She wasn't laughing, but she wasn't telling people to stop either. Seven shook her head as she stared at the witch who was supposed to be her best friend, and white-hot rage filled her body.

"Thorn's right. You probably banged your head, and we don't want you being any weirder than you already are," Valley said.

"Whatever. Let's just go," Seven said, feeling defeated.

"Oh, and, Seven?" Valley said. "I won the bet. So tomorrow we do things my way."

CHAPTER SIX

VALLEY PEPPERHORN
IS A BULLY

OF ALL THE WITCHES in all the world, Seven would never understand why she got stuck with the likes of Valley Pepperhorn. Seven kept an itemized list of all the torment and perceived slights from Valley, and the top three were as follows:

1. Rat in backpack (particularly heinous since Seven has a phobia)
2. Replacing shampoo with mayonnaise during PE, smelled worse than boiled cabbage for three days
3. Almost certainly the source of the rumor that Seven liked to kiss Edgar Allan Toad, leading to the infamous "toad kisser" incident/nickname

Seven struggled up the Hill, nervous and more than a little annoyed about having to go to Valley's house. She had spent most of the night before trying to learn more about the Nightbeast so she wouldn't embarrass herself again, but there was very little on the witchernet, so she had stopped at the library first thing that morning. Miss Dewey, Seven's favorite librarian, had done the best she could, considering nearly every book Seven might need had been checked out—including *every* book on the Nightbeast. And any books on previous impossible tasks were housed in a forbidden section, which you needed special permission to access. In her black rucksack were two books with high-level monstruo-focused protection spells (illegal) and one three-levels-above-her-magic-class (highly illegal) combat spells booklet tucked discreetly inside *So, You Lost Your Best Pal, Huh?*

"Just to hide the booklet. You can bring it back later," Miss Dewey had said of the sappy friendship book. But the books Seven had really wanted had already been checked out. Some of them by Valley, and the one book Seven wanted most of all, *The Nightbeast Archives*, was taken out by someone named B. Birch. Annoying.

"Seems they took it out and never returned it. They've got a hefty fine coming their way," said Miss Dewey.

At least the book of combat spells would come in handy. Of course, all Witchlings were required to learn basic magical self-defense from a very early age. You never know when you'll run into the odd monstruo on a walk home. But Seven only knew the very basic things, like the spell for dodging attacks—evitar—and a low-level striking spell—zarpazo. They also had some hand-to-hand combat training starting at the age of ten, and the school used those classes to try to identify new members of the Gran's Guard: a highly elite group of warrior witches who protected the Twelve Towns. Not that Seven would ever be a fighter. She was much too chicken for that. Seven figured if she ever did get into a fight, she'd just use the sombra spell, which made shadows look like monsters, and scare her opponents away. She was pretty good at it.

A flurry of papers and heavy-looking boxes seemed to be floating up the hill beside her, small grunts coming from behind the various packages. For a second, Seven thought it might be enchanted mail, but then she noticed the old brown dress shoes sticking out beneath the boxes.

"Need help?" she asked.

"Oh," a muffled voice came from behind the tower of mail, "that would be lovely."

Seven grabbed the top two boxes, and they were incredibly heavy.

"Oof, how are you carrying all of this? Why don't you use a feather spell—" Seven stopped herself. A feather spell was a level two point five, which was probably above what Spares were capable of, although Seven wasn't 100 percent sure what all the specific limitations were. "Oops, sorry," she said, her cheeks going hot.

"No, no." The young witch's eyes opened wide, and she shook her head. "It's okay. Some Spares *can* do the feather spell, just . . . my employers, the Dimblewits, don't allow it."

"Why not?" Seven asked.

"My fate as a Spare, I'm afraid. Can't really question the only person in town willing to give me work. Besides, Mrs. Dimblewit said it would build character."

A Spare. Seven had spoken to them in passing before, of course; she had always thought the way her neighbors treated Spares, like they were cursed or something, was cruel given they already had to deal with not having full purchase of their powers. But there were rumors about Spares being bad luck, and Ravenskillians were nothing if not superstitious.

"I hope this isn't rude," Seven asked as they trudged up the Hill, "but can I ask you a few questions about . . . being a Spare?"

The young witch looked shocked; then a look of understanding passed over her face.

"You're the young Spare from the other night!"

"Seven. That's me." Seven's face went hot.

"I'm Pixel Gibbons. Nice to meet you. Not often I get to talk to another Spare; we keep to ourselves mostly." Pixel was definitely older than the twelfth-year students at Seven's school, but not by much. She had a short, messy haircut and a nose like a button.

"There's no Spare coven meeting?" asked Seven. Every other coven held meetings four times a year to discuss secret coven things in their grand houses. She'd never considered that Spares didn't have their own meetings, but she supposed it made sense.

"Nope, none of that. No meetings, no special-colored robes like the other covens. We're pretty much on our own. I don't even talk to the other two Spares from my class; they don't leave their houses much. Too embarrassed."

"Is it really that bad?" asked Seven.

"*I* wouldn't stay indoors even if my job for the Dimblewits didn't afford me a bit more respect than the others. But the stares, the name-calling sometimes, the whispers . . . they *can* get tiring. Especially knowing there's no escape. *Once a Spare, always a Spare* is a saying for a reason."

A wave of sickness overtook Seven, and she took in a deep breath of crisp, cold air to keep from being ill. The thought of being treated that way made her upset and angry and very, very sad.

"You have to adjust your expectations. When I was younger, I wanted to be Town Uncle, but once I got my Spare assignment, I knew the best I could hope for was an assistant to a family on the Hill. If I were you, I'd try to get my foot in the door now; otherwise you'll end up cleaning toad sludge from the sewers for pennies at best."

Seven knew there was no shame in a cleaning job, but toad sludge smelled horrific and pennies weren't enough to live or eat on. Was this what she was fighting for?

Pixel's portaphone began to ring then, and she struggled to get it out of her pocket to answer.

"You're going to drop everything," Seven warned.

"It's Mrs. Dimblewit; if I don't answer, I could be fired!"

Pixel managed to get the phone out, prop it on the edge of one of the boxes beneath her chin, and press the answer button with her nose.

"Yes, Mrs. Dimblewit!" she answered cheerfully.

"It's been over *twenty* minutes, young lady, and for such a simple and easy task. Why?"

Mrs. Dimblewit's voice was steeped in cruel sarcasm. The boxes should've taken at least four people to carry, not just one.

"So sorry, ma'am." Pixel's face went bright red as she looked at Seven sheepishly. "The line at Gustav's was exceptionally long today."

"Excuses. You have exactly one minute to get my packages to the back door, or I will cut your food rations for the week."

"Please, ma'am!"

But Mrs. Dimblewit had already hung up.

Pixel's eyes watered then. "I can't go another week with

so little food. I'll faint again and get in even bigger trouble. Here, Seven, please give me those boxes."

"Are you sure? I don't mind helping."

"Please, if she sees you've helped, she'll be even angrier."

Seven carefully slid the two heavy boxes atop the pile in Pixel's arms and watched as she practically sprinted up the hill toward the side gate entrance of a bright orange house. Seven hoped she would be okay while guiltily feeling sorry for her future self if her fate looked anything like Pixel's.

Seven lumbered up the final stretch of the hill and wondered at how different things looked up here compared with the rest of Ravenskill. All the foliage was neatly trimmed, in bright, beautiful colors, the roads devoid of even one small weed and paved in fancy yellow brick that began down by the waterfront. Instead of house numbers like where Seven lived, signs reading things like *Mango Estate* and *Snowcap House* pointed to the various houses. It was less cold here too, a soft breeze warming the air around her. It even smelled nicer, and Seven wondered, quite angrily, if this whole section of town had been enchanted. She knew how much magic and effort that much enchantment took, and she could think of a few places where their resources would be of better use, especially if witches like Pixel were going hungry. Everything felt rigged and unfair, and Seven couldn't help but feel powerless.

Winded and annoyed, Seven finally reached the front gate

of Valley Pepperhorn's mansion. She couldn't remember ever feeling this discouraged. In the past, whenever she'd felt horrible, she'd just have a giant gossip fest with Poppy, but now when she needed her most, Poppy was too busy with her coven to care. Even after seeing Seven get thrown from a tree. She still hadn't answered Seven's text from the night of the ceremony. Seven stopped at the gate to catch her breath and, despite her anger, sent one more quick text. Seven had shut her phone off in annoyance the night before, not wanting to deal with any taunts from Valley. When she turned her portaphone back on, there were a bunch of notifications from both Valley and Thorn, which she quickly swiped away and ignored for now.

"Hey, Poppy, can we talk?"

Seven held her phone close to her chest and waited.

"Please, please, please message me back," she whispered.

She waited.

And waited.

And waited some more.

But nothing happened. She could normally count on one finger the number of seconds it took Poppy to write back, but now it was like Seven didn't even exist. She felt even *more* pathetic reaching out after how Poppy had snubbed her, but Seven really needed a friend right now.

"Fine," Seven muttered to herself, stuffing her phone in her pocket.

A plaque reading *Blood Rose Manor* in gold adorned the gate, and Seven scoffed. Before she could ring the doorbell at the front gate, her anger bubbling to the surface, a voice crackled over the intercom.

"Yeeeeees?"

"Uh, hello, I'm Seven Salazar and . . ." The gate buzzed open before she could finish, and Seven stomped all the way up the almost-vertical driveway.

"Listen here, Valley Pepperpoop. You might know more about monstruos than me, but we're supposed to be a team and I can be useful too," Seven practiced beneath her breath. She would tell Valley once and for all that she would not be pushed around by her anymore. It was bad enough Valley had bullied her for so long; now she was trying to make her look like a total warlock. Things were going to be different now, and this wasn't just about being a Spare; this was about everything Valley had ever put her through, about Poppy ignoring her, about every rotten thing that had happened, and Seven had had enough.

The Pepperhorn Estate was completely black and white. Even the roses had been enchanted so they were the oily black color of a raven's wings. Seven steeled herself and rang the doorbell, which played the Ravenskill funeral overture because of course it did. A shiver slithered down her back. The Pepperhorns were creepy creeps. The door creaked opened, and Valley smirked, crossing her arms and leaning sideways against the massive doorframe. She looked just like she did when she was about to make fun of Seven or demand her lunch money.

Suddenly Thorn was at the door beside Valley, a fistful of popcorn going into her mouth.

"Oh, hpphi, Veson," Thorn tried to say with her mouth full.

"Hi, Thorn." Seven tried not to be nervous, but she felt uncomfortable and weird and, annoyingly, homesick for Poppy. She couldn't believe she was at *Valley's* house.

"Are you coming in or not?" Valley asked.

Seven took a deep breath, trying to let the anger, embarrassment, the injustice of it all out when she exhaled, and crossed the threshold into Valley's house.

Valley's room was not what Seven expected it to be. Sure, there were skulls and faux ravens perched in every corner, but what girl didn't have a few skulls and black birds decorating her room? The unexpected part was all the boy band posters, the furry pink pillow that matched the rose tint of Valley's hair, the stuffed animals—even if one of them had moving beetles for eyes. There were also nail polishes in every color you could imagine in a glittery aquamarine bucket by her bed and stacks and stacks of *Tween Witch!* magazines littered throughout the room. The large volume of monster-related books was . . . less surprising.

Seven stared up at one of the ravens, enchanted to move its head side to side and blink creepily, and matched its confused stare.

"Whose room is this?" Seven asked.

"Mine, duh," responded Valley, plopping on her bed just as Thorn did the same.

Seven stood in the doorway, arms wrapped around her waist. None of this made sense. How was Valley's room this . . . *cool*? This cute? How had she managed to make Thorn, who Seven was sure would be on her side, her friend so quickly? Seven's eyes fell on a large book near Valley's bed, and her heart stopped. How in the froggin' hex did Valley Pepperhorn already have a copy of the latest Witches of Heartbreak Cove novel? It wasn't out for another six months! It was just sitting there next to the complete Monster Hunting & Identification textbook series like it was no big deal. Seven narrowed her eyes at the thick book and decided that she disliked Valley more than she'd originally thought.

"This isn't the Cursed Forest. You can come in," Valley said lazily.

"I know," Seven snapped, then took a big, much-needed deep breath. She'd been acting like Beefy with a fever: irrational, angry, immature. *This is my coven*, Seven reminded herself silently, *like it or not*.

And she most decidedly did not like it, but the longer she resisted the circle, the longer she'd be stuck a Witchling. There was nothing for it but to dive in. Seven removed her black booties carefully, placing them next to Thorn's and Valley's, and slid onto the bed, sitting stiffly.

"Viento." Valley flicked her wrist, and a small gust of wind shut her door.

"Whoa, how do you know that spell? We're not supposed to know it yet," Thorn whispered.

Valley smiled smugly. "I have my ways."

Seven narrowed her eyes at Valley and inched closer to the copy of Witches of Heartbreak Cove in the meantime. No harm in taking a little look.

"Maybe we can learn more about the Nightbeast with these," Thorn said, picking up one of Valley's many monstruo volumes.

"You don't need to bother reading those." Valley put her hands behind her head and smirked. "I know everything there is to know about those."

"Doubtful," Seven said.

Valley scowled and sat up straight. "I can name every monstruo in those encyclopedias over there: five classes, over two hundred species. I know that one hundred of those can kill the three of us no sweat, but only one can do it without making a sound. I know that you can stop a mega-owl from flying by feeding it purple honey, that Nightbeasts like snacking on baby witches, and that you can convince a siren to bring you to her house with dead man's fingers."

"A dead man's fingers?" whispered Thorn, scandalized.

"It's a kind of seaweed," Seven said. "I'm more worried about the baby thing."

"I know how to fight winged whippers, and trick faerie folk, *and* I know how to identify Nightbeast poop."

Thorn made a grossed-out face.

"Fine! You're a monster expert. But I doubt knowing all those facts about them will be the same thing as fighting one face-to-face."

Thorn made a strangled squeak of a noise and nearly knocked a tray of candles over. Seven shot her a confused look. Thorn was nice, but she was also really weird.

"It's better than nothing," Valley huffed.

"I wish we had *The Nightbeast Archives*. That book is supposed to have all the info on them," Seven said.

"I tried to take that one out too. Some butt-toad checked it out already though, and all the other Nightbeast books were checked out too. We'll have to wait to get them from the library once they're brought back in. There's another reason I asked you both here," Valley said. She ran to her bedroom door and pressed her ear to it. Then, turning around, she waved her hand at the wall beside her and whispered, "Exponer."

Right there where a poster of Kill Le Goose had been, a

small bookshelf appeared. There were five or so books on it, all ancient looking. In fact, they looked . . .

"Are these books from the forbidden section?" asked Thorn. Valley waved at her frantically, holding her finger up to her lips to be quiet.

There was an entire section in the library that was only open to adult witches with special permission from the Hill Society—the group that oversaw all Hill-resident business and who had built that entire section of special and rare books and therefore, infuriatingly, controlled it.

These books looked just like the ones from the forbidden section. They had black covers with gold writing on them and elaborate spines with flourishes and decorations. In other words, *expensive*. Valley grabbed one off the shelf and sat back down near the others.

"These are the most complete records of the most recent impossible task," Valley said. "1965: the Cursed Toads. I think the best way to not repeat the mistakes of the past is to learn all about their history."

Seven begrudgingly agreed. Knowing what the previous Spares had done, or not done, might help them avoid making the same mistakes.

"Isn't that all stuff we can just get from other, non-forbidden-section books?" Thorn asked nervously. Having these kinds of books without permission was a serious infraction. Like, *get thrown in the Tombs* serious.

Valley and Seven shook their heads at the same time.

"Not with *all* the information, no. The council voted a long time ago to keep impossible task records redacted except for absolutely necessary information," Seven said. "Tiordan Whisperbrew did a whole thing on it last year. The books are created in the Hall of Elders, then kept in the library's forbidden section."

"Yep, so those other books are incomplete. This book has what their task was and everything," said Valley.

"Whoa," Seven said, eyes wide. How did Valley even have these books? Maybe all families on the Hill had secret libraries with more information than everyone else. It would track with how everything else in this town worked. Rich witches had access to everything.

Valley cracked open one of the books and began to read.

"'October 8, 1965. Three Spares from the town of Ravenskill invoked the Clause of the Impossible Task for the first time in over one hundred years,'" read Valley.

"What else does it say about them?" asked Seven, scrambling closer to the book to get a better look.

"Maybe we'll find out if you stop interrupting," Valley said, before continuing to read. "'The Spares were given the customary twenty-one days to complete their task—to find the infamous poisoned trichotomous, three deadly plants that are invisible to the naked Witchling eye. On the twentieth night, they called a last-minute meeting with the Town Uncle since the Ravenskill Town Gran had been summoned to a nearby town to help with an emergency.'"

"What emergency?" asked Thorn as she scooched closer to Seven.

"There were fires in two of the other Twelve Towns, believed to be the work of some evil warlock or something," Valley said.

Seven had grown up hearing about the Cursed Toads. How they'd failed their impossible task and been turned into toads, though she never knew what their task was. Or about the fires.

"Does it say the Spares' names?" Thorn tried.

"I just snatched this one from my dad's private library and hoped it would have more information than the others, but it doesn't seem to. Hold on."

Ah, so that was where Valley had gotten her stash.

Valley muttered as she skimmed the rest of the passage. "Their names aren't here either." She sighed.

Spares mattered so little that even their names didn't matter, thought Seven. It was really bumming her out.

Valley continued reading. "'Many residents believed the Cursed Toads had solved the impossible task just under the wire, but the following evening, the town gathered and were informed that the Spares had not completed the task. They were sentenced to public punishment by toad. There were light protests following the toadification, with some activists calling the punishment archaic and cruel. The Cursed Toads resided in the Twelve Towns Museum of Magical Artifacts in their *Living Monuments* exhibit until their deaths in 1987, when their bodies were dipped in copper and preserved for future generations to observe and beware.'"

"That does not sound like fun," said Thorn.

"An understatement," said Seven, thinking of an eternity spent trapped in a museum next to Valley. "Look, there's even a picture of them."

The three Witchlings crowded together to look at the Cursed Toads. They were boys about their age, and they looked sullen and scared. Seven touched the picture carefully, her heart lurching.

Just then, the door swung open, startling the three Witchlings. Seven nearly fell off the bed, Valley let out a low growl as she hid the book under a pillow, and Thorn, the smallest of startled burps.

"Esconder," Valley whispered, and the bookshelf was suddenly gone.

"Valley," Mr. Pepperhorn said, stepping into the room. "Lift your pillow for me, please."

Seven's heart dropped. Valley's father was tall, so tall he had to duck to enter the room, and he wore a sour expression on his face, as if he'd smelled spoiled milk. Seven had never heard Mr. Pepperhorn speak before, but a wave of unease washed over her at his pipe-organ voice. Seven suddenly remembered Mr. Pepperhorn's knuckles gripping Valley's shoulder so tightly they turned white with pressure the night of the Black Moon Ceremony. How Valley had whispered, "Chispa"—the spell for static shock—and a small spark on her shoulder made Mr. Pepperhorn pull away angrily. The whole thing made her feel all squirmy inside.

"I'm busy," Valley said, turning her back to her dad. Thorn and Seven exchanged looks.

Mr. Pepperhorn clenched one fist briefly as if he were about to yell; his face went red. Then he released his hand and gave the girls a tight smile. "Little girls, go home now. Valley has familial obligations."

Mr. Pepperhorn flicked his wrist, and the pillow on top of the book they'd been reading flew off. Valley's face went bright red as Mr. Pepperhorn reached the bed in what seemed like a single stride and grabbed the book quickly. "Both of you go home. Now," he said, but his eyes were pinned to Valley. She was in *big* trouble.

"But we have to solve the impossible task, sir," protested Seven.

"I know. Thanks to you. Six, was it?"

Seven held back a forbidden word, trying not to lash out at this older man.

"Well, Six, I appreciate you trying to help, but I will handle my daughter's predicament myself. Please." He smiled smugly and stepped aside, gesturing for them to leave.

"Oh, all right," Thorn said. "See you soon, Valley?"

Valley only nodded, her eyes like daggers at her father as Seven and Thorn packed their things and made their way out.

Seven walked out, but before she did, she gathered her courage, looked up at Mr. Pepperhorn, and gave him the same look Beefy had before biting a raccoon once: a vicious one. "It's Seven," she said, storming off before he had the chance to reply. Valley might've been the worst, but her dad seemed like the king of the butt-toads, and a tiny, little, extremely small part of Seven, deep, deep down, began to feel sorry for Valley Pepperhorn.

CHAPTER SEVEN
BEEFY GETS LOST

"INCENDIO!" Seven intoned the spell for fire and nearly hit the burlap sack she'd tried to make look like a Nightbeast. She'd enchanted it to move around like a wolf might so that it would be more of a challenge, but it looked more like a half-melted bear, if she were being honest.

As part of the impossible task, they'd been given a few weeks off from the Goody Garlick Academy for Magic, so Seven and Thorn were practicing their combat spells at the school's empty toad racing track. They hadn't seen or heard from Valley since the forbidden book incident three days earlier, and Seven was beginning to worry.

Next Thorn tried and succeeded in hitting the burlap Nightbeast with the ice spell.

"Nice shot!"

A tinkling sound came from Seven's pocket, and she took

out her phone. But before she could say a word, her mother interjected, "Seven, your brother is gone again. We looked in all the usual spots, but can you check for him on your way home?"

"On it," said Seven, before they said their goodbyes and hung up.

"My brother is missing," she said casually, and Thorn raised her eyebrows in alarm.

"Oh, no, it's okay. He always does this; it's part of his magic manifesting. He can vanish and reappear in random places, and he obviously hasn't learned to control it, since he's a baby. I've gotta go home now and look for him on my way there."

Babies in Ravenskill were all in varying stages of magical manifestation and, therefore, chaos. Whenever a new power appeared in them, it was erratic and unstable, as magic tends to be at the start.

"I'll come with you." Thorn grabbed her rucksack from the frozen grass and slung it onto her back. "My house is just past yours anyway."

"Dope," said Seven, smiling.

"Dope," mimicked Thorn softly, as if she'd never said the word before.

"Encantamiento terminado," Seven said, pointing at the burlap Nightbeast. It shriveled like a deflating balloon. She stuffed it into her bag, and they made their way to find Beefy.

It was a crisp autumn night, and leaves danced in the

air, the threat of a storm whispering in the wind. Seven took the path alongside the Cursed Forest home, the one her mother had told her to check, with Thorn walking very closely behind her.

"You're going to make me trip," said Seven, looking over her shoulder.

"Sorry, it's just, um, scary here." Thorn caught up, walking next to Seven now.

"It's cool. There's nothing in these woods that can hurt us while we're in town. The Town Gran keeps Ravenskill sealed with powerful magic." But even as she said it, Seven knew this was no longer true. There *was* a monster in the woods. A monster they were meant to defeat.

Thorn nodded slowly, not looking very convinced herself.

"Past the row of giant Strangling Figs, that's where the Cursed Forest starts, remember? So long as we don't go past those, we're good."

"Noted," Thorn squeaked.

"What's your favorite movie?" Seven asked. Might as well try to get to know Thorn as they walked, and maybe it would calm her down so she wasn't walking literally on top of her.

"*Sea Sirens III: Sirens Strike Back*! Have you seen it?"

"Course, best one in the franchise. Solid choice. Mine is *Creatures*, even though I watched most of it like this." Seven held her slightly splayed hands up to her eyes.

Thorn giggled. "I already know your favorite books,

Witches of Heartbreak Cove. Mine is the same. Who is your favorite witch sister?"

Seven whistled. "Hard one. Everyone says Bianca Nightingale because she's the most popular and pretty, and I do love her, but I have a soft spot for Seraphina."

"Oh goats, Seraphina has *always* been my favorite!"

"Right? She can fight with fire, become invisible"—Seven ticked each thing off on her fingers—"and her familiar is—"

"A unicorn!" the girls said at the same time, just as a loud sound pitched through the woods. They whipped around in unison toward the dark forest, where the sound was coming from. Seven and Thorn looked at each other, the big, happy smiles on their faces fading. Then Seven heard it clearly: It was a baby crying.

"Beefy," choked out Seven before breaking into a run. They followed the sound of Beefy's voice, closer and closer, as Seven's chest got tighter and tighter. What if he was hurt? What if someone had gotten him? Beefy was not your average baby, of course. Like any baby in Ravenskill, he was born with magic, and he was also incredibly strong. Once, he nearly threw Talis over the sofa while they were playing, and Seven knew to be careful not to leave anything heavy lying around in case he picked it up and threw it at someone in an attempt at catch. But he was still a baby, and there was a Nightbeast on the loose.

"Does he normally cry like this?" asked Thorn.

"No, and he's never gone into the Cursed Forest." Seven stopped just at the edge of the forest. Beefy's magic only allowed him to travel places he'd been before, being a baby and all, so why, then, were his insistent cries coming from deep within the Cursed Forest? The knot in Seven's stomach grew. He was okay; Beefy had to be okay. She didn't know if she could handle it if he wasn't.

"Isn't this the same place we came with Valley to place the jelly bean fish pods? The Nightbeast might be here, Seven. We should get an adult," suggested Thorn.

"You can go. I need to get my brother," Seven said. She knew Thorn must be afraid; she was too, but she remembered what Valley had said—Nightbeasts liked to snack on babies. She had to go now, before she lost her nerve.

Seven stepped one foot over the line where the Cursed Forest began, and the night changed around her. The sky, once twinkling with stars, went completely dark, so Seven had to squint to see. The gnarled roots of the Strangling Figs made way for the two Witchlings to cross over into the pitch darkness. Thorn stood next to her, looking scared but determined.

"That's weird," whispered Thorn. She pointed up at the tree Valley had climbed. The jelly bean fish pods sat there, untouched.

Seven hoped they were untouched because the Nightbeast hadn't been here and not because they'd already eaten something else. Seven held out her hand and raised her eyebrows at Thorn. Thorn nodded her okay, so Seven took her hand and they walked deeper into the woods, following the sounds of Beefy's wails.

Seven felt she might be sick. There was really nothing worse than the thought of her baby brother being hurt and her not being able to do anything about it. They walked deeper into the woods, faster now, the initial hesitation gone as Beefy's cries grew louder, more insistent. Before long, they'd broken into a run, Seven pulling Thorn along. This was deeper than she'd ever been in the Cursed Forest. They were going much too fast for Seven to see much of anything around them, but every few minutes, something slinked out from the dark to watch them, a figure shrouded in moving shadows, something that only appeared in the darkest part of the forest.

Finally a small figure came into view.

"Luz," Seven said, snapping her fingers. A small blue light bloomed from her hand, and she could see Beefy, his purple blankie clutched in his chubby fingers, his mouth open wide as he cried in the middle of a clearing. Seven stopped abruptly, relieved, and Thorn panted at her side, hand still clutching Seven's.

Not running to him immediately felt to Seven like her insides were being pummeled with a hammer. But she had to be sure he wasn't a Shrouded, the shadow creatures that lurked in the Cursed Forest. Disguising themselves was one of their favorite tricks. Seven and Thorn were both silent, as if speaking would break the spell of the forest and the shadow figures would descend on them.

"You wouldn't happen to have any unveiling dust on you?" Seven whispered, her voice barely audible and much too loud all at once.

Thorn shook her head.

"I'm going to get him," Seven said.

"It's dangerous." Thorn's voice hitched. "What if it's a Shrouded? Or a trap?"

"Then I'm in a bog. But if it's him, my brother needs me, now." Seven launched herself into the center of the circle, grunting loudly as she scooped Beefy into her arms. She let out a sigh of relief: If he were a Shrouded, his disguise would've fallen away at her touch.

But he was Beefy. He grabbed on to a chunk of her hair and buried his wet face in her neck. Seven's heart broke into a million pieces.

Something screamed behind them, and Seven nearly fell over, fear ripping through her like a violent storm. They all shrieked, and Beefy buried his face deeper into Seven, his tears soaking the neck of her cloak. Thorn was there to catch her, helping her keep balance, and they ran toward the town line as fast as they could.

They panted as they ran, the promise of something terrible rushing behind them all the way to the edge of the woods.

They passed the barrier separating Ravenskill from the Cursed Forest, and instantly the pressure around them lifted. The night filled with the comforting sounds of Ravenskill after dark: soft music coming from the jazz club up the road, crickets and frogs singing their nightly lullabies, the faint sound of Ravenskillians talking in taverns and Evanora's Tea Room in the distance. Thorn doubled over, her hands on her knees, while Seven set Beefy on a bench to check for any wounds. He was trying to get a word out, and Seven felt her stomach drop at the thought of his first word being brought on by this horrible night.

"He looks okay," she said after inspecting every inch and fold of his skin.

"Mmmm, mmmmm," Beefy wailed, and Seven shushed him gently, stroking the little tuft of black hair on his head the way Fox and Talis did when putting him down for a nap. He'd been trying to say his first word, probably *Mama*, for weeks.

"Do you think your parents could come get us? I'm too freaked out to walk home in the dark," Thorn said, a slight tremble in her voice.

Seven put her hand on Thorn's shoulder and squeezed. "I'm sure they can. Why don't you sit here on the bench while we wait." She called her parents, who said they were on their way.

The bench was under a lamppost, flooded in merciful

light, and seemed miles and miles away from the Cursed Forest, though they were only a few toadstools away, if that. A few minutes later, Talis and Fox arrived in the old black buggy they took out sometimes. They rushed over to them, concern etching their faces.

"We're okay," Seven reassured them. "Beefy seems okay too."

"Thorn?" Talis asked, and Thorn just nodded, but she bit her lip at the same time and tears began spilling from her eyes.

"Come." Fox pulled Thorn in, holding her head as she sobbed.

Talis checked Seven, much like she'd checked Beefy, and then picked up the baby, who was still trying to get a word out.

"Is he . . . ?" Fox hitched an eyebrow as Beefy finally got the word out, his first word, a dark word. A terrible word.

Beefy whispered quietly, picking one chubby finger up and pointing it in the direction of the Cursed Forest. He repeated the word, three times, in his little voice. The hairs on Seven's arms stood up when she realized what he was saying, and Thorn sniffled as she looked at him.

"What did he say?" she asked.

"He said *monstruo*," Fox said gravely.

And everyone in Ravenskill, even baby Beefy now, knew that *monstruo* meant one thing:

Monster.

CHAPTER EIGHT
THE TROUBLE WITH THORN

SEVEN KNEW THAT just because they technically, by Witch Law, had three weeks to solve the impossible task didn't mean they'd last that long. Their task involved them finding the Nightbeast, but there was nothing to say that the Nightbeast could not find them first. And if what had happened with Beefy was any indication, things weren't looking good for them having much time. Seven had an awful feeling, like they were already being hunted. At least they had finally heard back from Valley, and had gotten together the first chance they had.

"So did the Gran find anything in Beefy's memory?" asked Valley as they trudged through the snow to the library the next day. The Gran and the Uncle had gone over to Seven's house the night before to make sure Beefy was okay and to ward the house with protection magic. Seven couldn't help but wonder why a monstruo would go through all the trouble of trying to take her brother. He was far from the only fat, magical baby in town. So what was so special about Beefy?

"Not yet," said Seven. "She just saw the woods around him and some freaky-looking shadows, but no monstruo. She's still looking though."

As they walked past the road that led to the Cursed Forest, Seven was reminded of their trap. "The jelly bean fish were untouched yesterday, but we should check on them again today."

"I already did early this morning," Valley said. "Staked them out for a good hour, but nothing."

"Rats," Thorn mumbled, looking down.

"It's really weird. Nightbeasts love jelly bean fish. Figured they'd disappear by now."

"Speaking of disappearance, where have you been the past couple of days?" Seven asked.

Valley's face went a weird gray color, and she shook her head. "I was sick."

Seven continued to look at her, suspicious of the answer but only because she was worried it was something worse.

"Oh no, you should be more bundled up, then!" Thorn pulled another hat and a fluffy scarf from her rucksack and flitted around Valley like a fairy, trying to wrap her in the thick green wool. By the time she was done, Valley looked like a scowling overstuffed burrito, and Seven couldn't help the small laugh that escaped as they confronted the front door of the library.

Seven had noticed that in the morning, the library door didn't like to be pressured or scolded into opening. Compliments worked best, so did a cheerful voice.

The door shivered, as if it were about to open but thought better of it because of the cold.

"Please, open!" said Thorn, and with a happy sigh, the door did just that.

"I guess it can tell you're not just pretending to be nice to it. That's why it opens so easily for you," Valley said when they were safely inside.

"You goats pretend?" Thorn asked.

Valley and Seven shared a giggle. Their first shared giggle in person. Heck had frozen over. There was at least one icicle.

The library was Seven's second-favorite place in the world after her own bedroom. It had high cathedral ceilings, books lining every wall from edge to edge, and sliding stairs where, on a busy day, librarians could be seen soaring from shelf to shelf. At the center of the library was Miss Dewey's station, adorned with colorful plants, fairy lights, and hidden compartments for snacks. It had a circular desk, which Miss Dewey glided around, tapping on the various MAKLs—magical archiving knowledge locators—and helping people find "that one book with the blue cover," or "that one mystery about the lady on the train." Miss Dewey had won the Best Darn Librarian Award in the Twelve Towns for three years running now, which didn't surprise Seven one bit. Seven hoped that when she was older, she could be this good at something.

Miss Dewey had called to let them know the Nightbeast books were back in the library and she had reserved them for the Witchlings—though unfortunately not *The Nightbeast Archives*. They headed right toward her station, where she was busy working. She gave a patron a thumbs-up, and a bright blue-and-pink bird emerged from somewhere behind her MAKL. Almanac, Miss Dewey's familiar/assistant, had wings made up of tiny glowing letters and numbers. He flew to the exposed second floor of the library and hovered near one of the books Miss Dewey had probably just looked up, just as he always did. Seven could see several other familiars already at work for other librarians and patrons. A neon-colored ferret slinked and climbed around the bookshelves and made its way toward the opposite end of the stacks, prob-ably locating a book for another reader. It was a perk of the job, since only librarians got familiars—a long-standing tra-dition of the Twelve Towns.

There were a few tables with witches from the Frog House coven already reading or working on homework. And one table, Seven noticed as her stomach sank, with members of House Hyacinth chatting and looking over spell books. Poppy was there too.

Seven cleared her throat as they passed. "Hi, Poppy."

Poppy looked up, surprised. Her face went red as one of her coven members plopped a giant book in front of their faces, blocking them from Seven's view.

"That wasn't very nice!" Thorn said, but Seven pulled her away.

"Don't bother," Seven said, feeling so miserable she could cry. "I shouldn't have said hi."

"Hello, girls," Miss Dewey greeted them. Miss Dewey sounded like . . . like a black-and-white movie. Her accent was unlike anyone else's in Ravenskill, and the only way Seven could think to describe it was old-timey.

"Hey, Miss Dewey," said Seven.

"I've set something special up for you. Follow me." Miss Dewey walked toward the back of the library with purpose, her favorite yellow scarf fluttering behind her.

The Witchlings followed, giving one another curious looks but not questioning their favorite librarian. When Moira Dewey said to do something, you did it.

At the back of the library, Miss Dewey took them through a discreet wooden door, to a room Seven had never seen before. Soft, comfortable reading lights illuminated the room, and two big comfy sofas sat facing each other, with a coffee table between them. To one side, mugs and a glass carafe filled to the brim with steaming hot cocoa sat next to a bowl of fluffy homemade marshmallows and a giant bag of those long, crispy orange snacks that left your fingers dusty and your throat craving fizzy drinks. On the walls were posters of every toad racing tournament in the past few years, including the upcoming match right here in Ravenskill. At the center sat a shiny crystal bell, and Seven wondered what it was for. Beneath the table sat a cooler, and Seven would bet her entire book collection it was full of their favorite sugary drinks.

"Fuel for important work," said Miss Dewey.

"This is so cool." Thorn sank into one of the sofas.

"You three need to focus."

"It's perfect! Thanks, Miss D," Seven said.

"Yeah, thanks. I love Cheesy-o's," said Valley.

"They are your favorite, according to your mom. And, Seven, you'll find your favorite purple fizzy cola in the cooler. Thorn, the hot cocoa is your grandma's special recipe." Miss Dewey pantomimed hitting a ball out of the park, and the three Witchlings cheered. Miss Dewey wasn't just the best darn librarian; she was on a whole other level.

"If you three need anything, I'll be just outside. I've left all the Nightbeast-related books there on the table." Miss Dewey pointed at a pile of heavy-looking books near one of the sofas. "But Almanac is on call to find you any books I might've missed; just ring that little crystal bell on the table, and he'll come to you."

Valley immediately went over and grabbed one of the Nightbeast books and began looking through it.

"Thanks again," said Thorn, waving to Miss Dewey as she left them in their private research room.

"This is awesome. I should come to the library more often," said Valley, stretching out on one of the sofas with the book she'd grabbed.

"Let's hope we don't get toadified, then," said Seven. The Witchlings sobered up at that. As cool as this room was, as delicious as the snacks looked, this might very well be one of their last meals not involving insects if they didn't stop the Nightbeast. That is, if they didn't become monstruo food themselves.

"We need to learn more about the Nightbeast." Seven eyed Valley, who had mentioned more than once now how much of a monster expert she was. Somehow, Seven doubted it, since (a) she had not taught them much about Nightbeasts and (b) Valley fell asleep in or never came to class.

"Well, that's why we're here. To learn more about the Nightbeast. Here." Valley passed books to Seven and Thorn, and the three Witchlings began to read.

After a few minutes, Valley jumped up from the sofa.

"What?!" Thorn and Seven asked in unison.

Valley looked at them, wide-eyed. "Listen to this: 'The Nightbeast, the most elusive of the monstruo class, is not without its quirks. Nightbeasts are particularly drawn to children showing the promise of power. The more powerful the witch, the more delicious it is to the monstruo,'" Valley read.

Seven shivered, reliving that awful night her brother had gone missing. Beefy *was* strong for his age, so that explained why the Nightbeast would want to take him, but there was still something Seven didn't understand.

"How did he get there though? I think my parents would have noticed if a Nightbeast broke into his nursery."

"When I heard Beefy was found in the Cursed Forest, I started thinking—he could never have gone there on his own, so someone or some*thing* must have brought him there . . ."

Valley sat back down, and sifted through the book on her lap. She found the section she was looking for and read in silence for a moment before looking up.

"Okay, I think I know how Beefy was taken into the Cursed Forest. It says here: 'Because they go through cycles of strength and weakness, Nightbeasts typically hibernate and gather strength upon their arrival to a new territory. They are very difficult to track during hibernation. The hibernation period can vary from three weeks to six months. During this hibernation period, they are dependent on a creature known as el cuco.

"'Cucos are not as strong as their leader but still deadly,'" Valley continued. "'They have powerful tracking magic, which aids in their job as hunters. They hunt and gather for the Nightbeast until it gains enough strength to emerge from its cave and attack whatever unlucky town it's descended upon.' See! If one of the cucos took Beefy, underestimating your brother's strength, he could've dispatched it," Valley said.

"I really doubt my brother, a literal baby, could beat a Nightbeast minion."

"He could if the cuco was a smaller, younger one. Look," said Valley, pointing at the book again. "The Nightbeast sometimes targets specific prey and depending on that prey can choose to send one of their smaller and therefore less-valuable-to-it cucos. All cucos are smaller than the Nightbeast, but they vary in size. So maybe Beefy appeared somewhere normal, like the edge of the forest, and our Nightbeast took advantage of the situation and sent a smaller cuco to take him but Beefy punched him or something."

"Or it saw us and realized it was outnumbered," said Seven.

"Some of the cucos are only a bit bigger than we are. Look." Valley turned the book around to show them. At the center of the page was the Nightbeast. It looked like some sort of wolf, if wolves were the size of teenage elephants and had not one but two snarling heads. Its fur looked slimy instead of soft and was a bloodred color. Its eyes were completely white. One paw was probably the size of Seven's head, and she shuddered to think what this creature could do with all four of them. Around him stood smaller creatures, skinny and tall, with matted fur stretched over visible bones. And rows and rows of teeth. The cucos. There were other animals lined up beside them for scale, and some of the cucos were in fact around Valley's height.

Thorn dropped her cup of chocolate, and it spilled everywhere.

"Oh no, oh no," she said, dropping down to dab at the mess.

"Thorn, are you okay?" Seven asked, crouching down to help Thorn. "How in the goose are we supposed to fight that thing?"

"I have some ideas. Nightbeasts are the most elusive of the monstruo class. They have no scent, not traceable by memory spells or potions. Even the most famous monster hunter of all time, Vega Mirabal, couldn't find one back in 1985." Valley had a weird twinkle in her eye. It was the same look Seven got when talking about famous witch reporters or V. V. Avenmora, the author of Witches of Heartbreak Cove. "Instead, the Nightbeast found her, and, well . . ." She ran a finger across her neck. Dead. "But we've discovered things about it since then: Like the kinds of droppings it leaves behind. That they use fallen trees to reinforce their lairs. The Nightbeast is hard to find, but it's not impossible.

"What's probably impossible is fighting it, for us anyway. If Vega couldn't, then there's not much hope for us," Valley said. "If we're going to have a chance, we have to take advantage of its biggest weakness."

Seven stopped helping Thorn for a moment and looked up at Valley expectantly.

"If it's still in its feeding-and-hibernation state, it won't fight, out of self-preservation. The closer it gets to full strength, the more it will venture out, but it won't fully expose itself until it feels every weakness is leached from its system. That's why it makes the cucos fight for it. The Nightbeast is a proud and selfish monstruo. Only worried about its own survival by any means necessary. We have to try to find it before it emerges; otherwise, our only choice is to figure out the day it's going to appear according to its usual pattern of behavior. It's quite fascinating, really."

"You obsessed with monsters, Pepperhorn?" Seven asked.

"What tipped you off?" Valley asked sarcastically, and Seven flinched. Every time she let her guard down even a little, she remembered that was a colossal mistake. Valley cleared her throat, and her voice changed a bit, became softer. "How do you think I know all this stuff? I want to be a monster hunter and keep Ravenskill and all the magic towns safe."

Funny, Seven always pictured Valley as the "let monsters loose on a town" type, not a protector. But if the past few days had taught her anything, it was that she didn't know the people in her life quite as well as she thought she did. Seven glanced at her phone, but nothing new from Poppy. It made her stomach sink, like she was gonna barf. She hadn't done anything wrong, at least not that she could remember, so why was her best friend in the world treating her like a phantom? Everything felt shaky and unsafe, like she was moments from tumbling from a broom high up in the clouds.

"So if we want to stop the Nightbeast," said Valley, "our best bet is to find it during its weakened state."

Seven and Thorn nodded.

Valley scrunched her face like she was deep in thought. "Problem is, there's not much intel on how to do that, considering that most people who fight them don't make it out alive."

"So we're toast?" Seven said.

"That doesn't mean we lie down and let it eat us. There are a lot of really scary monsters, ones nobody thought you could defeat, that ended up being defeated anyway. It's just a matter of finding the right battle plan," Valley said.

Valley rolled a big blackboard out in front of them from the other side of the room and wrote *Stupendous Spares Battle Plan* up top. Thorn smiled.

"Okay. It's time to learn how to hunt a Nightbeast."

The Spares spent the next few hours reading through the books and writing up everything they learned: how Nightbeasts could camouflage themselves in the woods, how their fangs could pierce almost anything, and how they had a love of long, luxurious naps and fat baby witches. They learned Nightbeasts operated in three phases: expedition to find their next lair with scouting help from cucos, hibernation and feeding, and lastly the hunt, when they left their den and attacked a town.

"I have an idea." Seven raised her hand.

Valley rolled her eyes. "You don't have to raise your hand—we're not in class."

Seven shrugged and put her hand down. "If the cucos bring them food, can we find one and follow it? Maybe they'll lead us to the Nightbeast."

Valley clapped. "Yes! You're smarter than you look. If the cucos are out hunting for the Nightbeast, they'll leave behind things like hair and droppings. Tracking them could also lead to the Nightbeast." She wrote *tracking* and then *using cucos* right beneath it on the blackboard, and Seven wasn't sure how to feel at the backhanded compliment. "We should also be on the lookout for dead flowers. Nightbeasts' presence makes it impossible for flowers to thrive near them. Any flowers that should be alive in winter and aren't might be a sign they're near." Valley wrote *dead flowers*, right beneath *using cucos*, on the board.

"Aren't most Ravenskill flowers dead in winter anyway?" asked Thorn.

A bit deflated, the Witchlings went silent for a few moments. Seven dove deep into her memories, trying to recall something, anything, she'd read in one of her many botánica books that might help them now. Something tickled the back of Seven's brain, and she snapped her fingers, took out a notebook from her backpack, and flipped through the pages. "Here, I cataloged this plant years ago but had almost forgotten. The Bayahíbe rose can withstand frigid cold temperatures and survive even the harshest of winters. They're pretty common in the areas surrounding the Cursed Forest too, including Oso Mountain, which also has caves. So kind of perfect."

"All right, then we start with looking for cucos to follow first, and keep the flowers in mind," Valley said.

"Will we be able to get *past* the cucos once we've followed them to the den?" asked Seven.

"There will likely be too many for us to fight at once, so we'll need to figure out a way to hold them off," Valley said.

"We can use poison foxglove or sleeping tonics if I can manage to make it into an aerosol," said Seven. "I also found something in my independent research that might help." Seven whipped out her trusty faux-dragon-scale notebook and read from her notes. "They're called shushrooms, and they almost completely silence your movements and steps. These might help us sneak up to the cucos or the Nightbeast."

Shushrooms were essential to any spell involving sneaking and quiet, and they grew exclusively along the marshy banks of the Boggy Crone River. The key was to ground the shushrooms up and eat one fingernail-sized bite. Any more than that and they'd be greener than Edgar Allan Toad, Seven explained.

Valley wrote that all on the board and kept talking. "Cucos usually, but not always, hunt at night, so we're most likely to find one at night, in the deep woods or along a river. We already know Nightbeasts like jelly bean fish, so we'll have to get some more of those and, I dunno, maybe spread them out. Or put them on ourselves like bait!" Valley said. "Cucos will try to gather them for the Nightbeast, so it could work."

Seven shivered at the thought of being Nightbeast bait, but it did make sense. "Isn't it kinda weird that the traps didn't work if they love jelly bean fish so much?"

Valley shrugged. "Lots of explanations for that. It could have enough food. The closer it comes to emerging, the bigger their appetite. Could just be a sign it wasn't hungry enough."

"I hate this," said Thorn. She was worrying the hem of her dress, and Valley looked at her intently.

"You okay?" Valley asked.

Thorn looked up, her eyes wet with tears. "I tried to fight a Nightbeast once."

"What?" Seven and Valley asked in unison.

Thorn nodded as Seven took her hand. Valley sat on the other side, doing the same.

"I . . . didn't tell you because I was worried it would make you not want to be my friends. Everyone back at home stopped talking to me after it happened, like I was cursed or something. But the reason we moved is because a Nightbeast tracked me home one night."

Valley gasped.

"There had been rumors that there was a monstruo on the loose in Boggs Ferry—that's my old town—for a few weeks, but most witches thought they were *just* rumors. Then, one night, I don't know why or how, but it followed me home and . . . it almost took me. My house was warded but it cut us off before we could run inside and my . . . my twin stepped in front of it."

Thorn had a twin? Seven and Valley exchanged looks as Thorn continued.

"His name was Petal. He was always braver than me. Somehow . . . he stopped it. I don't remember how, but I remember the Nightbeast was huge, with really sharp teeth, and it had a white stripe down one ear. It was the scariest thing I've ever seen. I remember I was screaming and trying to pull Petal back into the house, but he wouldn't listen. My brother pushed me out of the way, and I fell behind a rosebush; then he ran in the opposite direction. The Nightbeast tried to lunge at me and stopped, then ran after my brother and took him into the woods like he was just a little puppy. Grabbed him by the nape of his neck. He looked so helpless . . ." Thorn shook her head and then began to cry again. *Oh no*, thought Seven, *oh no, oh no*.

"I'm so sorry, Thorn." Seven pulled her into a hug.

"I'm cursed," said Thorn.

"You're not cursed. I reject this theory," said Seven.

"Then why is our task a Nightbeast? Why did it follow me here?"

"I'm pretty sure the rumors about the Nightbeast being here started before you moved to town," said Valley.

Seven nodded. "Right!"

It was not right. Seven seemed to recall the rumors began circulating on the message boards *after* Thorn had already moved. But now was not the time to say that, not when Thorn was just starting to calm down.

"You're not alone, Thorn. I'm scared too," Valley admitted.

Seven's eyes went wide with shock.

"As much as I want to hunt a Nightbeast, because, well, I'm me, I had, like, twenty separate nightmares about being eaten by one," Valley added.

"I had a dream about a Nightbeast too but it was super weird. It didn't eat me, but it turned into a baby and then I . . . rocked it to sleep?" Thorn said uncertainly.

The Witchlings exchanged silent looks, and then all at once, burst into laughter. Tears-streaming-down-their-faces laughter, the kind you can only share with people who are just as worried and anxious as you are.

"We need to be ready. I know how dangerous it is first-hand," said Thorn, wiping her eyes. "I'm going to try to be brave." She gave Seven and Valley a smile.

"I won't let anything happen to you, Thorn." Valley had that look on her face, the one she always got before one of her heinous pranks.

"If I were a Nightbeast, I'd be worried about that heckin' look," Seven blurted out before she could stop herself.

Valley let out a loud laugh, throwing herself back on the sofa, and Thorn's small smile turned into a giggle. If it weren't for the voice in the back of her head telling her Valley still didn't like her, Seven would almost think they were becoming friends. Lately that voice was getting a little less loud.

Valley got up and walked to the blackboard. "I'll get some more jelly bean fish," she said, writing it on the board.

"I'll gather the foxglove and sleeping tonic," said Seven.

"And I'll . . . hmm, maybe I can make us pouches to hold everything!" said Thorn.

Seven realized that they all had the strengths that might come in handy for this impossible task. Maybe the Oracle was right after all.

"There," said Valley, a satisfied smile on her face. No matter what, there was a bit of good news finally: They had a solid plan. Seven looked over the blackboard Valley had just finished writing on and committed it to memory—they would find the Nightbeast while it was still in its weak state by luring and following cucos. Once they found its den, they would use shushrooms to sneak up on the Nightbeast, then flood the den with sleeping tonic and dispatch any cucos that were awake with foxglove blow darts. They would also keep an eye out for dead Bayahíbe roses and, in turn, the Nightbeast's cave, just in case.

Seven felt a bit more prepared, a bit more like they knew what they were doing, and she had to admit a big part of that had to do with Valley. Even if she still didn't completely trust Valley, and part of her felt she would pull the rug out from under her at any moment, Seven was glad to have Valley on her team. It was way better than having Valley against her.

Seven closed her notebook and slapped it on the table with a *THUMP*. "Okay, we've got to get home and rest. We'll start tomorrow. I think we've researched and prepared about as much as any witch could."

"Agreed," said Thorn. Outside the library, their respective parents waited to drive them home. After the scare with Beefy the other night, they were all being extra careful. The three Witchlings stood outside the entrance awkwardly. It felt like the end of something or, maybe, the beginning.

"Are you goats as nervous about all this as I am?" asked Thorn.

"Yes, I am, and I'm not sure how I'm gonna sleep without dreaming of baby Nightbeasts," Valley said. Thorn giggled at that.

"I think it's normal to be nervous." Seven's next words came out slowly. But still, for their coven's sake, she said, "We're gonna prove every ugly butt-toad in this town wrong." Seven tried her very best to sound brave, but she did not feel brave. She felt doomed.

Thorn beamed, and Valley gave her a small nod.

"See you tomorrow, nerds," said Valley, getting into her family's fancy black car.

"Bye!" said Thorn, hopping onto the back of her mother's waiting motorcycle.

"See ya," said Seven, wanting nothing more than to make tonight last just a little bit longer. Because tomorrow night they would start, for realsies, to hunt the Nightbeast.

CHAPTER NINE
POISONS, BOOKS, AND QUARRELS

THE NEXT MORNING brought a clear, crisp day to Ravenskill. The ground was blanketed with fresh white snow as the Witchlings and one black wagon containing one cranky toad, pulled by Thorn, wound through town toward the Bruised Apple Bookshop. Seven had not taken Edgar Allan Toad out in a while, and he was even more of an absolute goose without fresh air, so she'd made sure to take him with her that morning.

"Do we get free books?" asked Valley.

"My parents let me borrow books from the used section sometimes, if I'm very, *very* careful," Thorn said.

"Come to think of it, do we have to pay for everything we need for the impossible task? I'm only twelve," said Valley.

"If we have to bankroll our own death, I'm coming back as a ghost and suing the Town Gran," Seven said. "I want to see if your shop has anything else on the Cursed Toads."

It had been bothering Seven for quite some time that they couldn't seem to find anything about those Spares of '65. Not their names, or their families. She refused to believe that Spares would be treated this way, forgotten so cruelly, and in part she was trying to reassure herself that no matter what the outcome, the entire town wouldn't just forget them. She was not loving her odds.

"Did you bring the foxglove liquid?" Valley asked Seven.

"Right here." Seven patted the front pocket of her coat, where she'd stored three vials of foxglove and the flora field map where she'd already begun marking all probable locations of the Bayahíbe rose according to their preferred environment, especially the spots in or around the Cursed Forest.

"Good, I brought the darts so we can load them and keep them on us all the time. Can't be too careful," Valley said.

Seven nodded, pushing down the fear that was becoming all too familiar now.

They entered the store, tiny bells tinkling as the door opened. The Bruised Apple was a small bookshop, with a second-floor loft and wall-to-wall books. There were pages floating everywhere, suspended in the air with magic, and twinkle lights cast a soft, warm glow over everything.

Thorn's father, Leaf Laroux, walked down the floating spiral stairs at the center of the bookshop. He had dark hair just like Thorn's and looked like he might be able to lift a building. He was almost as tall as Valley's dad, thought Seven. Every time she remembered how mean Mr. Pepperhorn had been that day at their mansion, she got mad all over again. Seven thought of her own dad and how different they seemed to be. She wondered what it was like to have a parent who was terrible to you all the time. She stole a glance at Valley and began wondering lots of things.

"How have you two been holding up?" Mr. Laroux asked.

"It's been . . . something," Valley said.

"Nightmares," said Seven.

"That's understandable." Mr. Laroux shot a concerned glance in Thorn's direction.

"Thorn, you told your coven about our rules for handling the books?" Mr. Laroux asked.

"Yes, Papa, I told them." Thorn smiled as her cheeks went bright pink. "We will be careful."

The bells tinkled as more customers came into the shop.

"Doesn't anybody work here?" a witch asked in a haughty voice, and Mr. Laroux shook his head.

"Be right there, ma'am. Help yourself to any books, girls. I'll be just over there if you need me." Mr. Laroux smiled warmly at the three Witchlings and left them to help the customer. Thorn led them to the back of the store.

"What he means by *help yourself to any books* is don't even think about taking any new ones," Thorn said.

"Fair, I think the book we need is kind of old anyway," Seven said. They'd had zero luck with finding Spare-related books at the library or even any specific information on the witchernet, so used books might be just what they needed.

"Before we start looking, come." Thorn gestured to Valley and Seven and led them over to a picture that hung next to the botánica book section. "This was Petal."

Seven looked up and saw a picture of what looked like Thorn with shorter, wavier hair. He had a sly smirk on his face and was holding flowers in his hands, which was customary for portraits of Witchlings.

"He looks like he was froggin' cool," said Seven.

Thorn's chest puffed out proudly.

"Yeah, he's kinda cute," Valley said.

"Hey! That means you think I am cute since we're twins." Thorn smiled.

"Maybe I do." Valley shrugged, and it sent the three Witchlings into quiet giggles. They were in a bookstore after all.

"Did he like fashion too?" Seven asked.

"Not as much. He loved botánica though, just like you, Seven. It's why we put his picture here in this section and why I am happy you're my friend. You're always talking about plants and good soil and stuff I don't really understand, but it reminds me a lot of Petal." Thorn smiled warmly.

Seven hoped she wasn't blushing, but her face was hot so she probably was.

"Thanks for showing us his picture," Valley said softly.

Thorn's eyes watered, and she smiled at Valley and Seven.

"I think Petal is real proud of you right now," said Seven. "You have two whole friends *at the same time*."

The Witchlings devolved into more giggles and then finally got to work. They began searching for the title Seven was so eager to find, *Spares Throughout History* by Lopez Montgomery.

"Have you read any of the WOHBC book?" Valley asked as they searched.

"I finished chapter fourteen last night," said Seven. "And personally I think Bianca is being a butt-toad."

"Queen of the butt-toads," said Thorn.

"I think she's trusting her gut. That's gotta mean something," Valley said.

"Yeah, but she's not trusting her coven," Seven said. "She's choosing a greasy boy over her coven members, and that's heinous!"

"I trust Bianca. She always has her reasons," said Valley.

"No spoilers!" screeched Seven.

"If the Wicked One betrays her, you owe us both two milkshakes and an order of fries," Thorn said.

Seven knew she was quite different from Valley and Thorn, but there was one thing they all had in common aside from being Spares: They were obsessed with the Witches of Heartbreak Cove series. Thorn and Seven had been reading the advance copy Valley had snuck into Seven's backpack together any chance they got. Valley had already read it, and it was a constant battle trying to stop her from spoiling the ending.

"I'm not worried. Zero worry on Team Bianca, the winning team," Valley was saying, when a voice made them look up in unison.

"This whole SPARE business is dreadful! Just embarrassing," a witch who looked like she was from the Hill was yelling, so close to the Witchlings there was no way she didn't know they were right there. It was the same customer who'd come in moments before. She wore a lime-green coat to match her hair, with leopard spots and purple shoes. Her eyes darted toward the Witchlings, and she sneered.

"And I'm not sure why Spares are even *allowed* in businesses. My Drascal will be bringing it up in the next town meeting," she sniffed.

The person with her smiled nervously at the Witchlings, seemingly apologetic but not defending them either. Seven looked at her more closely—it was Pixel. The Spare she'd met on her way to Valley's house. Her clothing looked old and thin and definitely not warm enough for the weather today. Her brown shoes were worn out—there was even a hole in one of them—and she carried a stack of books the mean woman was piling onto her arms. She looked tired and sad, with a fake smile painted on out of fear. Seven's heart felt heavier, her chest tightening with anxiety and worry. She gave Pixel a small smile, and she sent one back Seven's way.

This would be her fate someday—if she were lucky—living at the mercy of some rich butt-toad. She wished there was something she could do for other Spares, but mostly she just felt guilt that she'd never cared much about their lives until she became one of them.

"We've got as much right to be here as you," said Valley.

The woman looked shocked, as if she hadn't been purposely trying to goad the Witchlings. She looked around and, noticing the empty shop, narrowed her eyes at them.

"Don't you know who my husband is? Town Councilman Drascal. I'm sure your *father* has heard of him and would not be happy about you associating with these *Spares*." She wagged her finger at Valley.

Valley's cheeks went bright red. "*I'm* a Spare—what am I supposed to do?" she grumbled.

Mrs. Dimblewit, an apt name, nodded triumphantly, and Seven was about to tell her to eat rats when Thorn cleared her throat.

"I'm not sure how it's possible that your outfit not only clashes but that it's even louder than you," Thorn said in her politest voice.

Valley's mouth hung open. Seven let out a surprised laugh.

This was what Mrs. Dimblewit had been hoping for, a reason to unleash the true venom she had inside for the Spares.

"You are a nasty, dirty little rat of a witch who will likely be one of my assistants one day, just like Pixel here. Come to think of it, your face looks familiar. Weren't you the one who *killed* her twin brother?" Mrs. Dimblewit smiled cruelly, and Thorn's eyes filled with tears. "Figures you would come here and sully our town. Your kind should be illegal. Maybe you already are by the looks of you. That out-of-season dress, ha! Who are you to tell me about fashion?" the woman scoffed.

"She is my daughter," a voice with a smooth-flowing accent rang out from the top floor, where Mrs. Laroux, Thorn's mother, stood in a sharply cut powder-pink suit and a luxurious black cloak. She came down the stairs like it was a catwalk, her shiny aquamarine bob swinging as her gold-trimmed heels click-clacked toward them.

"I would suggest you get out of our store. Now. You're not welcome back," Mrs. Laroux said.

"Thimble, I didn't see you standing there. It was a harmless joke. Surely you're not *so* uptight as to not understand that."

Thimble Laroux smiled, put one hand in her pants pocket, and stepped closer to Mrs. Dimblewit. "Which part was supposed to be funny? When you called my daughter a dirty little rat witch? When you accused her of killing her own brother? When you bullied three little girls at your big, big age?"

Mrs. Dimblewit became the bright red of a cherry tomato.

"My Drascal—"

"Yes, yes. Your Drascal this and your Drascal that. Enough with your ridiculous threats. We know your husband is on the town council, but do not forget"—Mrs. Laroux leaned closer to the woman's face—"I am too. Au revoir." Mrs. Laroux pointed at the door and turned away from Mrs. Dimblewit.

"I will be telling my—you will not just speak to me however you want. We'll see about this store of yours." Mrs. Dimblewit looked around as if the bookshop smelled but also like she was appraising it. There was a threat in her movements. She whipped toward Pixel. "Let's go. Leave those books there," she said, walking toward the exit.

Pixel looked around frantically. "I should put these back," she said, barely audibly to Mrs. Dimblewit's back.

Mrs. Dimblewit whipped around, her face shaking with rage and almost purple now. "LEAVE THEM THERE!"

Pixel, hands trembling, placed the pile of books on the nearest coffee table.

"I'm so, so sorry," she whispered.

She kept her eyes down as she tried to leave, but Mrs. Laroux took her by the hand. "Look at me," she said softly.

Pixel raised her face slowly and looked at Mrs. Laroux. Thorn's mother smiled at the Spare.

"You ever want to leave there, I have a job for you here. I will treat you with dignity, like a witch and not just a puppy dog to follow me around."

Pixel dropped her eyes and shook her head. "I couldn't. Mrs. Dimblewit would never allow—"

"There is no law that says you cannot switch employers. Just remember that—"

Pixel's whole body jerked back violently. Mrs. Dimblewit held one hand up and sneered.

"You either obey or I force you to obey." The woman waved her hand again and said, "Halar." The spell to pull or tug on something, usually an object, never ever used on a person.

"I'm so sorry," Pixel whispered again, and right before she turned to go, Mrs. Dimblewit intoned another spell. "Arrastrar," she said cooly, and Pixel's body fell like a plank of wood to the ground and was dragged all the way to the exit of the store.

"Stop this!" Mrs. Laroux said, putting her hands up.

Mrs. Dimblewit raised an eyebrow. "You surely do not want to have a magical duel here in your shop! Why, something like that could get you permanently shut down." She sneered again and then opened the door. "You'll follow me home this way, and I hope it teaches you a lesson," she said to Pixel, and as she walked out into the snow, Pixel followed helplessly from the ground like she was Seven's wagon and not a witch.

"No, stop!" Seven got up and tried to run after them, but Valley held her back.

"It'll only make her hurt Pixel more," Valley said.

"We can't just let her do this!" Seven's stomach hurt. She had never seen a Spare treated that way before. She knew they were sort of outcasts in town, but this was more than that. This was more than funny looks and whispers; this was abuse.

Mrs. Laroux let out an exasperated scream as she slammed the bookshop door. "People like her should not be allowed to be employers, that poor witch. I am going to raise hell at the next town meeting. Are you girls okay?" she asked, as if she'd just remembered they were there.

"You were froggin' cool," said Valley.

Thorn smiled proudly but then looked at her mother in concern. "Maman, will Pixel be in trouble now?"

Mrs. Laroux ruffled her perfect hair as if she were thinking, and angry, and plotting. "I will do what I can to get her out of that house, but there is no telling what Mrs. Dimblewit and her awful husband are capable of. They've been discussing terrible things in the latest meetings and—I have to find a way to stop them." Her eyes were pinned to the window.

"What kinds of things?" Seven asked.

Mrs. Laroux looked down at the girls. "You have enough

to worry about. This is unrelated to your task; you must focus on that. Let me take care of this. Teamwork, okay?" She raised an eyebrow and smiled.

Mrs. Laroux *was* froggin' cool.

The Witchlings all nodded.

"Good; now, if you see that lady around town, don't interact with her; you just walk away. She will have a grudge now, and she's cowardly enough to try to settle it with you," Mrs. Laroux said. "Did you find the book you were looking for?"

"No luck. We better get going before it gets any later," Seven said.

The Witchlings left, waving their goodbyes and yelling thank-yous to Mrs. Laroux as they ran out into the cold on their next mission: finding the shushrooms they'd need to sneak up on the Nightbeast. As Seven's boots crunched down on the icy snow, she couldn't help but notice the jagged path Pixel's body had made. It was already disappearing with newly fallen snow.

* * *

The place where the Boggy Crone River ran alongside the train tracks that led to Stormville and the other magical towns was called Pavoroso Passage. It was a beautiful place, with its enormous willow trees and wild, colorful flowers, but it could also be creepy and isolated. There were long, dark alleyways between the historical buildings, hidden paths, secret entrances, and a few unsavory occult shops where only the most mysterious villagers seemed to congregate. Seven was glad she wasn't going alone. They neared a group of abandoned train cars, and Seven pinched her nose.

"Gross. What is that smell?" Valley asked.

"Look," Thorn said. In one of the train cars, giant hunks of meat, covered in flies, were piled almost to the ceiling.

"I guess they just forgot this was here." Seven shrugged.

Valley cocked her head to the side and narrowed her eyes, as if she were deep in thought.

"Come on, let's go this way. I'm gonna barf," Seven said.

They made their way toward the shushroom patches and, mercifully, away from the horrid stench of meat. The marshy lands were as quiet and out of the way as Seven remembered. They crossed a row of yellow bricks and reached the shushroom patch on the other side. A heavy feeling overtook Seven as they crossed, maybe because them being here, gathering all the supplies they needed, meant they were really doing this. They were really hunting a Nightbeast.

"Do you think this is worth it?" said Seven, knowing it didn't matter. They couldn't take the impossible task back now.

"You'd rather be a Forever Witchling?" asked Valley.

"Than a toad? Yes," said Seven.

"Toads are pretty cool," said Valley.

"Have you met Edgar?" Seven gestured toward the small glass mushroom tank in their wagon that held a scowling Edgar Allan Toad. His mustache looked especially slimy today.

"He's not so bad. You're just touchy," said Valley.

"Maybe so. But *you've* never had to race with him and stay after school till he crossed the finish line!" said Seven.

"Fair."

They picked shushrooms until the sun began to dip between the mountains. The darker it got, the more Seven hoped Valley or Thorn would suggest they go home. She even faked a few yawns, hoping they'd take the hint, but nobody said anything. Seven didn't want to look like a giant baby, but the truth was, she was frightened of her own shadow right now. They were close to the road with fading yellow bricks when Seven stopped cold.

"Hey, goats," she said. "Come see this."

She was looking down at . . . she wasn't sure what she was looking down at. At what she was standing in. Because at first glance it just seemed like a small hole in the ground, except it was weird there was no snow there. There were one, two, three smaller holes bordering the top of the hole where Seven stood. Almost like . . .

"A print," said Valley. "Get out of there, Seven. Now."

Seven jumped back, and Thorn held on to her arm as Valley checked out the print. She walked around it, inspecting it closely.

"This doesn't look like a Nightbeast print," said Valley.

Thorn let out a breath of relief.

"These are cuco marks," Valley continued. "At least two."

"Oh, rats," said Thorn.

"We should hide." Valley ran behind a train car; Seven, Thorn, and their wagon followed.

"A week has already passed; we only have fourteen more days till we're toads," Valley said. "We've gotten lucky. This is our chance to follow a cuco to the Nightbeast's cave."

Seven shook her head. "We're going home. Now."

"We aren't ready, Valley," said Thorn. She shrunk away from the other two Witchlings, shaking her head. "I'm with Seven."

"Our task is to fell a Nightbeast. They are really hard to find, and once they find you, it's usually too late. This is our chance to get to it while it's weak." Valley gestured to the print. She had a fierce twinkle in her eye, and Seven almost felt emboldened enough to follow her lead. But she was too scared. Everything was happening too fast. "Please?" Valley asked. "Just this one time, listen to me."

Seven sighed. "Fine. But I still think this is too risky with more than one cuco."

A shriek tore through the night sky, loud and high and piercing. The Witchlings jumped, nearly crashing into one another.

"What was that?" asked Thorn.

"A cuco cry. They're close," said Valley.

"How hard are these things to beat? On a scale of one to we're-burnt-toast-on-a-greasy-skillet?" asked Seven.

"Slightly burnt toast, no grease."

"Please, please, stop talking about toast. I haven't eaten, and my stomach grumbles loudly," said Thorn.

Another shriek, and Thorn buried her head in the cloth of Seven's hood.

"Thorn, if you want to go back . . ."

"No way I'm going anywhere alone."

"Then we stick together and follow it. We can grind these shushrooms up and eat one fingernail-sized bite a piece. No more, or we'll be sick for a week," said Seven.

"We should have the blow darts ready just in case, but the idea is to follow, not fight," said Valley. "For now. Just make sure you don't let them take anything of yours."

Seven took the vials out of her coat pocket as Valley pulled out five blow darts and began filling them with the dangerous purple poison. Once she was done, Valley grabbed two skinny cylinders and handed them to Seven and Thorn carefully. "You put this end on your lips and blow in the cuco's direction. If you get them anywhere on their body, it'll slow their heart."

"If there's more than one cuco, we should try to take them out. That way we only have to fight one if it catches us tailing them," Seven said.

"There's no way the other one won't notice," said Valley.

"We could . . . lure them away from one another. Make sure they're too far to notice if the other goes down."

"Or we can just follow them and not engage, which is our best bet," Valley said. "Trust me."

Seven wasn't sure how she felt about trusting Valley. Even the thought of it made her feel weird. She let out a frustrated breath. "I still think my idea is better."

"As much as I'd like to prove you don't know it all, we're gonna lose our shot if we don't act fast," Valley said.

"You goats shouldn't be fighting right now!" Thorn said.

Seven's face went hot with anger. She was *not* a know-it-all. Valley was just mean.

As she opened her mouth to say that, a creature bounded out from behind a train car a few toadstools away as quick as a rat, and the Witchlings crouched low behind the car just in the nick of time.

"Do you think it saw us?" Thorn asked.

"I don't think so," Valley whispered. "Let's stay down and wait it out. When it's about twenty toadstools away, we'll start following."

"What if it ambushes us? Then what?" Seven asked. "You saw two prints—what if there are more?"

"All the more reason not to fight them," said Valley.

"Wait . . . wait . . . we never took the shushrooms," Thorn whispered in a panic.

The Witchlings opened their eyes wide. The cucos could hear them.

Just as they realized this, the monstruo landed in front of them with a *thump*.

It was at least as tall as a small tree but doubled over like it was picking something up, bringing its head closer to the ground. Its limbs were long and veiny and covered in bite marks and slashes. It looked almost like an enormous, rabid hyena. The cuco.

The Witchlings screamed in unison as the cuco knocked their wagon aside with a brush of one long gray hand and sent everything in it flying across the station tracks.

"Edgar!" screamed Seven, but there was no time to wait. She turned back to the cuco and shot her poison dart, aiming for its oversized eyes. The dart went right over its head, and it came even closer.

"Where's Valley?!" asked Thorn.

Seven whipped around, but Valley was nowhere to be found. Rats. Rats on a boat! Of course Valley bolted the moment things got bad. Seven *knew* they couldn't trust her. She just knew it.

"Thorn, it's up to you. Can you shoot it?" Seven had to try to stay calm, even though the monster was mere toadstools from them now, and she was beginning to think their task would end them before they could even begin it.

Thorn nodded and pressed the foxglove dart to her lips,

shooting it out and landing it right in front of the monster.

In the dirt.

"Okay, so we run. Let's go!" Seven grabbed Thorn's hand just like she had in the Cursed Forest that night, and they took off toward the town. Her heart was pounding and she kept looking around for Valley, but she had completely vanished. Had Valley shown her true colors and ditched them right when things got dangerous? Or had another cuco gotten her?

As if she'd conjured it from her thoughts, another slender gray creature, slimy and covered in what looked like sticky, prickly fur, blocked their path forward. Now they were well and truly trapped. The cucos stalked toward them slowly, growling horribly and licking their long tongues over their jagged teeth.

So many teeth.

And the Witchlings had no darts, no weapons, only a pocket full of shushrooms and each other. Seven pushed her anger aside and looked at Thorn, who was wearing one of her many black hats. A hat filled with pins. Seven's mind raced. Maybe they could use the pins as weapons, put them in their gloves, swipe at the cucos' eyes, and make a run for it. But before she could explain it to Thorn, a third cuco, taller than the others, emerged from the shadows.

It had blood streaked across its body.

Seven had to force herself not to collapse right then and there. The creature made horrible *click, click, click* noises like an enormous, slow-motion cicada. It bared its teeth in a gruesome smile, and it was clear this one was in charge. They were done for.

The monster bounded on Seven and Thorn, both enormous arms raised and ready to attack, when from the top of the train car a figure came flying at the creature and Valley Pepperhorn rained down on the cucos like a firestorm.

CHAPTER TEN
WITCHLINGS ON TOAST

"VOLCÁN!" SCREAMED VALLEY, and a burst of flame erupted from her hands.

There was blood coating the tips of Valley's hair and a gash on her hand. She had come flying from the top of a yellow train car, the waning sun lighting her up like a stained-glass window. The sight of the blood had made Seven's stomach turn, her fear becoming desperate worry. For *Valley*.

"Valley!" cried Thorn and Seven in unison, running over to her.

The biggest cuco howled as Valley's level-two fire spell lit up all around it. The other two cucos weren't as lucky. The spell slashed across their spindly bodies, and they bolted behind another train car.

"I'm okay, I'm okay." Valley was already getting up, brushing snow and soil off her cape and black jeans.

The snow beneath her was red.

"Are you hurt?" Thorn asked.

"It's just a scratch on my hand, maybe one on my leg; I'm okay. But look." Valley's eyes narrowed, and Thorn and Seven turned to follow her gaze.

The cuco was catching fire. Valley's spell had created a circle of molten lava around the monstruo, and it was closing in on the cuco. Its enormous shoulders heaved up and down like it was having a hard time breathing. The monstruo glared at them, baring its pointy teeth, saliva dripping from its open mouth.

"What now?" asked Thorn.

"We run before the other two recover. I got in some hits and slowed them down, but they're coming," said Valley. "The last thing we want to do is kill *all* the Nightbeast's cucos. It'll be much harder to find it before it leaves hibernation if we do."

We should've run in the first place, thought Seven, but Valley was hurt and Seven's commentary wasn't going to help.

Just as the Witchlings began to make a run for it, the cuco shrieked loudly and ran through the lava, straight at them. Fear prickled every inch of Seven's skin as the cuco, which was now very much on fire, growled and snapped just inches from their heads.

"Go, go, go!" yelled Valley, but in a flash, the other two cucos were on their heels as well.

"They're too fast!" screamed Seven.

"We can't fight them!" said Thorn.

Seven's legs burned as she ran, Thorn and Valley at her side. She looked back, and they were doing it—they were losing the cucos!

"Come on, we're almost in the clear!" said Seven.

"Uh, spoke too soon!" said Thorn.

The other two cucos rounded a corner, skidding and kicking up gravel and snow as they joined the first. They were bleeding in a few spots but not on fire anymore, and much, much faster. They would never be able to outrun these two. Seven had to do something, and fast.

She let Thorn and Valley pull ahead, gritted her teeth, and turned around, hands up.

"Viento!"

"Seven, no!" Valley said, but it was too late.

A strong wind whooshed around them and pushed the two cucos nearest them back. They careened against the cuco that was on fire, and their fur caught like a well-oiled wick.

"Yes!" said Seven when the viento spell rebounded and came back in her direction, bringing the fire with it.

"Oh my goats!" Seven turned to run when the fire caught the edge of her cloak.

"Ahhh!" Valley screamed as fire lit up her pink hair. Thorn ran over to try to help, when her own cape burst into flames. Now all three Witchlings were on fire and running in circles, trying—and failing at—spells to put the fire out.

Seven tried to think of how to put them all out at once. She briefly contemplated jumping in the Boggy Crone River, before remembering it was frozen. *Snow,* she thought.

"Jump in the snow!" she screamed, and lunged into an embankment of snow, putting the fire out. Thorn and Valley must've done the same, because the next thing Seven knew, the three Witchlings were side by side, smoke rising from them as they sat up.

"The cucos," Seven said, panicked and scrambling to get to her feet.

"Chill," said Valley. "Look."

From the embankment, they could see two piles of ash and large towers of smoke billowing in the wind. One of the cucos, the smallest, was dragging itself not in their direction but in the direction of the woods, a trail of dark, gooey blood in its wake. They had somehow managed to kill two of the cucos, with the third on its way to meet the same fate. And now their plan was well and truly cooked.

Seven began to cough—her insides were too hot. Blowback.

Something wet landed with a thump on Seven's foot, and she jumped.

"Edgar!" she cried, picking up the toad and kissing him without thinking.

"So the rumors *were* true," said Valley.

"This is no time for jokes! The cucos are gone, which means we can't follow them to the den," Seven said. "Now what?" She was lightheaded, and exhausted, and her skin felt like it was on fire. She buried her head in her hands.

"We're toast," said Valley, sounding defeated.

Thorn's stomach rumbled loudly.

CHAPTER ELEVEN
LIGHT AS A FEATHER

SOMEWHERE BETWEEN realizing the cucos were dead and the dread of their situation sinking in, Seven passed out right there in the snow. By then, some townsfolk had gathered near the scene of their battle, the fire from the cucos' charred and lifeless bodies creating a smoke signal. Not one of them stepped forward to help or see if the Witchlings were okay.

"Step ASIDE!" The Town Gran's voice broke through the crowd. The Town Uncle held on to his furry green hat as he ran beside her and toward the Witchlings.

"What happened?" The Gran picked Seven's head up off the ground. She wasn't unconscious, but she was barely holding on.

"Cucos, three of them. One was a mega cuco," Valley said.

"Did any of them take a shoe or a sock?" the Gran asked as she cradled Seven's head in her arms. She was reciting some sort of incantation between questions, probably something to give Seven strength.

"No, no clothing. Right?" Valley asked Thorn.

Thorn shook her head. "He did whack me into a train car and scratched us some, but that's it."

"Good. That at least is good."

"Also, my hands . . ." Valley held her hands out, and they were blistering and red.

"Rulean!" The Gran instructed the Uncle as he rubbed something on Valley's burned palms.

Seven was regaining a bit of strength now and began to cough. The Gran pulled a vial of something green and murky-looking from her cape.

"Drink, drink, quickly." She tipped the vial into Seven's mouth, and the green sludge slithered down her throat like a family of worms.

"I'm gonna barf," said Seven as she sat up.

The world around her had lost its color; everything looked gray and cloudy like a smudged watercolor painting.

"What's happening to me? Everything looks weird," said Seven.

"By chance, have you been using any magic above your proficiency level?" asked the Town Uncle.

Seven could feel her cheeks going hot, and she looked at Valley and Thorn, who were standing just off to one side of them. Their eyes opened wide with fear.

"That is *very* serious. Very serious indeed," the Uncle said.

Just then, the Gran broke into a coughing fit, sending the Uncle into a panic.

"Agua!" He conjured water but forgot the glass, and it rained down on his furry green hat, making it look like wet moss.

"Seven, do you think you can stand up?" the Gran whispered. Her coughing fit had stopped abruptly, although the Uncle was still fussing over her and oblivious to her suspicious recovery.

"I think so," Seven said.

The Gran stood up, holding her hand out for Seven. Seven planted one foot on the ground and then another, but when she grabbed the Gran's hand and tried to get up, her legs gave out from under her and she tumbled to the cold, snowy ground.

"We can carry her," Valley said, but the Gran waved her away. "You're in bad shape yourself. You might have to see the witch doctor for those hands." Seven glanced over at her coven, and both Valley and Thorn looked like they'd rolled around in a fireplace. Everything from their hair to their cheeks was covered in soot, and Seven had a feeling she looked just like them.

The Gran pulled her wand from her sleeve and pointed it at Seven. "Light as a feather."

A small stream of white light shot from the wand, and

Seven floated up, looking around in amazement as she did. She was enveloped in a softly glowing orb of light. It might be the closest she'd ever get to flying, she thought.

"Follow me," the Gran said to no one in particular, and they headed out in the direction of Twilight Square.

"Are you all right?" Thorn asked Seven.

It was weird. Seven was in a sitting position, floating in the air beside Valley and Thorn as they walked.

"Yeah, trying to figure out how I can float around in this bubble forever."

"You're making bad jokes, so that's a good sign that you're A-okay," Thorn said.

They passed the edge of the forest, the same spot where Thorn and Seven had entered the other night to save Beefy, when a wet, gravelly growl stopped them in their tracks.

"Stay back." The Town Gran moved at warp speed, pushing the Witchlings behind her. "Don't move."

"What was that?" Thorn asked anxiously.

"If I had to guess, I'd say the cuco that got away," Valley whispered. "The littlest one. It must have survived."

A shadow grew in the forest. The group took a step back. It was a small shadow at first, maybe a squirrel or a chipmunk, but then it grew larger and larger, quicker than any natural shadow could grow, until it loomed over them.

"Easy, easy. We do not want to lure it into town. Rulean, follow my lead and do not—"

"Acometer!" the Town Uncle cried out, and his body rushed forward toward the shadow.

"RULEAN!" called the Gran, but it was too late.

In the darkness of the forest, the Town Uncle cried out, and terrible ripping and crunching sounds emerged. Like he was being eaten.

"Witchlings, stay here!" cried the Gran. As she rushed into the forest, her glittering cape lit up the air around her, and a million tiny stars swirled and grew in the dark velvet fabric.

Silence hung in the air, but before they could think to speak, the Gran emerged from the Cursed Forest with the Town Uncle in her arms.

"It—it—it tried to eat me." The Town Uncle was crying as the Gran put him down. She was scowling.

"It didn't even scratch you," she pointed out. "Let's go. Now. To my cottage." The Gran made a circle around them with her wand. "Veloz," she said, and as they walked, and Seven floated, Ravenskill zoomed by them.

In just moments, they had reached Hallow Lane. They climbed the high steps that led to the Gran's home in record time, and Seven was grateful to be floating instead of being on foot.

"You'll wait here for your parents while I make sure none of you were hurt or infected," said the Gran, standing in front of the ivy-covered door to her home. They were actually going into her home, a place known as Starlight Cottage that few were allowed to enter. It was the most concentrated area of magic in all of Ravenskill. The safest place in all of Ravenskill too, Seven knew. It was the right place to recover after a monstruo attack.

"Wait," said Thorn as the Gran's hand turned the crystal knob on her door. "Where is the Uncle's hat?"

CHAPTER TWELVE
STARLIGHT COTTAGE

THE GRAN AND THE UNCLE exchanged a look.

The door to the Gran's cabin opened, and she ushered everyone inside with a wave of her hands. "Quickly," she said as Seven's bubble floated inside.

The three Witchlings looked up in unison as they entered the main room of Starlight Cottage.

"Whoa," Seven said.

From the outside, Starlight Cottage looked like a two-story townhome, covered in ivy and surrounded by flowers and a cobblestone sidewalk. Not much different from many of the homes in downtown Ravenskill. But Starlight Cottage was unlike anything Seven had ever seen. Instead of a second floor, the ceilings shot all the way up, and somehow every wall was made of sparkling glass. There were giant crystal bookcases along one wall, and like a scene out of one of

Seven's dreams, black planters with every kind of plant and flower you could think of hanging from the ceilings. Seven knew the Gran's home was high above the town, but it looked even higher from inside. In a crystal case at the top of the far wall sat the most powerful weapon in all of Ravenskill, and maybe the whole Twelve Towns: the Celestial Sword. The gem-covered blade was sharp enough to cut through a mountain, legend said, and only the Ravenskill Gran, as the eldest of all the Twelve Towns leaders, could use it safely. If anyone else tried to wield it, the sword would slowly burn them from the inside out.

"Holy rats," Seven said, staring at the sword.

"You can see all of Ravenskill!" squealed Thorn. She ran to one of the glass walls and placed her hands against the crystal surface.

"Yes, it is quite impressive." The Town Uncle beamed as he flitted around the room preparing tea. He still looked a bit sick, but overall he seemed okay. Seven wasn't sure what the significance of his hat going missing was, but she did remember Valley telling them not to lose any items to the cuco. She just wasn't sure why.

"You should see it when there is a waning moon," the Uncle said almost wistfully. "That is when you can truly appreciate its magic."

Valley and Seven joined Thorn at the windows. The Gran had a perfect 360-degree view of everything from their homes to the town to the Cursed Forest and the Boggy Crone River. They stopped on the right side of the room, where the train station was. The lights of Ravenskill glittered beneath them, smoke came from chimneys, and Seven could even see most of the mansions on the Hill from this side of the house. The glass itself had a beautiful iridescent sheen, as if it had been washed in the finish of mermaid pearls. The moonlight made streaks of rainbow across Starlight Cottage, and Seven realized suddenly how late it was.

"I must warn you," the Gran said. "This is the last time I can intercede on your behalf in such a direct way. My emotions got the better of me this time, seeing you Witchlings hurt . . . Well, it's been a long time since there's been an impossible task so dangerous. I wish there was more I could do, but alas. At least your parents will be arriving shortly, I imagine."

"My parents as well?" Valley asked.

"Your father, yes," the Gran said.

Valley shifted uncomfortably, and Seven's stomach dropped. She felt guilty for not trusting Valley earlier, and now, seeing how afraid Valley looked at the mention of her father, she felt even worse. Seven wished she could know what she was thinking or at least help her feel less afraid than she looked. Thorn reached out slowly for her hand, and Valley pulled away, shaking her head.

"I'm fine," she whispered.

"Did the cuco mark the Uncle?" Valley asked the Gran.

"I imagine that was the point of taking his hat, yes. I believe it meant to eat him, but when I arrived, it did the next best thing. We will not know for sure until . . . other events occur."

"What events? What does 'mark' mean? Can you let me out of here, Gran? Please?" Seven asked.

The Gran raised one hand and sent Seven's bubble over to the large white sofas at the center of the room. With a *POP*, the bubble burst like it were made of soap, and Seven fell gently onto the cushiony sofa.

"Do not get up. I have to inspect your limbs," the Gran said.

"My limbs are okay. I've been floating in a bubble for the past hour!"

"Marked . . . for tracking?" Thorn said. "Maman makes anti-tracking clothing sometimes for special clients. The cuco either wants to find the Uncle again later or find someone who's touched the hat . . ."

"Oh . . . oh no." Seven's hand flew to her mouth. Her mind flew back to the night of the Black Moon Ceremony. The Town Uncle crouching close to Beefy, the baby grabbing his hat, Seven taking it from her baby brother and handing it back. What if the remaining cuco was still looking for Beefy?

"The night of the Black Moon Ceremony, my baby brother touched the hat," Seven said in a daze. "I did too."

"My goodness," said the Uncle, his hands shaking.

The Gran nodded, not meeting Seven's eyes. "Their tracking magic is incredibly potent. All they need to do is be near an item touched by a mark to sense it. It's likely the cuco was near the edge of the forest, and when the Uncle, or more specifically his hat, came closer, the cuco believed it was Beefy. It either did not hurt Rulean because it realized he wasn't Beefy or because it knew I was close by and it was too hurt to fight both of us. Either way, you were incredibly lucky, and we will have to be vigilant so that you are safe." The Gran addressed the Uncle, whose face had gone whiter than the snow outside.

"Why does the Nightbeast want my brother?" asked Seven. He had almost been taken into the Cursed Forest once, and now this.

"Beefy is incredibly powerful for a baby. Maybe even destined for the Guard," said the Gran. "If the cucos are after him, it's so they can feed him to the Nightbeast. The stronger the witch, the more power the monstruo can absorb for itself and the more . . . delicious it is for the Nightbeast."

Seven shivered.

The cucos were after Beefy for his power, and the only thing standing in their way was Seven and her coven. It was all on their shoulders.

"I will make sure Beefy is safe. Do not worry," the Gran said.

"Now that I think of it, Beefy being tracked should've been a help to us," said Valley.

Seven narrowed her eyes.

"No, listen: If the cucos were after Beefy, that means all we had to do was wait for one to come get him, make sure it didn't, then follow it back to the Nightbeast."

"That seems risky," Thorn said.

"And we killed two of them . . ." said Seven. "*I* killed them."

"I do not think the last cuco survived either," the Gran said.

Valley shrugged. "Which is why I said *should've*. You know, nothing about how the Nightbeast or the cucos are behaving is normal: the jelly bean fish being untouched, trying to grab the Uncle when it was hurt. All uncharacteristic."

"There *is* something strange about this impossible task. First, your punishment of toadification . . . that should not be. Every task is different, every punishment as well. The Cursed Toads were the last to invoke the task and fail and they were toadified, so it stands to reason you should have gotten a new punishment altogether," the Gran said.

"Gran," said Seven, suddenly remembering something she had been wanting to ask, "do you remember the Cursed Toads' names?"

"I—" The Gran paused and stared off into the distance. "It's the weirdest thing . . . I can't say that I do. That time was very tumultuous. There were fires spreading across the towns, and I had a lot on my plate. Between the Spares, the fires . . . and Rulean getting sick."

"It was an awful time," the Uncle said, his cheeks red. "I am sorry I made it even harder, Gran."

"Do not be silly, Rulean," the Gran said, and turned back to the Witchlings. "You see, when the Spares of '65 were toadified, Rulean was inconsolable. He was sick for a very long time, because he had tried so hard to help those Spares. Within the boundaries of the impossible task, of course. It took many months before he was himself again."

"The impossible task is a pointless tradition," erupted Valley.

Thorn gasped, Seven stared at Valley with her mouth agape, and then they both looked at the Gran, waiting for her to respond. Would she make Valley's eyebrows grow uncontrollably? Seal her lips shut with frog glue? Banish her to the Cursed Forest?

"I cannot say I disagree with you," the Gran said. "But that belief will not keep it from happening."

Seven blinked. "*You* think the impossible task is pointless?"

The Gran smiled. "I didn't create the thing. But I have no choice but to uphold it if someone invokes it. Rulean, will you show Valley and Thorn the crystal sphere? I need to speak to Seven for a moment."

Seven's face went red. The Uncle nodded and ushered Valley and Thorn from the room.

When they were out of the room, the Gran sat beside Seven on the sofa. "Seven, there is something I want to give you." The Gran rotated one hand around the other and then turned her palm up. In it sat a ceramic bird. She nodded at Seven to pick it up, and she did. She turned the bright pink-and-blue bird over in her hand, and it came to life suddenly, shaking its feathers and chirping a beautiful song. Seven nearly dropped it in surprise. The Gran smiled, and the bird turned to ceramic once more.

"This is an ave. A very special item that should only be used in the direst of circumstances. If you hold it up to your mouth and blow, it will take a message to anyone of your choosing. It will only work once, and you must be incredibly careful about when you use it."

Seven nodded, not quite sure why the Gran was giving it to her and why she'd asked the other two to leave the room in order to do it. Was the Gran playing favorites?

"Listen carefully now. Only other Grans or Uncles can use an ave without being hurt; if you need to use it, you must be ready for the consequences."

"What consequences?" Seven was more confused than before.

"Using this will drain you of all your power. If you are hurt in battle, it will likely kill you. But if you are out of options, if there is nothing else to do, and all you *can* hope to do is save

Valley or Thorn"—the Gran gestured at the ave—"then use that."

"Why is this a secret? Why'd you send Thorn and Valley away?"

"You may tell them if you wish. But possessing this item, and having to use it if the time comes, is a heavy burden. Valley and Thorn are dealing with some pretty heavy burdens of their own. I did not want to add another. You've shown yourself to be capable of making hard decisions, Seven. The impossible task is not for the faint of heart, and it was invoked because of your bravery. I have a strong inkling you can handle this."

"I don't know if I can do it on my own," Seven said.

The Gran looked right into Seven's eyes. "You don't have to do it on your own, Seven. You are never alone—remember that. Even if the people you love and count on can't be by your side, they are always in your heart. We will all keep a closer eye on Beefy and his magic; there are ways to keep him close to home. I know you will figure out the impossible task with Thorn and Valley. Let them help you."

The Uncle came back into the room with Valley and Thorn, talking loudly about the wonders of crystal spheres, and Seven hid the bird in her cloak. She felt terrible about being singled out. She didn't want to be responsible for making that kind of choice. It was a lot to put on her shoulders.

"Rulean, come. We must prepare healing tonics for the

Witchlings to take tonight so their wounds don't get infected." A staircase appeared in the ground, and she floated down to some unknown room, the Town Uncle following close behind. The moment they'd left, Valley erupted.

"Great, another thing to worry about," Valley said.

"We should've had stronger capes on. That would've helped," said Thorn.

"What did the Gran want?" Valley asked Seven.

Seven's face went red. "Um, just to talk about the impossible task. How it was a big responsibility and blah, blah." Seven wanted to sink into quicksand. She wanted her shoes to sprout into a broom and take her away.

"Maybe if we weren't backed into a corner, we wouldn't have to make decisions like that. We're just kids!" Valley's eyes were narrowed, and she faced not just the town but the Hill, Seven realized.

"What else were we supposed to do, huh? Just be okay with a future as a Spare or Forever Witchlings with no magic? This town treats Spares like they've got badger boils; imagine if we couldn't even perform basic spells! We'd be the biggest outcasts in the history of the Twelve Towns. I'd rather be a toad," Seven said.

Valley turned around; her face was bright red, and her hands were balled into fists. She looked angry enough to explode. Her eyes darted around the room and landed on a side table next to the sofa. She stomped over to it, picked up an expensive-looking ceramic dish that was holding some sort of candies, and flung it at the window.

"Valley!" Thorn and Seven yelled in unison. The dish shattered, and the candy scattered everywhere. Seven hopped up from the sofa, but the moment she attempted to run toward Valley, her legs gave out and she fell to the floor.

"Oh, oh." Thorn stood between the two Witchlings now, not sure what direction to go in.

"Owwwwww." Seven grabbed her legs and groaned, the pain as sharp as porcupine needles. She should have listened to the Gran.

Thorn began to cry, which made tears stream down Seven's face too.

"Sorry, sorry!" Valley seemed to snap out of her rage and scrambled to pick up the broken pieces of the dish, also wiping tears from her own eyes. The Gran and the Uncle returned to a room in chaos, vials of tonic in their hands.

"I was gone for *less than two minutes*," the Gran sighed.

Thorn rushed over to help Seven back onto the sofa, and Seven watched as the Gran's eyes fell on Valley.

"Valley," she said, "come with me."

"It slipped. It was a mistake," Valley said quickly.

"We can talk about it here or in private; it's up to you," the Gran said calmly.

Valley dropped her head and followed the Gran downstairs. Seven desperately wanted to listen to what was going on. She was sure the Gran would ask Valley if she was okay or if there were troubles at home. Whenever a witch got in trouble at their school, that was one of the questions they asked, and Seven knew that firsthand—her run-ins with Valley hadn't come without the occasional visit to the Head Supreme's office.

"I hope Valley is okay," Seven said, then her hand flew to her mouth.

Thorn smiled and nodded. "Might as well stop pretending you aren't friends already."

"Whoa, whoa! I wouldn't take it that far." Seven held her hands up. "We're *not* friends. Not even close."

Thorn grabbed a pillow from the Gran's sofa and threw it at Seven. "Do you know how hard it is trying to make sure the two of you don't start fighting all the time? I'm very sleepy, Seven; you goats tire me out. But lately, it's just been nice. The air feels less sticky and heavy now that you're starting to get along. Don't mess it up." Thorn smoothed her skirt, not looking at Seven but not appearing afraid or shy either.

Seven smirked. Thorn was different than she'd first thought, or maybe she was changing, but Seven liked this side of her. Thorn should stand up to her and Valley. They *could* be butt-toads sometimes.

"And I hope she is okay too," Thorn said. Seven nodded. Friend or not, she was really worried about Valley.

That night in her room, Seven reinforced the wards her parents had helped her construct at her window.

"Acorazar," she whispered as she held her hands up toward the window, and a gold light sealed her room.

Seven flopped onto her bed and hugged a pillow, thinking of the very long day she'd just had. It was after midnight, and she still couldn't sleep.

Seven took the ceramic bird from her bedside table and turned it over in her hand. The Gran had assured her Beefy would be safe, but if the cuco was tracking her . . . and she was home . . . then that meant not just Beefy but her parents too would be in harm's way. She eyed Valley's copy of the latest Witches of Heartbreak Cove. She was itching to read it, and she really needed a distraction, but somehow, she couldn't even stomach fun right now. Instead, she grabbed her phone from her nightstand.

"Why not try for a little rejection instead," she said to herself cheerily, and typed out another message to Poppy.

"Hey Poppy . . . still alive?"

Seven bit her lip as she stared at her phone screen, nerves crawling like a billion bugs all over her skin. The phone in their kitchen rang its loud trill, and Seven's heart dropped. Late phone calls always made her think of bad news. When her own gran had passed, it had come with a phone call in the middle of the night.

Then Seven's portaphone lit up and Seven jumped, her heart racing at what Poppy might say.

But it was Valley.

"Are you awake?"

"What happened?" Seven wrote back.

"They took the Town Uncle. The cuco came for him. He's gone."

CHAPTER THIRTEEN
THE NIGHTBEAST'S CAVE

THE GRAN HAD BEEN ANGRIER than Seven had ever seen her when she announced via telecast that the Uncle had been taken. They'd found only one shoe, a trail of blood, and a half-eaten bog-pickle-and-chili-mustard sandwich. The Gran had left Ravenskill on the very night he'd gone missing, meeting with the Twelve Towns' council and combining their efforts to try to find him.

The telecast had run a story on the Uncle's life. Rulean Pennyfeather was an old man now, but he had been under the Gran's mentorship since he'd been chosen as an Uncle when he was thirteen, the customary age. A bluebird had been the first animal to ever speak to him, which was why his Uncle brooch was of the bird. The bluebird had sat on his shoulder, the story went, and warned him that he was about to step in a pile of goose poop. He'd run all the way to the

Gran's home, the bluebird clasped gently in his hands, and told her he'd been chosen as the next Uncle. In his excitement, he'd stepped in the goose poop anyway.

It was a job second only to the Gran and an incredible honor. His parents had been proud, his coven—Frog House—had risen in fame, and now, by just about every estimation, he was probably dead. Seven shivered at the thought and hoped all the town gossip was wrong.

On a more promising note, Seven had a new theory. "Our talk at the Gran's cottage got me thinking. If the Nightbeast doesn't have most of its minions anymore, it's the perfect time to strike. You said it yourself, Valley—that last cuco was nearly dead, so we'd only have to fight a weakened, hibernating Nightbeast and an injured, smaller cuco," she had messaged Valley and Thorn the night before.

"That's actually good thinking for once," Valley had responded. "And if it was willing to risk its life to take the Uncle, it might mean that the Nightbeast is getting hungrier for grown witches."

"And that could mean it's almost time for it to emerge," Thorn added.

"Exactly. We should go as soon as we can, super early morning before the Cursed Forest creatures wake from their sleep," Valley said.

"So we can go search tomorrow. Be ready," Seven had said.

The Witchlings were up before the sun on the very next day.

"We can start right here. Where the Uncle was nearly taken yesterday, and where you both found Beefy," Valley said as they stood at the edge of the Cursed Forest. It was foggy and cold out and still so dark you could see the stars and a sliver of the moon, but soon, the sun would rise over the Boggy Crone River.

It was time to execute their plan: visit all the known locations of the Bayahíbe rose, in hopes that one might point them to the Nightbeast. If they found it and it was daylight, they would come back to fight it, but at the very least, they'd know where to go.

Seven pulled out her flora field map, where she'd marked all the places they could find the flower beyond the Cursed Forest. "There are fields of Bayahíbe roses just beyond the Spector Lagoon," Seven said. "That's the first place to look since it's the closest to town. If the Nightbeast passed by this field when it arrived in Ravenskill, the flowers will be dead and we'll have an idea of at least a part of its path."

"Like breadcrumbs but dead flowers," said Valley.

"The Spector Lagoon . . ." said Thorn. "Is it filled with . . . ghosts?" She whispered the last word.

Seven smiled nervously. "Well, yeah. But no need to be scared. Most ghosts are real nice."

Thorn clapped once and smiled. "I *love* ghosts."

Seven and Valley exchanged a look.

"Just when you think you know a witch," said Seven.

They each took a small nibble of shushroom to quiet their steps and crossed over into the Cursed Forest.

It was much colder in the Cursed Forest, and as if on instinct, the Witchlings pulled closer together. Seven flinched when Valley's shoulder touched hers, but she was too cold and too scared to pull away. They walked quickly and without a sound, passing long shadows and the ominous snicker of the mischievous duendes who could take your rucksack just as easily as they could steal your memories. Seven's fear rose with every second that passed. For what seemed like the two hundredth time, she went over their plan, she touched her pockets to be sure she had her foxglove darts, she recited their combat spells under her breath. They had been walking for over twenty minutes now, the woods thick and dark despite the daylight that must be approaching outside it. It was like they were in a massive empty room with thick curtains pulled all around them. As they walked, Valley inspected tree after tree, looking for Nightbeast or cuco hairs and poking at animal droppings and shaking her head at Seven and Thorn.

"No luck. The Nightbeast should've left some trace when it traveled into Ravenskill, the cucos should leave traces whenever they venture out of their den, but it's like they're hairless and don't poop or something," Valley said.

"We're almost there," said Seven, conferring with her

map by the waning light of the moon and stars. "The lagoon is at the edge of the Cursed Forest; just beyond it should be a big field with our flower."

The Witchlings picked up their pace, which was proving difficult as their boots sank into the dark red mud.

"Just a little farther," Seven said. "I can see the light breaking through the trees up ahead."

It was the deepest into this forest Seven had ever been, and she begrudgingly admitted to herself that Valley *had* had a point about their timing. She never imagined they'd get through the Cursed Forest so quickly and without incident. A blue light pierced through a wall of brambles ahead and pulled Seven from her thoughts. The Spector Lagoon. They'd reached the edge of the Cursed Forest.

"How are we going to get through these brambles? They look painful," Thorn asked.

"We can find another path," Valley answered. "It might take longer, but—"

"There *is* no other path to the Bayahíbe roses. There'll be brambles anywhere between this side of the Cursed Forest and the fields," said Seven confidently. "We can try a spell. The machete spell is silent."

"Oh, you're right!" Thorn said.

"It's not a good idea, Salazar. Trust me."

Seven resisted the urge to scoff. Trust Valley? Yeah, right. It had been her idea to follow the cucos before they were prepared, and look how that turned out. Seven knew the only way to get something done was to do it her way.

"I'm gonna try it," Seven said. She threw up her arms dramatically and tilted her face toward the sky, trying to pull as much magic into the level-four spell as possible.

"Wait, Seven, don't!" Valley said, but it was too late.

"Machete!" Seven said, making a cutting motion with one arm.

Red light cut across the air right in front of them with a loud crack, throwing them back and into the mud. It made the air so hot, Seven's curls were plastered to her forehead in an instant.

But it had worked. The brambles that once stood before them were completely gone, the trees on either side of them charred. Had the spell not thrown them back, they would have been charred too.

"Holy rats," said Thorn. "That was cool."

"Are you bonkers, Salazar?" Valley seethed. "You almost got us all killed, and you probably alerted every monstruo in Ravenskill."

Valley struggled to her feet, slipping in the mud as Thorn got up and helped Seven do the same.

"I didn't think it would actually *work*," said Seven. "I've tried that spell a dozen times . . ."

"But never in the Cursed Forest. Magic here is corrupted and weird, and it's not safe to use it if you haven't completely mastered it." Valley was wiping the mud from her coat.

"At least the brambles are cut. Look." Thorn pointed ahead, and there, through the now open path, was a lagoon, shining with beautiful crystal-clear waters and what looked like hundreds of blue lightning bugs.

"The Spector Lagoon," said Seven. "Come on!"

They ran toward the edge of the forest, and all at once, the mud began pulling them down. What was left of the brambles and the trees around them reached out and caught on their cloaks and rucksacks.

"What's happening?" yelled Thorn.

"The forest is trying to keep us from leaving. Don't try that little trick again, Seven, or you'll barbecue the three of us."

"Can we fight about this later? I'm up to my knees in cursed mud!" Seven said.

Indeed, both Seven and Valley had been so busy scowling at each other that they hadn't noticed the moment they'd sunk, almost to their knees, in the thick red mud. Thorn had managed to grab on to a vine from the Spector Lagoon and was pulling herself out.

"Hold on!" she yelled as, with a great effort, she got out of the mud and onto solid ground. The Cursed Forest made a smacking noise like lips closing, and Thorn shivered. "Gross. Here, hold on!" She stretched over and passed the vine to Seven and Valley, and heaved.

"Unghhhhh." Thorn pulled, and Seven tried to find

purchase somehow, but there was just nothing to anchor herself to. The mud was too heavy, and it was sucking them both under.

"Give me more of the vine—I can't get a good grip!" Valley said.

"I can't! There's no more!" said Thorn desperately.

Valley tugged hard anyway, pulling Seven deeper into the mud.

"Stop!" Seven yelled, but it was too late.

The vine snapped, and Thorn tumbled over with half of it still uselessly gripped in her hands.

"Quick," Seven gasped. "Do we know any spells that might help?" The mud was almost up to her shoulders now.

"My mind is goose poop right now. I can't think of a thing," Valley said.

As Seven and Valley struggled in the mud, Thorn scrambled around, trying to find another vine to throw to them—but there was nothing. She threw her hat off in frustration, her face red and streaked with tears. "I don't know what to do! I can't do this again!" She looked around desperately and then began to yell, "Help! Somebody help!"

Seven highly doubted that anyone would come to help them all the way at the edge of the Cursed Forest.

"I'll be right back!" Thorn ran the few toadstools toward the Spector Lagoon, and as she entered through the curtain of the willows surrounding the area, what looked like hundreds of red eyes opened and blinked at once.

"Thorn!" Valley called out. But she was gone.

The mud was touching Seven's chin now. Her heart was beating so hard she was sure every creature in the Cursed Forest could hear it. All around them, the forest was waking up after the few short hours of rest; soon they would have more than the mud to worry about. If they didn't drown first.

Just as Seven was beginning to worry Thorn wasn't coming back, she emerged from the Spector Lagoon, with a stream of ghosts behind her. They were glowing a brilliant blue, with red eyes. The swarm of ghosts descended on Valley and Seven, and Seven couldn't help but scream.

She could hear Thorn yell from the other side but couldn't see; the light from the ghosts all around them was too bright. Suddenly she was being pushed up and out of the mud and was flying in the air. Both Seven and Valley landed with a *thud* on the hard ground on the other side of the Cursed Forest mud trap—scared but alive.

Thorn was doubled over, her hands on her knees and shaking. "Don't do that again. I thought you goats were rat food."

The swarm of ghosts floated back into the lagoon, and Seven struggled to her feet. "Thorn, that was fast thinking. Thanks. Are you all right?"

Thorn straightened up and nodded, and Seven couldn't help but think how hard it must be for Thorn to watch people she cared about almost croak. Just like she'd watched her brother be taken.

"We have to keep going before it gets any later," Valley said.

"Yeah," Seven said, still annoyed at Valley. "Let's go."

They ran through the Spector Lagoon, where ghosts were yawning awake and chatting with one another. The lagoon was glittering and beautiful, with hundreds of sparkling lights and glowing plants. They ran along the edge of the lagoon on the—thankfully—solid ground. Some ghosts were sleeping in the boughs of the trees, while others looked at them curiously. There were ghosts with hair rollers in and others making what looked like glowing coffee, and one very animated ghost exercise class. Seven held in a laugh. It wasn't often you spotted a ghost in Ravenskill, but she had seen a few here and there. Never in tights and dancing to sick drumbeats though.

"Thanks," said Seven, waving as they passed.

"Noooo prooooblem," they all said in unison.

The Witchlings broke through the lagoon to the other side, and they were officially out of the Cursed Forest.

"We almost didn't make it." Valley scowled.

"But we did, so chill," said Seven.

"You two are so busy fighting, you never notice anything," said Thorn. "Look."

Before them was an enormous field of Bayahíbe flowers. And they were very much alive. The flowers looked like a sea of pink, undulating in the wind. They looked almost holographic, like they were glowing from within.

"Rats!" cried Seven.

"All that for nothing," Valley said. "But there are more flower patches to check."

Seven knew Valley was right. And it would've been too lucky to find a trace of the Nightbeast on their first try. But she was still disappointed, and now they'd have to go all the way back through the Cursed Forest.

"I've never seen glowing flowers like this before," said Thorn. "They're pretty."

"I . . . don't think they're supposed to glow. Maybe these do because of how close they are to the Cursed Forest," Valley said.

"Hmmm." Seven quirked an eyebrow. "Hold on."

Seven crouched down near one of the flowers and touched its petals softly. She pulled a small vial from her rucksack and poured two droplets of a clear, glittering substance onto one of its petals. The flower shivered, and the pink of its petals began to run like it was melting.

"Oh my goats," said Thorn.

As the color drained completely from the flower, it withered from a glowing pink to a dusty gray. It *was* dead.

"The flowers aren't alive," Seven said. "They've just been enchanted to look that way."

"Who would go through the trouble of enchanting a whole field of flowers?" Thorn asked.

"Someone who wanted to conceal the Nightbeast," Valley said.

"Can Nightbeasts cast spells?" Thorn asked.

Valley solemnly shook her head no.

The Witchlings were silent for a few moments. "We can figure that all out later. We know the Nightbeast is probably around here somewhere. Let's go find it," Seven said.

"I don't know . . . I'm afraid we've made too much noise already. We were supposed to surprise it, remember?"

"We could at least find its hiding place," said Seven.

Valley shook her head and sighed. "Fine. But we have to be as quiet as possible."

Thorn zipped her lips and threw away the key.

"We all know *that* doesn't work," Seven said, and they began to walk through the field and toward the mountains.

"The Nightbeast will likely pick a cave, some sort of enclosed space, to gather strength. The caves at the base of Oso Mountain are our best chance," Valley said.

There were hundreds of caves in Oso Mountain, but with the enchanted flowers here, it was a sure bet that they were close.

They walked carefully through the field, the shushrooms quieting their steps. When they reached the edge, they crept toward the closest cave.

"Prints," Valley said, pointing in front of them. "This is it. Get your sleeping tonic ready, Seven. We flood the cave with tonic, then attack."

"It feels kinda wrong attacking a sleeping monstruo," said Seven.

Valley gave a small laugh. "The tonic will make it woozy at best. Don't worry, we'll still be at a disadvantage."

"I'm just glad we don't have to deal with that big cuco," Thorn said.

Valley and Seven nodded in agreement.

"I'll go ahead," Seven whispered, and they scaled the wall of the mountain toward the opening of the first cave.

This was it. They were going to face the Nightbeast. Seven was sure they could stop it and save Beefy from being eaten and themselves from being toads. They could save their whole town. They reached the mouth of the cave, and Seven looked back at Thorn and Valley.

"Ready?"

"Born ready," said Valley.

Thorn just nodded, but her face was white as a sheet. They were all afraid, Seven knew, but she worried the most for Thorn.

"Don't worry," Seven whispered. "I won't let it get you."

She swung the sleeping tonic into the mouth of the cave and waited. One, two, three seconds. It should take about ten to permeate any space and knock out anything within.

"Masks," Seven whispered, and they pulled the enchanted anti-sleeping masks, courtesy of Thorn, over their faces. "Let's go."

They crept into the cave, their eyes adjusting to the darkness, but when they reached the far wall, they realized . . .

"Empty!" Valley threw her witch's hat to the ground.

"We were so close," said Seven, deflated.

"We were, and it escaped." Valley ran to another, smaller entrance to the cave a few toadstools away and pointed at the ground. "Look, fresh prints, going out of the cave." She ran out, following the tracks, with Seven and Thorn trailing her. They followed the prints for a few seconds until they reached the field and a fresh path of dead roses.

"It must've just taken off!" Valley said. "And look. More cuco prints."

"Let's follow the tracks," said Seven.

They walked through the field in single file, following the giant prints. Seven thought all three of them could fit inside one print at a time.

"Stop," Valley said. "Get down."

The Witchlings crouched in the field. A swarm of shadows danced in and out of view on the path just ahead.

"Shoot, Shroudeds," said Thorn.

"Is there a way around them?" Seven asked.

The three Witchlings looked around for a way to bypass the Shroudeds and still follow the prints, but they were bordered by Oso Mountain on one side and a marsh on the other. There was no way forward. They doubled back and out of the Shroudeds' path.

"We could've fought them!" Seven said. "We were so close."

"No way we could take on Shroudeds if the Nightbeast also joined in the fight. And, yes, we *were* so close," Valley said, spinning on Seven. "And it got away because of you!"

"Me?!" Seven was offended. "What did I do?"

"You used that bonkers machete spell! The plan was to catch it by surprise, and instead you alerted everyone we were here!"

"How was I supposed to know it would make noise? It was supposed to be a silent spell!"

"Stop fighting!" Thorn yelled, but Valley and Seven were too heated to listen. The fight felt like all the horrible things they'd ever felt about each other bubbling over like a bad potion in a cauldron.

"I told you. I told you not to do it! And you didn't listen because you're a know-it-all!"

Seven stepped back. Ouch.

"It's a fact that spell is supposed to be a quiet one, or I would've never tried it."

"If you would've just listened to me, we would be fighting the Nightbeast right now. Instead we have to start from scratch, our time's running out, and it's all on you!"

"That's not fair!" Seven said.

"What's it going to take for you to start trusting me, Seven? How many times do I have to prove myself?" Valley was screaming now.

Angry tears streamed down Seven's face. "I don't know.

Can you erase everything you did to me? Make all the hurt I felt go away magically? If you have a spell for that, go for it! You want me to suddenly start trusting you after you played mean tricks on me for years?"

Valley went silent at that, and the three Witchlings stood there awkwardly.

"Maybe we can talk about this later, when you both aren't so angry?" Thorn tried.

"Fine by me. I don't particularly feel like talking to Seven anyway," Valley said, and stomped off angrily in the direction of the Cursed Forest.

"You okay?" Thorn asked Seven, who was wiping away her tears.

"Let's just go home. I've had enough of Nightbeast tracking to last my whole life."

CHAPTER FOURTEEN
SO, YOU LOST YOUR BEST PAL, HUH?

"HEY, WAIT UP!"

Seven's heart caught in her throat at the sound of that voice. *Poppy.*

Seven turned around as Poppy caught up to her, cheeks bright pink like she was either out of breath or embarrassed. Seven was on her way home after the failed Nightbeast tracking that morning.

Now Seven was standing face-to-face with her best friend. Or ex–best friend. She really wasn't sure anymore.

"How ya doing?" Poppy asked.

"Oh, you know, I'm a Spare witch, with an impossible task and a Nightbeast to defeat." *And a friend who keeps ignoring me,* Seven thought but didn't say out loud. "So I'm doing pretty fantastic."

Poppy frowned. "I'm sorry I haven't been around much

since the ceremony. You wouldn't believe the stuff they make you do for House Hyacinth. There's an entire course on the past covens, with super-secret info and banquets and flying lessons, and it hasn't even been two weeks yet. I've been *so* busy."

Seven tried, very hard, not to scream. It wasn't that Seven wasn't happy for her—begrudgingly, but she was. At least one of them had made it into their dream coven. But Poppy was . . . being a total warlock. She tried not to let the anger show on her face, but Poppy seemed to notice.

"Sorry, sorry. How's it been with *Valley*?" Poppy asked.

"Believe it or not, she hasn't been the worst part of this whole thing. But I don't want to talk about Valley right now," Seven said, remembering with a painful pang the fight they'd just gotten into. Instead, Seven gathered all her strength, and then just let out the thing she'd been wanting to say. "I'm . . . I'm mad at you, Poppy."

Poppy took a step back; she looked shocked. "Why are you mad at me?"

"Because you ditched me. The second you got placed in House Hyacinth, it was like I was a ghost. You haven't sent me messages or called or anything!"

"Seven, I just told you I was really busy. You're being selfish."

"*I'm* being selfish? Me? You mean your former best friend who is a Spare and *might die* because she has to fight a murderous Nightbeast and you haven't even checked on me, once, because . . . let me check my notes . . . you were going to banquets?!" Seven's face was hot, her whole body was hot. With anger and sadness and indignation.

Poppy had always been the leader, the more popular one, the one adults trusted more, and Seven was always second best. She still was. But she hadn't thought that mattered, not so long as they were friends, but maybe they weren't friends anymore. Maybe they never were.

"It's not my fault you're a Spare. Or that you invoked the impossible task. It was rotten luck, but don't take it out on me!"

"I just . . . thought you'd be there for me. That's all. I thought you'd still be my friend even if we weren't in the same coven."

"We are still friends . . ."

"Friends talk to each other! They don't run away when things get hard. You left me behind, Poppy!"

"Because . . . I just feel weird around you and I don't know why."

"Oh." The words were like ice water, so cold it stung. A lot.

They stood there in excruciating silence, and Seven wished a dragon would come and eat her alive. Or maybe pick her up and throw her over one of the mountains around their town. Anything but this. Tears streamed down Poppy's face now, and Seven did not reach out and hug her like she had so many times before.

"You don't have to feel weird. I'm still the same Seven."

"And I'm still the same Poppy," Poppy said. "We're just on different paths now."

Seven nodded and tried to hold back tears. She wasn't sure how much more crumminess she could take. She couldn't deal with getting into yet another fight today. She felt like everything was coming down all around her, and she didn't know how to fix any of it.

"I've gotta split," Seven said coldly. "Sorry about . . . everything."

"It's okay. I'm sorry too." Poppy wiped her tears just as two of her coven members walked up to them, hooking their arms in Poppy's, their luxurious purple capes billowing softly in the crisp morning breeze.

"We're going for waffles, Poppy. Wanna come?" asked one of her coven mates, eyeing Seven with interest but not unkindly.

"Sure." Poppy eyed Seven sadly. "See ya."

"See ya," Seven said. As she watched Poppy walk off with her coven, skipping toward one of the mansions on the Hill and talking animatedly, Seven knew they weren't just on different paths: They were in two separate worlds.

CHAPTER FIFTEEN
BOGGS FERRY RACCOONS VS. STORMVILLE LIGHTNING FORKS

WHEN SEVEN ARRIVED AT THORN'S two days after their expedition, it had been a bit awkward, with nobody daring to bring up their fight. Valley was acting as if nothing had happened, and Seven did the same. It was easier that way. Her nerves getting the best of her, Seven began to talk nonstop and, over Thorn's grandma Lilou's famous fluffy pancakes, recounted the epic fight of the day before. Now they were on their way to a toad race in town. They had agreed they needed a day off. Just one day to forget about the task, and their fighting, and the Nightbeast.

"Forget Poppy Fairweather," Valley said on their way to the toad race.

"Poppy Mayweather, and I can't just forget her. We've been best friends since diaper days," Seven said.

"Sounds like the queen of the butt-toads to me," Thorn said.

"Thorn, you've been hanging out with Valley too much."

"I heard that from you, actually." Thorn blushed.

"Roasted," said Valley with a triumphant smile, high-fiving Thorn.

Seven put a brave face on, joking around and pretending her world wasn't completely upside down. The argument with Valley and then Poppy immediately after had given her a stomachache that not even her father's soothing guinea-hen-weed tea could help. It was hard to focus on . . . anything. Seven felt like she was a balloon with way too much air in it and that any moment she might burst. At least they could just have fun today.

"How are we still having a match? There is a crisis afoot!" one witch in the crowd walking to the race said.

"She has a point," Seven whispered to Thorn and Valley.

It had been nearly three days since the Town Uncle was snatched from his bed in the middle of the night, and the town had been in absolute chaos ever since, which only seemed to add to the electricity in the air for the race.

Every four years, the Twelve Towns had a magic tournament—the Golden Frog Games, where the towns would compete in everything from toad racing to spell casting to enchanted dressmaking. The tournament wasn't for another year, but there was a series of friendlies—matches that got the crowds excited for the oncoming competitions—throughout the year before. Today there was a toad racing match, and the Stormville racers had arrived to pit their toads against the team from Boggs Ferry—Thorn's old town. Seven was just glad Edgar Allan Toad had absolutely nothing to do with the competitions. They would lose *for sure*.

"Can't wait to see these toads race. It would take Edgar a week to complete a lap here," Seven said with a chuckle.

"How is Edgar Allan Toad doing, by the way?" Valley asked.

"Cranky and slow—same old. It was like nothing happened the other day with the cuco, even though he went flying, like, twenty toadstools! But the Uncle spoke to him before he got, uh, taken. And he's fine," said Seven. "He did ask for spicier flies though." Seven smirked, and Thorn and Valley laughed.

In the winter, every town sport took place in the Ravenskill Sports Egg. It was, like its name suggested, shaped like an egg on its side. It was white and gleaming, and the pride of Ravenskill, a town that took sports and competition very, very seriously. Seven was excited to watch the match and get a break from fighting monstruos and getting stuck in cursed mud.

Teams from the other Twelve Towns often came to the Ravenskill Sports Egg, or the Spegg as it was sometimes called, to practice, and often inter-town matches took place there even when Ravenskill wasn't one of the teams playing. A big crowd was gathered outside the Spegg, waiting for the doors to open before the match.

"Oh good, we're not too late for the rush," Seven said.

The rush was how seats were picked. Witches ran like mad to try to get the best ones.

"The key is," Seven said, gesturing the movements with her hands and explaining to Thorn, who had never been to a match at the Spegg, "to run *under* grown-ups' legs and get to the front of the line. You've gotta crouch sometimes, but it's worth it. Sometimes witches cheat and use spells, but once you're inside, spells only work for team members and only spells that are allowed for the scheduled sport. If you try to do anything else—"

"You smell like rotten eggs," Valley finished, her smirk widening. "But that doesn't mean we can't use a spell *now*."

Before Seven could protest, Valley whispered, "Veloz," waving her hand across all three of their feet. The spell moved quickly, like its name suggested, and took the Witchlings faster than fast toward the front of the line, ducking and crawling under grown-ups' legs as they did.

"Hey!" "Cheaters!" "It's the soggy Spares!" yelled some of the other spectators, and Seven's cheeks went hot from the name-calling. But the moment they reached the front of the line, the doors opened. The crowd rushed into the stadium, a stampede to get the best seats.

"Who's soggy now?" Seven said as they ran into the arena and snagged courtside seats.

They settled into the big, comfy seats and high-fived one another.

"I've never gotten seats this good!" Seven said.

"Stick with me." Valley smiled.

Food vendors walked up and down the aisle yelling, "Granpopcorn, popcorn just like your grandpa use to make!" or "Fairy floss!" and Seven's stomach grumbled.

"I'll go get us snacks," Thorn said, and the other two Witchlings nodded enthusiastically.

Thorn was halfway up the stairs and running after a vendor when Seven realized she'd been left alone with Valley. All day, Thorn had been there, so it wasn't too bad. But now it was just them. Awkward Town, population: 2.

Seven looked out onto the racetrack, but there was nobody there but a lone witch spraying anti-cheating mist onto the asphalt. She was trying her hardest to avoid looking at Valley and avoid breaking the spell of whatever had kept them from going at each other's throats that morning.

Thorn was like a magical buffer. It was hard not to be friendly when Thorn was around, if only because it made Seven feel like a crummy witch to be mean or have not-nice thoughts. Seven fully intended not to speak, but then Valley cleared her throat.

"I've been meaning to talk to you."

Oh no, here it was. The confession that Valley still hated Seven. That she had been pretending to be so nice for so long because of the coven. That the moment their circle was sealed, it was back to pranks and cruel jokes.

"I wanted to say . . ." Valley paused, squeezing her eyes shut tight as if she were gathering courage, before opening them and looking right at Seven. "I wanted to say I'm sorry."

Seven opened both eyes wide in disbelief. "You're *sorry*?"

"I think . . . I mean . . . okay. I'm not great at making friends. And I think you've got the wrong idea about me."

"You've been bullying me for two years straight," Seven said.

"They were more like misunderstandings."

"You mean the rat in my backpack when you know I'm scared of them? The mayo in my shampoo? What about stealing my lunch money?" Seven asked. "Those misunderstandings? And what about the fight the other day? You . . . said really mean things about me."

Valley took another deep breath. "I overheard you telling Poppy you wanted a pet. I had an extra pet rat and thought you'd like it. His name is Cotton Swab, and he's actually really nice. I trained him to find nightshade and doll's eyes since we're low on poisonous plants in Ravenskill and I know you like plants. Also he knows how to roll over."

Seven's mouth fell open. "Wha—"

"The mayo was because you were complaining to Poppy that your hair was really frizzy because of the humidity. I read in my mom's magazine article that mayonnaise helps make your hair shiny, so that's why I put it in your shampoo."

Seven shook her head. No, no, no, she couldn't have been

jumping to conclusions this whole time! "But you also said mean things about me! That I'm a know-it-all. And that I loved kissing Edgar Allan Toad!"

"Which is why I'm apologizing. I'm not perfect."

"Why didn't you just talk to me? Tell me about the mayo and Cotton Swab instead of sneaking?" Seven asked.

"I tried to surprise you with Cotton Swab and that had *not* worked." Valley looked down, and Seven's cheeks turned red, remembering how angry she'd gotten. How she'd yelled at Valley for it. "I didn't think you'd listen about the mayo either, but I swear I didn't think it would make you smell like boiled gym socks! You always just seemed so . . . popular. I was scared if I tried to talk to you, you'd laugh at me."

"I had a grand total of one good friend at school," Seven said, and her stomach turned at the use of the word *had*. Poppy *had* been her friend. Not anymore.

"That's one more than I ever had," Valley said, her cheeks bright pink.

Seven still thought Valley should've told her. Just because she hadn't meant to hurt her didn't mean she hadn't. Seven still had a right to be upset, but she could tell by the look on Valley's face now that she hadn't meant to bully her. At least not in those two instances.

"What about the lunch money?" Seven asked.

"The lunch money was because . . ." Valley took a deep

breath again, and her voice hitched with the next sentence. "My dad took food away for a bit as punishment for a bad grade. I was just really hungry and not thinking straight. But that's no excuse. I shouldn't have taken your money, and for that, I am sorry and I will pay you back, promise." Valley held her head up, much like she had at the Black Moon Ceremony, and Seven's heart felt like it had just shattered into a million pieces.

"I didn't start the thing about your toad. Honest. Although I did laugh when someone else said it in class and gossiped about it with some other kids. I just wanted to be your friend but kept messing up and it made me angry. I shouldn't have done any of those things though or yelled at you yesterday and called you a know-it-all. It wasn't nice and I'm sorry about that too."

Things finally started making sense. The way Valley would run away after one of her pranks, how she never seemed to gloat in the moment. How she'd brush Seven off after, when really she was just trying to get away. It was not because she was a bully; it was because she was afraid. Because she was hungry.

"How long did your dad keep you from eating?" Seven asked softly.

"Two days." Valley looked down at her black boots. "It's okay. He said he was sorry."

"Does your mom know?"

Valley hesitated. "No. She was out of town for a book thing that week, and my dad told me not to tell her. Things are better now, promise. It only happened once, and it was because I didn't do well on a test. It was my fault."

"Valley, that's never okay. You should always get to eat. Are you sure your mom . . . ?"

"She can't know. Please, can we just drop it? I don't want to upset Thorn."

"But, Valley—"

"Please, Seven?" Valley looked desperate.

"Fine, okay," Seven said. After a few moments of awkward silence, she cleared her throat. "I'm . . . I'm sorry too. About not listening to you out in the Cursed Forest. I really didn't know about how the magic there would affect the machete spell, but I shouldn't have been such a butt-toad."

"Yeah, you kinda were." Valley smirked.

"Okay, okay." Seven smiled.

"But I was too. Let's not be like that anymore. Let's try to, like, work together maybe?" Valley said.

"Deal," Seven said.

She felt warmer toward Valley than she probably ever had, but her mind was lingering on what Valley had said about her dad. Something told Seven she had to talk to someone about it. It wasn't the kind of thing you kept a secret.

Just then, Thorn came back with an armful of snacks.

"What did I miss!" Thorn's voice was muffled in cardboard and plastic wrapping. Valley and Seven helped her, and they all settled in for the race.

As they ate their granpopcorn and chocolate-covered goose eggs, Seven looked up to the nosebleed seats. They were way, way up, and she knew that after they'd solved, or failed, the impossible task, they'd never be able to sit this close to a game again. It wasn't illegal, as a Spare, to sit courtside or to switch jobs like Mrs. Laroux had said, but that didn't mean it was done. Spares usually came to games with their employers because they couldn't function without their assistants, but were relegated to the farthest, most uncomfortable seats. Even if there was room closer to the court.

Seven took a bite of the sweet, sweet fairy floss (it was onion-and-bean-flavored, Seven's favorite) and sighed. There were a million little things she never considered about being a Spare because she never thought it could happen to her. Now that it had, those things were crashing down on her, hard and fast. It was painful to know that even if they survived the Nightbeast, even if they solved the task and avoided being toadified, their lives would still be worse than rats on a boat.

"Let's just enjoy today, like we said," Thorn said softly. Seven had been staring at the three Spares sitting in the nosebleed seats, her eyes watering, and she guessed Thorn had noticed.

Seven swallowed a big chunk of fairy floss. "You're right. No despair for the day."

She smiled at Thorn and turned back to the court just as the teams made their way out of the locker rooms.

"I've never seen the Stormville Lightning Forks play," Thorn said excitedly.

A song by Kill Le Goose started playing, one of Seven's favorites to get her pumped before a test, and the lighting in the stadium went darker.

"I love this song," said Valley.

"Me too!" Thorn said.

"Le Goose is one of my favorite bands," the Witchlings said in unison, and then began to laugh.

As the rapid guitar riff went off, the Boggs Ferry Raccoons emerged, their gray-and-black uniforms sparkling in the disco lights.

"Oh, oh, that's Tia Stardust," said Thorn, pointing at their star racer, her eyes welling up.

A second later, the announcer said, "NUMBER FOUR! TIAAAA STARDUST and her toad BOB!" The crowd cheered wildly, and Thorn whooped and waved her witch's hat in the air.

Tia waved at the cheering crowd as she ran in place, a number four forming in midair in sparkling lights courtesy of trained fireflies. Her jet-black hair was cut in a short, blunt bob, just like Thorn's. Seven looked over, and Thorn was mesmerized. Tia was clearly her idol.

The rest of the teams were introduced and cheered on by the crowd, and finally it was time for the race to begin. It would be a relay-style toad race today, with each toad hopping

131 toadstools before passing a baton to their teammate. Ten toads total were racing for each team, and the first to reach the finish line would be the winner of the race. It was the very first friendly, which often set the tone for the rest of the games for the year to come. Whoever came out as the favorite after the friendly matches was often a crowd favorite and, in any case, would have all eyes on them.

The racers got into place and waited for the official song to be announced. All toads might not be as mean as Edgar Allan Toad, but they *were* all just as finicky. Toads only raced to music, specifically classical music, and winning depended not just on speed but on how much they could keep pace with the rhythm of a song. They didn't hop or run a race so much as spun and danced their way to the finish line. It was no wonder Seven's toad was the worst; he hated music and croaked loudly whenever she tried to train him using any of the approved classical music for training. Much of it was from the humdrum (what witches called non-magical humans) world, and today's race would be no different. The announcer said Overture (Suite) No. 2 in B Minor by Johann Sebastian Bach would be the racing song of choice.

"Oh, this should be good," Seven said, rubbing her hands together as the racers got into place.

Stormville's number eight, Rifky Highmore, was the starting runner, while Boggs Ferry had La Sala Sparrow as their starter. They crouched in place, sizing each other up before carefully placing their toads on the rubber rainbow track but not letting go just yet. Each toad held a baton, sparkling with the prismatic light of anti-cheating magic.

"On your marks, get set, TOAD!" The announcer's voice boomed over the loudspeaker just as the music began to play, and the toads were off.

The toads pirouetted and leapt gracefully with the music as they made their way to their team members. The crowd cheered wildly; Thorn, Valley, and Seven screamed and clapped as each toad completed its run. To pass the baton, a toad grabbed the edge of the baton with its mouth and then wiggled till it was holding it at its center. One wrong move, and the baton would fall or go flying, which would mean precious seconds off their time. Each transition moved smoothly until the unthinkable happened.

The Stormville toad dropped its baton in the very last second, and the crowd gasped in unison. Bob, the Boggs Ferry toad, took the lead. The final Stormville toad, Jessica, scrambled to recover while the Boggs Ferry toad took off at a ferocious pace. The witch team members ran alongside the toads on the inside of the track, yelling dance moves and encouragement to their toads, sometimes splashing them with small amounts of water to keep them moisturized and limber.

"Oh my goats, oh my goats!" Thorn screamed as all three Witchlings leapt to their feet and leaned over the railing. By now, almost the whole crowd was standing and so loud, you could barely hear the music.

Bob raced expertly toward the finish line, spinning into several brisés before taking huge, graceful leaps, just moments away from snagging the win, when Jessica unexpectedly zoomed forward with a series of masterful dance steps, tightening the impossible gap between them. The crowd exploded with excitement. Tia and Plip Flapper, the Stormville witch, waited on the other side of the finish line, crouched down, screaming support for each of their toads.

"It looks like this race is NOT over yet!" the announcer narrated over the loudspeaker. "Will Bob come out on top again, or will the scrappy Jessica snatch victory from his clammy hands?!"

The toads pranced and twirled and shimmied to the finish line where, with one final croak and sidestep, Bob passed the red ribbon, victorious.

"Tia! Tia! Tia!" the crowd chanted in unison. Thorn jumped up and down, screaming so hard her face was red as she hugged Seven, and then Valley, until all three Witchlings were jumping and screaming together. Breathless and sweaty and not thinking about anything but the happiness of this moment.

Tia Stardust met Bob with a tiny high five as he hopped into her waiting hand, and she picked him up and waved at the wildly cheering crowd. A microphone rose from the ground, and Tia went over to meet the announcer in the center of the arena.

"What a rousing race!" the announcer declared. "Congratulations to the Boggs Ferry Raccoons on this amazing win. An exciting start to the gaming season! Normally our Town Gran or Uncle would present the prize for first place but"—the announcer shifted uncomfortably, and conspiratorial murmurs spread throughout the stadium—"they cannot be with us at present, so I'm afraid I will have to do!" He held out a small stone trophy in Tia's direction, and as soon as she grabbed it, Bob jumped inside it.

"Thank you, thank you, Ravenskill and the Toad Race League!" Tia said, holding the trophy close to her chest now as she leaned toward the mic. "I know that there are some dark times falling on the Twelve Towns right now, but together we can overcome anything. I believe in us all and want to give a special message to my coven, House Hyacinth— you have helped make me who I am, and for that, it's only right that I'll be bringing home the Twelve Towns Cup next year!"

A wave of purple capes roared in the audience as House Hyacinth celebrated their champion. Seven tried not to feel jealous, and she tried not to look for Poppy in the large patch of purple in the crowd but she couldn't help it. Thorn squeezed her hand, and Valley shoved her lightly.

Seven smiled, grateful for Thorn and Valley.

"Come on. Let's get out of here before the rush," Seven said.

As the Witchlings made their way through the still-cheering crowd and toward the exit, Seven couldn't help but wonder if there was more to Tia's comment about dark times in the Twelve Towns, and she wondered if there was any chance the fear prickling up her spine was right. Because Seven had a very bad feeling that, whatever it was, it had to do with them.

CHAPTER SIXTEEN
THE TRUTH ABOUT BOGGS FERRY

SNOW WAS COMING DOWN on Ravenskill. Again.

"Doesn't the snow get sick of coming here? Try some new towns for once!" Seven shouted at the sky as snowflakes clung to her eyelashes and melted on her skin. The Witchlings were walking to the center of town from the toad race, their hearts still racing with adrenaline as they went over the match in detail, weighing in on what they thought were the Boggs Ferry team's weaknesses.

"We all know there's no way they're beating Ravenskill. Tia will be eating her words when she's up against Holo Vexx, and I, for one, would go ahead and put Holo first. Let him take the lead, and they won't be able to make it up," said Valley.

"No way! If anything goes wrong, I'd rather have Holo at the END—that way he can make up for lost time!" said Seven. "His toad, Lorenzo, is good under pressure."

"What do you know? Your toad is a dud," Valley scoffed.

"You don't even HAVE A TOAD!" screeched Seven, to which Valley responded with a snowball launched squarely into Seven's forehead.

Thorn looked nervous until the two Witchlings began to laugh, and she breathed a sigh of relief. Seven felt guilty; she knew Thorn worried about them fighting, but she was starting to understand this was just how she and Valley joked around. One thing was for sure, and it was one thing Seven never thought she'd admit or feel in her entire life: She really liked Valley Pepperhorn. Seven laughed, wiping the snow off her face, when a voice called out behind them.

"Thorn? Thorn Laroux?"

Thorn's face went every shade of pink on the planet.

"If you wanna run, just say the word," Seven said, guessing Thorn might be worried about seeing witches from her old town, but Thorn just shook her head no.

"It's okay," she said softly. "I have to face them sooner or later."

They all stopped and turned around, Thorn lifting her chin up like Valley had taught her to. She looked defiant, not quite tough, but getting there. And then her face softened.

"October?"

An older witch, maybe sixteen or so, was jogging toward them with a huge smile on her face. She was wearing a Boggs Ferry Raccoons uniform and had long, curly red hair.

She also wasn't alone. Running with her, hand in hand, was Tia Stardust.

Thorn whispered a string of *oh-my-goats-oh-my-goats-oh-my-goats*, until October and Tia were standing face-to-face with the Witchlings. October opened her arms and shrugged when Thorn ran to her, hugging the older witch tight.

"I didn't notice you on the track," Thorn said, pulling away. "Your hair got so long I didn't even recognize you."

"I was moving too fast; that's the problem." October laughed. "Oh, sorry, this is Tia Stardust, my girlfriend. I don't think you two ever met. Tia, this is Thorn. I used to tutor her back in Boggs Ferry."

Tia waved at the Witchlings. "Nice to meet you!"

"You too. You were great out there," Valley said, blushing.

"Thanks. It was all Bob. He's resting in his tank back at the Spegg, but you can meet him later if you want. We'll be here till tomorrow."

Thorn clapped her hands together. "Oh, will you? Where are you staying? Do you want to stay in my house? You must be exhausted. Tia-I-love-you-oh-my-goats. Are you hungry?" Thorn said breathlessly.

"She's short-circuiting," Seven whispered to Valley.

October laughed. "We are actually starving and wouldn't mind some quiet time away from the team. Want to join us at Evanora's?"

Thorn smiled. "I love their cakes!"

"We'll meet you there, then. Just going to get changed out of these uniforms. We smell like week-old shushrooms."

"Speak for yourself. I smell worse," Tia said, and the two witches took off in the direction of House Hyacinth's Grand House. Coven houses had luxurious guest rooms with showers and any kind of beauty treatment or ointment you could want for their members. Another thing to add to the list of stuff she'd never get, thought Seven.

But that didn't matter right now because they were about to have lunch with Tia Stardust, and Seven was excited for a different reason than Thorn. Tia's speech had been really bugging Seven. The Gran had been called away to another town, the Uncle indisposed, just like they had been during the impossible task in 1965. Maybe it was nothing, but if there *was* something fishy going on in Ravenskill, maybe there was something happening in Boggs Ferry too. And it was the perfect opportunity for Seven to find out.

❖ ❖ ❖

Evanora's Tea Room was tucked between a witch doctor's office and a clothing shop for toads and other familiars. The small restaurant was covered in ivy, and *Evanora's Tea Room* was written in gold flourishes on one giant, exposed window.

"The window seats are free," Seven said, running inside before someone else took the coveted location.

The three Witchlings and the two older witches settled

into cushiony floral chairs around a table covered with an old-fashioned doily tablecloth. They ordered seaweed-crusted sandwiches, and fried cheese, and strawberry shortcakes with the singing kind of berries, not the regular kind. *Fancy.* There was a handful of other witches in the small café, sipping on tea and nibbling on dainty cakes in the shape of different animals. There were none of the mean people Seven had come to recognize from the Hill, and a wave of relief washed over her. Every time they went into a shop, or a library, or walked through town, the anxiety of having someone call them Spare scum or having to defend herself or Valley or Thorn made Seven want to stay locked up in her house forever.

Thorn and the two racers talked excitedly about Boggs Ferry and the school year, and although Seven was almost positive they knew Thorn was a Spare, they kindly avoided any sorting talk and tried to keep the conversation cheerful. Seven learned that October was Seven's potions tutor in Boggs Ferry and they had become friends, according to the older girl, which made Thorn blush. Clearly, she hadn't known October considered her a friend. They were nice, these two witches, and Seven hoped they'd also be blabbermouths. But just in case they didn't volunteer the information she was curious about, she had a plan.

Seven took her black wool cape off and pushed the sleeves of her sweater up just so. "It got hot all of a sudden," she said, and waited. She made sure her scratched forearms from their run-in with the cucos were on full display, even reaching over the table (rudely) to grab another strawberry-filled marshmallow goose.

"Oh," said Tia. "What happened to your arm?"

Seven had to work especially hard to hold back a smile. Valley rolled her eyes.

"Cuco attack," Seven said gravely. "We were lucky we got out alive, actually."

Tia and October exchanged looks. Then October leaned in close and whispered, "They've been happening here too?"

"Too?!" Thorn clasped one hand over her mouth, then brought her voice down to a whisper. "What do you mean *too*?"

They were all leaning close now, speaking softly. "There was a string of cuco attacks in Boggs Ferry last month. Before that there hadn't been a cuco sighting in years and years," Tia said, and immediately covered her mouth. She and October both looked surprised.

"Oh!" said October excitedly.

"But one night, there were ten sightings in ten different parts of town. The next night twenty. By the next week, we had fifty of them and . . ." The older witches exchanged looks again. "Three witches were killed. And our Town Uncle was taken."

Now it was the Witchlings' turn to exchange looks. How

was this possible? And how hadn't they heard about it? Petal was taken in spring; that was months ago. It made sense for the cucos and the Nightbeast to pass Boggs Ferry on their way to Ravenskill; it *didn't* make sense for them to go back.

"Why isn't this in the *Squawking Crow*?" asked Seven, indignant. She diligently read the Twelve Towns' paper every week and followed everything their star journalist, Tiordan Whisperbrew, wrote. She prided herself on being informed, and the paper not covering the Boggs Ferry attacks was unacceptable. Not to mention, this was crucial information for them if they were going to find the Nightbeast.

"Well, that's the other thing. Our Town Gran put a shush order on us so we wouldn't be able to tell other witches. Which is why I was so surprised I could tell you any of this. I'm not sure why we can tell you though," Tia said.

Seven smiled. "Probably because we're not really witches, and not Forever Witchlings either. We're somewhere in between till the task gets solved. We're the only ones in this state of magic." The shush order probably didn't account for that.

"But shush orders are illegal," Thorn said.

Shush orders were an arcane type of magic, something their ancestors had used to keep dissenters quiet back when only the wealthiest had any rights. That particular kind of magic—and it was a hex, really—had been outlawed hundreds of years ago. Using it to keep any witch quiet now was considered a most heinous offense. Seven had never heard of it used against an entire town though. That was infinitely worse.

"There's corruption everywhere, Thorn," Seven said, still upset herself.

"That's what we've been saying too. Well, what we've been *wanting* to say. But we haven't been able to talk about it till now." October rubbed her throat.

"We'll have to find a way to tell our Town Gran about this," Seven said. "Our Uncle went missing too."

"We heard. When did it happen?" Tia asked.

"Just about three nights ago now. After we were attacked— we beat the cucos, by the way." Valley smiled smugly.

"But only by accident," said Thorn.

"And the Gran and Uncle came to help us, since Seven passed out and all—" Valley said.

"Only for a moment!" Seven interjected.

"And then a shadow appeared in the woods, and when the Uncle went to confront it, they took his hat," Thorn said. "That same night he disappeared."

"When did the first cuco attack happen? Do you remember the date?" Seven took out a small notebook and pen from her black cape, prepared to jot down the information like any good reporter would. If the *Squawking Crow* wasn't on the job, then she would have to be. She would find a way to get this information to Tiordan Whisperbrew if she had to.

"It happened on the fourth day of fall. I remember because it was our first practice since summer and I had awful cramps," October said. "I had to sit out most of the practice, and our coach freaked out and sent us all home because of the news."

"Yeah, it was definitely on that night. I remember too," Tia said.

"Do you remember when your Town Uncle disappeared?" Seven asked.

"Just about three days ago," October said. "Same as yours."

Seven wrote it down in her notebook and nodded. Tia and October weren't sure of the exact dates of the other cuco attacks, but maybe that would be enough to get Seven started. She had some research to do, that was for sure.

"Thanks for helping us with all this," Thorn said shyly.

"Of course. Once a raccoon, always a raccoon, right?" October smiled at Thorn.

"We have to go. We have a team meeting in five minutes," Tia said. "It was really nice meeting you three. Good luck with . . . everything, okay?"

The Witchlings smiled, knowing that *everything* meant the impossible task. And they'd need all the luck they could get.

CHAPTER SEVENTEEN
AN UNFORTUNATE DISCOVERY

THAT NIGHT, cucos invaded Stormville.

The townspeople fought them off, but three witches were badly injured.

Seven stayed up late watching the telecast report and messaging Valley and Thorn in their group chat. Something was definitely wrong. Unless there was another Nightbeast in Stormville, cucos shouldn't have been attacking there too. But that was almost impossible, insisted Valley. Nightbeasts were rare and didn't hunt in close proximity to one another. There had to be some other explanation, but what? One thing was for sure: The three cucos the Witchlings had fought off weren't the only ones. Not even close.

Valley and Thorn both had family stuff the next morning, and alone with her thoughts, Seven felt anxiety creep in. She was overwhelmed and afraid. It was one thing to fight a

Nightbeast and a handful of cucos, but what if there was more than one? What if, like Tia and October had told them, there were fifty cucos like there had been in Boggs Ferry? They were no closer to finding the Nightbeast, and there were only eleven days left before they were turned into toads. Seven felt completely helpless, but then she remembered there was one thing she could do on her own. One thing she was really good at.

She walked to her parents' room, where she knew her dad was sewing holes in his socks using mending spells, and knocked.

"Come in," Talis said.

"Dad? Can I use your scroller?"

Talis had a scroller, which he used for his job selling insurance for magical disasters, and it had the latest in searching capabilities and thousands of books loaded in it.

"If you're careful, of course." Talis smiled. "Coser," he said at the waiting needle and thread suspended in midair, and it began to mend a pair of red-and-black-striped socks as he took the scroller from his wooden nightstand and handed it to Seven.

"How are you feeling, kiddo?" he said, ruffling her curls.

"All right," Seven said. "Considering."

"Understandable. I'm here and so is your mom if you need us," her dad said.

"Where is Mom anyway?"

"Setting up for tonight's council meeting," Talis said, and

got back to his sewing. "Just put the scroller back in the drawer when you finish. And don't drop it. Beefy broke the last one, and my boss won't be happy if I break another."

"Sure thing, Dad. Thanks." Seven went to her room and punched in the date Tia had told her, the one when the cuco attacks had begun, along with the words *Boggs Ferry*. The very first hit took her to an article that said there had been a Boggs Ferry town council meeting that night. She kept reading: They'd been voting on something called Amendment S.

"What's Amendment S?" Seven wondered aloud while typing it into the scroller. Another string of articles popped up on the black-and-white screen, and Seven's eyes opened wide as she read the first one.

> *The long-contested tradition of Spares has come under fire with the introduction of Amendment S, a bill that would expand Spare rights.*
>
> *The bill was introduced by the Boggs Ferry Town Gran herself with the help of the bill's original creator, Knox Kosmos, the Ravenskill Town Gran. It will be voted on the fourth day of fall and is expected to reach other Twelve Towns next month.*

Seven sat back against her pillows slowly. So, their Town Gran had drafted this bill originally. She couldn't believe that some witches wanted to give Spares more rights. Something like that could've really come in handy a few weeks ago. She read the article over again, something catching her attention. The night the Boggs Ferry town council was supposed to vote on this amendment, there had been the first cuco attacks. It said other towns were going to vote on it the month after . . .

Seven typed *Stormville, Amendment S*, and the article that popped up made Seven slap her hand over her mouth: It said that the Stormville council had been set to vote on Amendment S too. Last night. So two cuco attacks, nearly a month apart, both on the night town councils were set to vote on a bill about Spares. Strange coincidence.

Seven ran back to her parents' room.

"Dad," she said, breathless. "What is the council meeting about tonight?"

Talis looked up at her from his sock collection. "We are . . . voting on this thing." He looked like he was struggling for words.

"Amendment S—is that what you're voting on?" Seven asked.

Talis opened his eyes wide. "How did you . . . ?" He sighed. "Yes, it is. Seven, I don't want you to get your hopes up. Unfortunately, there are some powerful witches who oppose the amendment."

Seven explained her theory to her father: Someone was using the cucos, or working with them, to sabotage the vote to help Spares. If there was going to be an attack, at least

188

Ravenskill could be ready. Talis was on the phone in a flash, hammering out a plan with the other council members. Meanwhile, Seven began to formulate a plan of her own. If cucos were attacking her town tonight, and she was pretty sure they were going to, this was the Witchlings' chance to follow a cuco that would lead them to the Nightbeast.

CHAPTER EIGHTEEN
A PERILOUS, CHAOTIC, AND KINDA FUN SLUMBER PARTY

"I CAN'T BELIEVE we're using your baby brother as bait," Thorn said.

The Witchlings were having a sleepover that was really a cover for something else: a trap. Tonight was the vote on Amendment S in Ravenskill, and if Seven's theory was correct, there would be another string of cuco attacks—making this the perfect time for the Witchlings to strike. They had created a trail of jelly bean fish in the trees, starting with the Cursed Forest and leading to Seven's backyard, where they had installed a series of bells to alert them to the cuco's presence. There, they had placed another lure: an enchanted burlap-sack Beefy, complete with his clothes, so the monstruo would be able to smell him. Once the cuco realized it was a fake Beefy, it would leave, and the Witchlings would follow it right to the Nightbeast's den.

"It's not *actually* Beefy," said Valley. "Plus the Gran warded Seven's house and put extra protections on Beefy's room. He'll be safe."

"These smell like farts," Seven said, putting another fish in a pod and handing it to Valley.

Valley shimmied up the weeping willow in Seven's backyard, placed the pod, and slid down with the grace of a jaguar. "It's probably your breath."

Seven gave Valley a sarcastic smile. "Okay, that was the last pod."

They walked through Seven's yard, the sun making rainbows against the crystal wind chimes hanging from the trees. It would be at least four hours before it was dark and the cucos came out. So they made their way up to Seven's room to wait.

"Oh, I almost forgot. I have a surprise for you, goats. I'll be right back." Thorn dashed out the door, and they heard a door downstairs creak open, then shut. Thorn's footsteps raced back up the stairs seconds later.

"Okay," she said, out of breath. "I asked your mom to put these in the coat closet so it wouldn't spoil the surprise."

"You ever considered trying out for running club?" asked Valley. "You were froggin' fast."

Thorn blushed. In her arms were three large garment bags made of what looked like fancy yet sturdy materials.

"I worked on these for days. I really hope you like them." She laid the bags out on Seven's bed. "This one is yours, Seven." She pointed to the first bag. "The middle one is Valley's, and this is mine. We should all open them at the same time!" Thorn was jumping up and down and clapping, and her cheeks were bright red. She looked happier than Seven had ever remembered seeing her.

"Okay, don't short-circuit." Seven smiled and walked over to her bag. Valley and Thorn did the same, standing in front of their respective bags.

"On the count of three, we open the zippers *carefully*, okay?" Thorn asked.

Valley and Seven nodded, and Thorn began to count.

"One."

They put their hands on the zippers.

"Two."

They pulled down in unison.

"Three!"

They pushed the fabric of the garment bag aside, and Seven's mouth was agape in wonder. Inside the bags were beautiful red outfits, the color of their Witchling pendants, but . . . somehow Thorn had made the color Seven always thought to be ugly and muddy . . . absolutely stunning. Seven reached out to touch her outfit, and her eyes welled with tears. A thick, shimmering red thread stitched every piece into place. The fabric was supple and luxurious feeling. Each outfit came with a cape, dark red pants (except for Thorn's ensemble since she usually only wore skirts), and a matching shirt and vest. Each vest came fashioned with a harness that held small vials for Seven, holsters for Valley's blades, and darts for the three of them. Thorn's outfit had gloves with needlelike spikes that sprung up from the knuckles, and Seven's had a small golden dagger that gleamed in the light.

"These are incredible, Thorn!" Seven said. "We're going to look so dope."

Thorn's eyes lit up. "I was hoping you'd say that."

"These remind me of a humdrum story my mother told me about." Valley picked up her cape, spun it around and onto her shoulders expertly, and buttoned the brass button at the neck. "'Little Red Riding Hood.' The story goes that a young girl is going to her grandmother's house but stops to pick flowers on her way even though her mother told her to go straight there. She's tricked and almost eaten, until a woodsman saves her. I want to try the whole thing on!"

"What tries to eat her?" Seven asked.

"Hmmm, I don't remember. It was something ugly."

"We should try these on to make sure the measurements are all okay and also to take a picture," Thorn said excitedly.

Valley and Seven both groaned in unison.

"Must we document everything?" asked Seven.

"Yep! I'll change in the bathroom!" Thorn grabbed her garment bag and sprinted out the door.

"I'll go in the closet." Seven took her outfit into the large closet in her room, leaving Valley to change in the room.

"These feel so nice," Seven said, slipping the pants on. "I don't think I've ever worn anything this expensive. I'm scared to rip it." Her face went red, suddenly thinking how silly she must sound to Valley. She probably wore expensive stuff like this all the time, being from the Hill and all.

"I know. It feels like wearing a marshmallow," Valley said.

A bit of the embarrassment Seven felt waned, and she put on the rest of her outfit. There was even a hat, she noticed, and she picked up the short red witch's hat and put it on. Everything fit like a glove, and once again, Seven found herself in awe of her new friend's talent.

"Are you both dressed? Seven, don't you dare come out of the closet yet," Thorn yelled from the hall.

"Yep!" Valley and Seven said in unison.

"She's still in there. Don't worry," Valley said.

"Okay, on three I walk in and Seven walks out. Valley, you . . . just stand there!"

Seven giggled. Thorn was *so* excited, and it made her happy that despite everything they were going through, despite the reason for needing these outfits in the first place, they could still find pockets of joy and pride. It made her hopeful that they'd be able to find happiness no matter what their fate. Together, they could find happiness, in the most unexpected places.

"One, two, three!" Thorn opened the door at the same time as Seven, and they both stepped in the room. Their suits matched perfectly, and each one complemented the others in a way that, without knowing exactly why, you knew you needed all three suits to be complete. It was some sort of magic Thorn had infused in them. Seven knew because she suddenly felt braver than she ever had. Shivers ran over Seven's whole body. They looked better than cool, they looked formidable, and prepared, and like . . .

"We look like a coven," Valley said.

"I was just gonna say that," Seven said.

"I'm so happy!" Thorn said, sobbing.

Seven and Valley ran to Thorn and threw their arms around her, which meant *they* were also hugging. For a second, Seven thought about pulling away, but when she noticed Valley didn't so much as flinch, she hugged the still-crying Thorn even tighter.

"Do they fit okay?" Thorn asked between post-sob hiccups.

"Perfectly," said Valley.

"Thorn, you really did a kick-toad job on these. I'm especially surprised by the color."

"I know you thought the red in our pendants was ugly, but . . . I wanted to show you that in another light, it could be quite beautiful."

Seven smiled, knowing exactly what Thorn meant.

"Hey," Thorn said, wiping her eyes as she pointed in the direction of Seven's plants. "Speaking of beautiful. I didn't know plants could be see-through."

Seven ran over to her plant collection. And then she screamed.

"What?!" Valley asked, startled.

"I've been trying to grow this plant for MONTHS," Seven said. The opal-haworthia had been the most elusive of Seven's plant projects. She'd tried everything from changing its position every twenty-seven minutes one weekend, to feeding it worm guts. Nothing had worked, so Seven had just watered the plant every morning, in hopes of a miracle. It had just sprouted a very small leaf the other night, but Seven had not noticed that it had grown to full size.

"I can use these to create invisibility potions. They won't work for very long and you cannot tell my parents because I'm not even supposed to have this plant." Seven chuckled. "I can't believe it finally worked!"

Seven screamed again just as Fox called them down to dinner. They reluctantly changed out of their outfits, but not before modeling them for Seven's whooping parents. Dinner was mashed plantains with butter and fried cheese, Seven's favorite.

"We shouldn't be long," Talis said as they were clearing the dishes after dinner.

"Will you be okay?" Seven asked.

"Yes, the Gran's Guard is stationed all around town and at the Hall of Elders. If anything does happen, we'll be ready. Ingrelda next door will come over to make sure you girls are okay while we're gone too."

"We don't need a babysitter. No offense to Mrs. Villalobos, but we're too old," Seven said. Also? If their plan worked, they would end up having to defend *her* and not the other way around, Seven thought but did not say. Mrs. Villalobos was a real nice witch, but she was not a fighter.

"Well, just humor us, then." Fox winked at Seven. "Because we're *not* asking; we're telling you."

Seven cringed. "Yes, ma'am."

"Roasted," whispered Valley, smiling as she helped dry the dishes.

Seven's parents left for town after putting Beefy to bed, and Mrs. Villalobos had come over and promptly fallen asleep in front of the telecast of *Real Witch Wives of Hastings-on-Pumpkins*. Ha. Some protection she was. The Witchlings waited until she was snoring deeply and got back into their outfits.

"I feel like a warrior," said Seven, putting both hands on her hips. They were taking turns examining themselves in the mirror.

"We still need to take a picture—don't forget!" said Thorn.

"I'm feeling kind of sleepy, come to think of it," said Valley.

Seven gave a big, exaggerated yawn. "Me too."

Thorn put her hands on her hips. "I know you goats are faking. And we can't go to sleep—the cucos are coming."

The Witchlings shivered.

"Okay, okay, one pic." Seven put her hand over Thorn's shoulder and posed. Valley slid over to Thorn's other side, hands crossed in front of her chest.

"Say geese!" Thorn held up her portaphone and snapped a picture of the three of them. Valley didn't change her position, but she had shifted a bit closer to Thorn and there was a small, shy smirk on her face. Seven had her tongue out on one side, holding up two fingers like she'd seen humdrums do in a textbook once, and Thorn smiled wide. She snapped about fifteen quick pictures of them.

"You said one," Valley protested when Thorn had finally given them the go-ahead to relax.

"We need *options*." Thorn was already sifting happily through the pictures on Seven's bed.

"All jokes aside, we should get ready to stand watch," said Seven, looking out her window. The sun had dipped behind the mountains, and soon darkness would fall.

"Gonna go check on Beefy, and then we can go wait by the patio door. I am pretty sure I can hear Mrs. Villalobos snoring downstairs." Seven shook her head before stepping out into the hall. As she tiptoed toward Beefy's room,

Mrs. Villalobos's snores were so loud, the floor was shaking. *Wow, she must've had a really long day or something.* But the closer Seven got to Beefy's room, the more the floor shook. That was really weird. Her heart skipped a beat not from excitement but from fear. She picked up the pace. Even though Beefy's room was just at the end of the hall, the distance seemed to stretch out infinitely. The walls grew larger, the lights dimmed, the floor beneath her feet extended for miles and miles. Seven could not get to Beefy's room quickly enough because what she heard wasn't snoring.

It was growling.

Seven threw open the door of her baby brother's room and found a cuco standing over his crib. The large double windows in Beefy's room were flung open, his white curtains fluttering in the night wind. Somehow the cuco had gotten in, despite the bells, despite all her parents' protections. Despite the Gran's protections.

Beefy was fast asleep, and the cuco's outstretched hands were just inches from his chubby face. Seven had one chance to catch it off guard before it grabbed her brother, and she did the only thing she could think to do in that moment: She lunged at it.

The cuco roared as Seven crashed into its body. Its fur felt like icicles and it smelled like a dead animal, and Seven scrambled away from it as the cuco did the same in the opposite direction.

Beefy cooed, waking up as Seven struggled to get a blow dart from her harness. The cuco stood up and growled, baring its sharp teeth at Seven. It was smaller than the ones they'd seen by the river, and it had no signs of injury anywhere. That meant there were definitely more than three of them and there could be more on the way. Seven ran with a blow dart in hand, to make sure she did not miss this time. The cuco was too fast, however, and sent her flying to the other side of the room with a thud.

Moving quicker than lightning, the cuco whipped around to Beefy's crib, trying to grab the baby. But Beefy lashed out, much like he did when he threw a tantrum—arms and legs flailing, and screaming at the top of his lungs—but this time each flail and kick landed squarely on the cuco's face and body. The cuco snapped, growling and drooling all over Beefy's crib, but the baby did not look scared. Beefy looked mad. He balled up his tiny fists and pummeled the cuco with forceful blows. And the monstruo actually whined, holding its injured snout.

Seven got to her feet, the room spinning around her. She felt something cold and wet at the back of her head, and she was pretty sure she was bleeding. The cuco bent its head down toward the crib and growled, but Beefy kicked the monstruo with one bare foot, his cute toes wiggling in the air. Then Beefy climbed onto the far railing of his crib, jumped, and came down hard on the cuco's head, pummeling it with punch after punch.

"Seven, Beefy!" Valley ran into the room and immediately charged toward the cuco.

"Are you okay?" Thorn was just behind her. She helped Seven up from the floor, her hands shaking.

"Yeah!" Seven got up and ran toward the cuco, then with both hands grabbed its tail and pulled it back and away from Beefy and Valley, who were fighting it off together. Taken aback from the sudden force, the cuco stumbled backward. Thorn grunted as she picked Beefy up and placed him back in his crib, and Valley moved quicker than lightning, slashing the cuco's shoulder with her twin blades from behind.

"Do the shrouded spell, Seven!" Valley said.

Seven raised her hands, about to intone a spell that made shadows look like monstruos, when the cuco let out a piercing scream and spun around toward Seven. It was breathing heavily, its muscled shoulders going up and down and up and down as the room shook from the force of its growls. Seven froze in fear.

Thorn stepped in front of Seven, her hands up to intone the spell, and the cuco snarled and swiped at her face, leaving three lines across her cheek. Thorn's head whipped to the right, and her hand flew up to protect her face too late. Seven jumped in front of her right as the cuco stretched its long snout out, opened its mouth, and CHOMPED. It came away with a chunk of Seven's hair, and one of its teeth had grazed her arm, but it hadn't done much more. Beefy was trying to climb out of his crib and complained in unintelligible baby talk except for one word: *monstruo*. Valley thrust her weapon at the cuco, and it leaned back to dodge, but Beefy caught it square in the ear with a right hook.

Finally Seven raised her hands and screamed, "Silueta!" She weaved her hands in and out, making the shape of what she imagined a Nightbeast might look like, and the shadow of the beast grew and grew on Beefy's wall like a hand puppet show gone wrong. Drool fell from its mouth, its eyes burned red, and even though Seven knew this was not the Nightbeast, her heart still thumped with fear. Seven directed the shadow to the window, and now was the moment of truth. Would the cuco follow?

The cuco turned toward the shadow, sniffed the air, and let out a bloodcurdling scream. It turned back to Valley, who hit and slashed the monster's leg, bobbing and weaving like a boxer. Thorn stood near Beefy, hands up and ready to protect him if the cuco came too close.

"TRONIDO!" Seven screamed. If they couldn't make it follow their shadow monster, they would scare it.

A loud crash exploded all around them, like thunder times a thousand. The cuco covered its pointed ears and shook its head violently as Beefy began to cry. But it still didn't run.

Okay, then, Seven thought. They had to take it down.

"Change of plans!" Seven said.

She began to treat the monstruo like a pinball—any direction it went, it was met with another hit. The other Witchlings followed her lead. Thorn slashed at its side; Valley plunged her weapon into its leg, Seven struck out with her dagger, and Beefy punched the monster's head like it was a boxing bag, back and forth and back and forth. They did three more rounds of hit, hit, slash, punch, duck, and weave to avoid the cuco's counterattacks. But no matter how hard they hit it, the cuco wasn't going down.

"Why isn't it dying?!" Thorn screamed between attacks.

"And where in the froggin' swamp is our BABYSITTER?" Seven asked. "Cover me—I'm gonna end this now."

"Seven, we can push it out the window. The three of us can keep attacking till it falls!" Thorn said.

"No! I'm gonna kill it now. I can do this," Seven said.

"Thorn's right!" Valley yelled between hits. "If we push it out, it might survive and we can follow it if it leaves. And if it dies, at least Beefy is safe!"

"RAAAAAAH!" the cuco roared, lashing out. Seven's head spun. She was about to shake her head no again, to tell her coven she could do it, when she remembered the Gran's words.

Let them help you.

"Okay," Seven said. "You're right. Let's push it out!"

Valley gave the cuco one good kick of her boot, and the

cuco went flying backward while she and Thorn ran to Seven's side. They stood shoulder to shoulder, hands up.

"On three, we do the viento spell. One, two . . ." Seven took a deep breath, steadied herself, and shot. "Three!"

"VIENTO!" the Witchlings screamed at once, and the room erupted into full-blown chaos.

The cuco went completely feral, trying to hold on to anything it could as the strong wind spell pushed it toward the window. It smashed Beefy's dresser, pulled the wallpaper from the walls.

"It's almost out!" Thorn yelled.

"Don't put your hands down!" added Valley.

"Seriously, *where* is our babysitter?!" Seven screamed, and with one final gust of wind, the cuco was up off the ground and through the window. It landed outside with a bone-crackling *THUMP*, and the Witchlings ran to see if they could follow it, but there would be no tracking tonight.

"Aw, nuts, we killed it again," said Thorn.

There was a small knock at the door, and the head of an old lady peeped in.

"Do you girls want any cookies?" Mrs. Villalobos asked with a smile. She seemed not to notice that there was blood everywhere and three Witchlings slumped by the window in various states of injury.

"You have *got* to be kidding me," Seven said.

"Can you please call our parents?" Valley asked, and

Mrs. Villalobos nodded and left the room, seemingly unfazed.

"Beefy's A-okay," Thorn said, picking up Beefy, who was holding out his arms. "Oh goats, you're heavy."

"Beefy's his name for a reason," Seven said, still trying to catch her breath.

"I remember what the thing was," Valley gasped from the floor.

"What thing?" Seven asked, also out of breath.

"From the story, the monstruo from the 'Little Red Riding Hood' story. It was a wolf."

The Gran returned to Ravenskill the morning after the cuco attacks. Attacks with an *s* because there had been more than the one at Seven's house. In total, four families had been targeted throughout town that night, though thankfully, nobody had been hurt too seriously. Except for one witch.

Somewhere between Elvanfoot Yarns & Thingamajigs and her home, Perdita Elvanfoot was snatched from the snowy and well-lit path, Seven read in the *Squawking Crow* the next day. *Cuco tracks were found along the path, with droplets of blood confirmed by the local witch doctor to be a match for the victim.*

Seven shook her head as she put the newspaper down. Tia and October had said this was also happening in Boggs Ferry but that reporters were banned from writing about it by the Gran and Uncle of that town. The Gran had only arrived this morning, and perhaps she did not come back in time to stop the reporters from writing about it, but if she had, would she have used a shush order too? And why were the town leaders interfering with news the public had every right to know?

The Witchlings were supposed to be hunting a Nightbeast right now, and Seven knew that's what her focus should be, but what if . . . what if it was all connected somehow? Whatever the truth was, Seven had a plan to find out.

CHAPTER NINETEEN
TOTALLY SPIES

THAT DAY, Seven, Thorn, and Valley huddled by the side entrance of the Ravenskill Hall of Elders and schemed. They each had on wigs, glasses, and what Seven could only describe as prairie-like dresses, courtesy of Thorn.

"This wig is itchy," Valley said, scratching her head. "And we look like nerds."

"Yes, well, rat beard wigs will do that sometimes," Thorn said. "We were in a pinch!"

Seven winced at the mention of rat beard. "Pretending I never heard that."

"Okay," Valley said, "we're gonna go in there, ask to see the town records of the meeting, and see what's what."

Two cuco attacks in two towns, during a vote involving Spares, was fishy enough on its own, but three was a conspiracy. At least, that's what Seven had told Valley and

Thorn that morning when she shared her suspicions.

"It's more than just the attacks," Seven had said. "It's also the fact that the cuco was able to get past wards put in place by the Gran and Uncle. That there are no traces of a Nightbeast ever arriving in Ravenskill except the cucos. There should've been traces, tracks, fallen trees, poops! Not to mention, the dead flowers that were enchanted to look alive."

"And then there's the untouched jelly bean fish," Valley had added.

"Exactly. Someone is using cucos to sabotage the vote on Amendment S, and it seems like someone is helping the Nightbeast go undetected. I think it might be the same someone. Whoever it is, we should be able to find out by reading the meeting records and seeing who is against Spare rights."

They had come up with the plan to disguise themselves and get the information from the Hall of Elders, and now they were putting that plan in motion.

"But what if they say no?" Thorn asked.

"They won't," Valley said. "It's public info. My dad gets stuff like that all the time."

Seven and Thorn exchanged doubtful looks.

"The thing is, your dad is on the Hill. Not everybody gets the same treatment. We're *Witchling Spares*," said Seven.

"Oh." Valley's cheeks went red.

"Don't feel bad. I just learned last week that there is no *N* in *cemetery*," said Thorn.

"Wait," Valley said, opening her eyes wide.

Seven burst out laughing. "Anyway," she said. "That's why we have the disguises. And if it doesn't work—" Seven smirked and held up a small vial. "Las veras potion. We'll make them tell us the truth."

"You're scary," Valley said.

"Now you know how I felt! All right, if they say no, you two distract them while I pour a few drops of this in their mudbean juice. Older witches always drink mudbean juice at work."

"Got it." Thorn nodded.

The three Witchlings went inside the ornate Hall of Elders, where all government business was handled and the council kept their records and held their meetings. It was one of the most beautiful buildings in Ravenskill, with onion domes and high spires that looked like they reached the clouds sometimes. There were large archways and intricate etchings that told the story of the Twelve Towns' origins. They followed the signs pointing them toward the Ravenskill Records Room.

The Hall of Elders was run mostly by crones, the oldest witches in Ravenskill, but there was also a ghost, and a few fae folk who looked just like witches but were twice as tricky (and had lovely pointy ears). Seven hoped for the ghost. Ghosts were mostly friendly and less likely to see through their disguises than witches since, weary from their alive days, they tended to pay less attention to the living. If they got a fae clerk, they'd be done for. Like, toast.

"Follow me," Seven whispered, her straight blond wig shining in the colorful light from the stained-glass windows.

A curly ginger Valley and a brunette Thorn nodded and followed Seven to the desk of a shiny blue see-through clerk. A ghost. Seven searched his desk, and sure enough, a cup of steaming liquid was right next to his workstation. Flingo.

As they approached, the ghost smiled at them.

"Hello, Alaric," Seven said, peering at his slightly melted-looking name tag.

"Hello! Have you come to file a complaint or observation?" A clipboard rose from the desk, ready to begin taking notes.

"Huh?" the Witchlings asked in unison.

"Silly me. We keep records of everything, and I mean absolutely everything. So, when there's something amiss during an impossible task, or you've made some sort of progress, we record it here! For posterity. In the olden days, we used to assign Hall of Elders employees to follow Spares who invoked the impossible task around and record everything they did, but that became too difficult, so now it's your responsibility to come to us. Didn't the Gran tell you?! Oh, wait, maybe *I* was supposed to tell you . . ." Alaric held one ghostly hand to his chest, a concerned look on his face as he stared into the distance as if he were trying to remember.

"We're not Spares," said Thorn, horrified.

Alaric blinked a bunch of times, twisting his mouth to the side in a poor attempt at being discreet.

"Of course, of course you aren't. What can I help you with instead?" he said, winking, like, twelve times.

Seven bit her lip. If the Hall of Elders held records of everything, even impossible tasks, maybe they would find new information about the Cursed Toads too. It was still bothering her that so little information was available about them. That they had been so easily forgotten. Alaric seemed to know who they were anyway. So much for the disguises. Seven took the chance.

"Two things," Seven said.

Valley and Thorn raised their eyebrows.

"One, do you have the, um, any records about the Cursed Toads? The Spares of '65?"

Seven's cheeks were hot as Alaric tried, unsuccessfully, to hold back an amused smirk.

"Definitely not a Spare," he whispered. "Unfortunately, those records were lost in the great fire of '65. I know a bit about it off the top of my head, but I'm not sure it would be very helpful or accurate. That was a fraught night for me, you see." Alaric touched his half-melted name tag, and Seven knew for sure he had died that night.

"Sorry, didn't meant to bring up your death day," she said.

Alaric waved his hand and smiled. "Don't worry about it. I'm used to it by now!"

Seven had a thought just then, something that had been bothering her. "Alaric, do you remember their names? The Cursed Toads?"

Alaric stared off into the distance for a long while, then finally looked back at the Witchlings. "You know, it's the weirdest thing, but I can't seem to remember at all."

The Witchlings exchanged looks.

"What was the second thing you needed?" Alaric asked.

"We're doing a school project on local government. Would we be able to see some records from a council meeting?" Seven asked.

"Oh, sure!" Alaric said cheerfully, swooping through his desk. Ghost perks. He floated toward a big open room with rows and rows of filing cabinets as the Witchlings followed behind. "What year were you looking for? We have the records archived in a MAKL, of course, but there's nothing quite like seeing the old records up close. Gives you a real"—Alaric shimmied his ghostly shoulders—"*feel* for the history, you know?"

Seven did not know, but she still nodded and smiled.

"I love history," Valley lied. Seven nodded at Valley and Thorn and then quietly backtracked the few toadstools to Alaric's desk. Valley and Thorn chatted happily as they followed Alaric into the archives room. Seven looked around to make sure nobody was looking and deftly put two drops of las veras potion into the mudbean juice on his desk. She then ran to catch up with them and gave Valley a small thumbs-up.

"Actually, we were hoping for something pretty recent," Valley said.

Alaric stopped and turned around toward them, raising his eyebrows. "Oh?"

"Like, from a day ago?" Thorn asked hopefully.

"Oh," Alaric said again, but this time, he looked worried. "I'm afraid that isn't possible. You see, we're still processing the data." Alaric's voice cracked. Even without the potion, Seven could tell he was lying.

"Can you tell us which dates are available?" Valley asked.

"Of course!" Alaric floated back toward, and through, his workstation. "Now let's see . . ." He began typing on the MAKL. "We have any of the past three hundred meetings right here, except for the one two days ago." He laughed nervously.

"When will those records be done? We really need them. We can wait," Seven said.

Alaric loosened the collar of his ghost shirt, which, despite being see-through like the rest of him, was clearly bedazzled. "You see . . . the records, they . . ." Alaric picked up his mud-bean juice. *Yes, yes,* Seven thought, her eyes glued to the cup. Alaric brought it to his lips, and the Witchlings leaned forward in anticipation. He put the cup down gently.

"I'm afraid they just won't be processed for a while. But I assure you there are much more exciting meetings to peruse! There was a rousing one about toad race regulations just two weeks ago, and if you're in the mood for something older, we can look at the disco dance-off of '78, or even the great fire of '65! We have options with a capital *O*!"

"We really need the last council meeting records. We might fail if we don't get them." Thorn opened her eyes like a sad puppy dog.

Wow, she can use her cuteness for evil, thought Seven.

Alaric looked like he was going to faint, and Seven almost felt bad. But then his hand went to his mudbean juice and all her focus went to the cup again. He brought his shaking hands up to his face, and again the Witchlings leaned forward. Just as he was about to take a sip, Alaric put the cup down on the table dramatically and threw his head to the side.

"I can't lie. I have never been good at it. Oh dear, okay. A quick sneak peek, but no more. And you tell no one of this. Got it?" Alaric raised one ghostly eyebrow.

"Got it," the Witchlings said in unison.

Alaric pursed his lips and looked around before opening a drawer behind him with a skeleton key. "Jonafren, I love your tie!" he said to a fae who was filing something close by. The fae hitched an eyebrow and looked down. He was not wearing a tie.

Rats. If Alaric didn't pull it together, he was gonna give them away. The Witchlings exchanged nervous glances as Jonafren meandered toward them, eyebrows hitched. Alaric took a few files from a folder in the drawer and switched them over to another so swiftly even Seven almost missed it. Jonafren picked up the pace and was nearly beside Alaric now. The ghost closed the drawer with his key and handed over a green folder, his ghost hands shaking slightly.

"There you go, little witches. That will explain every-thing you need to know about how your local government works," Alaric said a little too loudly.

Jonafren stopped beside Alaric at the workstation and seemed to relax a bit at those words. Sheesh, whatever was in those files must be something they *really* didn't want anyone to see.

"Thank you, Alaric," Thorn said.

"Ha ha, for what?! I barely did a thing. Just gave you a packet of premade info. Good thing I thought to make those for the schoolkids."

Jonafren smiled tightly and picked up Alaric's cup, sniff-ing it. Oh no, oh no, oh no.

The fae brought it up to his lips and took a long, hard gulp. Seven's eyes went wide; Valley and Thorn looked at her, panicked. Would the fae know it was enchanted? Would they go to the Tombs? What was the penalty for something like this? Jonafren put the mug down and smiled.

"You know. At first I believed that project was quite use-less, as you are sometimes quite useless, Alaric, but now I realize it was actually clever," Jonafren said, and he opened his eyes wide. Oops.

Alaric looked madder than a toad on a hot lily pad. He grabbed the cup and threw the contents of it back, finishing it off and putting it down on the desk with a bang.

"Thank you," Alaric said with a wide smile. "I am often underestimated, but I strive to prove warlocks like you wrong."

"Is that so? Well, did you know I am often envious of your bedazzled ghost clothing?"

"As you should be. You wear the exact same utility pants every day. You are a fae, for rat's sake. Have some dignity!"

"Let's get out of here," Valley said, and the Witchlings took advantage of the truth fight and ran for it.

The Witchlings held on to their wigs as they hustled out of the Hall of Elders and to the nearest mudbean shop. The Ravenskill Mudbean House was on the bottom floor of a flatiron-shaped building. Big windows adorned three full walls, so you could sip your hot drink and use the nosy-nelly spell, chisme, to observe your neighbors at the same time. The intricate molding on the copper ceiling sparkled in the afternoon sun, and the comforting smell of mudbean juice filled the air.

The mudbean house was mostly empty at this time of day, as adult witches were busy at work and younger witches were still at school. Seven tried hard not to think about how much she missed school and getting the best grades in her class. She missed her teachers, and the smell of her old schoolbooks, and even the cafeteria food. There was no use in being sad about it now though, Seven thought. Plus, there would be plenty of time to reach the top of their year again if they survived. But right now, they had a mystery to solve.

"Come on, there is a booth in the back I do homework in sometimes," Seven said, and Thorn and Valley followed.

"I'm taking this thing off. It's itching like a chili pepper ant," Valley said as they slid into the tall seafoam-green booth. She yanked her wig off and started to stuff it into her backpack.

"Gentle!" Thorn said, an anxious edge to her voice. "These wigs are premium rat beard." Thorn took her wig off and gently placed it alongside Seven's and Valley's and zipped it up in a hot-pink bag with a hanger attached. She then folded the wig and placed it into her own rucksack carefully.

"Don't you think it's weird that Alaric can't remember the Cursed Toads' names? Not even the Gran can," Seven whispered conspiratorially.

"My mom either," said Valley. "It's totally weird."

Seven thought about the shush orders Tia had told them about. She had a suspicion, but she needed more info first before she could be sure. A barista witch slid up to their table. He had piercings in his nose and about five on each ear, cool braided hair, and lots of tattoos. He looked at the Witchlings suspiciously. "Didn't you have different hair when you walked in?"

"Ha, oh, that . . . um." Seven struggled for words.

"We just have weird winter hats." Thorn nodded.

"Got it." The barista winked. "Can I get you something?"

"Hot ponches, extra bogmellows, and bat-butter-and-toad-jelly sandwiches?" Seven looked at Thorn and Valley, who nodded enthusiastically.

"Coming right up," said the barista witch before walking back to the counter to make their lunch.

"Okay," Seven said. "First of all, excellent work back there. It was a close call."

"Can't believe Alaric cracked without even drinking the potion." Valley smirked.

"I hope we haven't caused an unmendable rift between coworkers," said Thorn, worrying the collar of her prairie dress.

"I'm sure they'll be fine. Let's read these papers before Jonafren comes looking for us," Seven said, taking the file from inside her cloak and placing it on the table.

They sifted through the big pile of records Alaric had given them. Seven pulled a pack of neon markers from her bag and began to highlight furiously. After just a few minutes, she'd gone through all the pages.

The barista brought them their food, and they sipped on their ponche and ate sandwiches as they talked.

"Well?" Valley asked impatiently.

"Okay, so as we know, Amendment S was supposed to be

voted on last night," Seven said. "They didn't get to the vote because of two things: One, some members of the council kept objecting and trying to introduce counter-amendments, and by the time they finally got everyone settled, they were alerted to the cuco attacks. They concluded the meeting abruptly around nine thirty."

"Does it say who objected?" Valley asked.

Seven shook her head no.

"If the cucos were trying to stop the vote, why didn't they just attack the Hall of Elders?" asked Thorn, scratching her head.

"That place is fortified with really strong magic and is guarded by the Gran's Guard at night. Especially during meetings. It would be harder for cucos to get in there than a normal house," Valley said.

"Do we know who else they *did* attack?" Thorn asked.

"I think the names are in the *Squawking Crow* article, hold on." Seven pulled out her dragon-scale notebook and read the names out. "Aside from Perdita Elvanfoot, and my house, there were attacks on the Grimsbane and Barlow families. I don't recognize those last names."

Valley's face went whiter than usual. "I do. Last summer, there was a thingy on the Hill, and I had to help my mom make these name cards for the tables. We painted the little cards by hand and alphabetized them, so I remember their names . . . Those are people on the council."

"Holy rats," said Seven.

"Perdita isn't on the council, her son is. Why wouldn't they just attack the council members themselves though?" Valley asked.

"When my family got attacked, we left Boggs Ferry because we were so scared. Maybe the cucos didn't want to hurt the council members. Maybe they just wanted to scare them," Thorn said.

Seven snapped her fingers. "Exactly. This all fits. It would be good to know if the council members' families were attacked in Boggs Ferry too."

"I can message Tia." Thorn blushed. "She gave me her portaphone number!"

Thorn typed into her portaphone, and a few seconds later it lit up with a message from Tia. Thorn held it up so they could see.

"Yep," Tia's message said, "all council family members."

The three Witchlings looked at one another, eyes wide. Someone really was working alongside the cucos and the Nightbeast.

"I think whoever is working with the Nightbeast brought it to the Twelve Towns specifically for this," Seven said. "To try to stop Spares from getting more rights." She leaned back in her seat.

Their impossible task had been to kill the Nightbeast, but this was bigger than they'd ever imagined. There wasn't just a monster on the loose—there were witches working with it—working against them.

If the only reason the Nightbeast had come to Ravenskill in the first place was because of a witch, if they could find out who that witch was, maybe they could stop it. But who in the Twelve Towns would ever do something so heinous? And who *could*? Nightbeasts didn't exactly bend to the will of witches. Seven couldn't think of any spell strong enough to make that happen, but then again, she didn't know every powerful spell. She was just a Witchling. Whoever was behind all this was someone really powerful.

"Who has the most to lose by not having Spares around to do their dirty work?" Seven wondered aloud. Her cheeks went red, realizing what she'd just said, and what the answer was. Thankfully, Valley spoke before Seven even had to.

"It must be someone from the Hill."

CHAPTER TWENTY
A SECRET POTION

THORN THREW A RAT TAIL into a cauldron between them and jumped back when the potion in progress squealed and turned green.

Thorn and Seven had snuck into their school's potions room five days after their spy mission and were mixing ingredients together for a particularly volatile enchantment. A memory potion. The school was empty, as everyone had gone home for the day, and the potions room was filled with ingredients even Seven didn't have access to.

Seven had heard from her parents that the town council had rescheduled the vote on Amendment S for tonight. They planned to attend. There, they could find a suspect among the council members opposing the bill. And with this potion—which would allow them to see their suspect's memories—they'd know for sure.

She mixed the potion with a big wooden spoon as it bubbled and, horrifyingly, cackled softly. Roba recuerdos potions like the one Seven was working on grabbed a witch's memories from any item they'd recently worn. It wasn't super potent and the memories might be muddled, but it would have to be enough. They would need to steal something from their suspect, then drop it into the cauldron with the potion.

"This is going to be real tricky," said Thorn as she helped Seven stir the potion. "I hope we can pull it off without getting turned into toads. No offense, Edgar." Thorn smiled at the toad, who was sitting in his little mushroom-shaped traveling tank atop a desk. Edgar turned around to face the wall in response. Seven laughed and turned back to the cauldron, stirring it as the potion bubbled.

"You know, there is a counterspell to this one, sort of. It makes you forget things, but it's super hard to do and, if you mess it up, you can set the subject on fire," Seven said. "Magic is finicky that way. It doesn't always turn out how you mean it to."

Thorn paused for a few moments. "What if the whole thing, bringing the Nightbeast here, was like a magic accident too, then? It's hard to believe any witch would go that far just to hurt Spares," Thorn said.

Seven scoffed. "You're too nice. Have you seen how they treat Spares? Spares . . . we, are the most vulnerable witches in this town because we don't have powerful magic. We can't protect ourselves against big threats. We're at a disadvantage, so they should help us because we're supposed to be a community, like we've been taught since we were littles. The same way we help make sure elderly witches are warm on the coldest winter nights, how we protect baby witches like Beefy. Spares are pushed to the sides and not protected because people on the Hill are more concerned with being able to treat their assistants like goose poop and to pay them only a handful of coins. They won't let go of that power, so we have to pay the price. We have more than enough magic and potions to help all Ravenskill residents live comfortably, but they just won't, for no good reason other than hate. I wouldn't put *anything* past witches like that."

Thorn's eyes opened wide. "Seven, you should write an article for the *Squawking Crow* about that. I think a lot of witches would agree with you."

Seven's face went hot. "I don't think they'd take a piece from me. I'm a Spare."

"So what? You're smarter than any other witch I know, fancy coven or not. They'd be warlocks not to run something you wrote."

Seven looked down; she was embarrassed and proud all at once, and she wondered . . . what if she still tried to write for her favorite newspaper? It wouldn't be the first time she ignored the rules and followed her heart. Why not with her biggest, most important dream?

"What are you goats talking about?" Valley asked, walking into the room with a handful of toads from the toad tank.

"Injustices," Seven said, still angry. "Thanks. Put them down over there. We just need some slime from their bodies to complete the potion. Edgar didn't have enough." Seven eyed her toad, who was sitting happily in his travel tank eating a ceramic dish full of spicy flies.

"Is this actually gonna work?" Valley asked, wiping her hands on Seven's cloak.

"Hey! Quit it," Seven protested. "And we won't know till we try."

Valley rolled her eyes, and Thorn caught her up on their conversation.

"If our theory is right and a witch is helping the Nightbeast, this is all gonna be twenty times harder," Thorn said.

"No way. In my opinion, if we're right, this is *good* news. Our mission is to fell a Nightbeast, right? So if the Nightbeast is only attacking the town because witches are making it, and we find out who they are, maybe the Gran can get involved since she wouldn't be directly fighting the Nightbeast. It means we maybe only have to stop a few witches as opposed to, you know, a giant wolf monster that wants to eat my baby brother," Seven said.

Thorn whispered at Seven through the side of her mouth, "But what if it's Valley's dad?"

Seven shook her head and held a finger up to her lips, eyes wide with panic that Valley might hear.

"If it's my dad, we'll turn him in. It wouldn't be the first time he did something terrible," Valley said.

Seven cringed, and the potion made a large *POOF* sound before settling to a soft lilac color.

"Welp, the potion is done. Let's pack up and head to the Hall of Elders. We have a traitor to catch."

CHAPTER TWENTY-ONE
LITTLE OLD WITCHLINGS

"IF I STAY AN OLD LADY, you're coming with me to flingo night," Valley said.

"Deal." Seven held in a laugh.

"I play flingo with Grandma Lilou every Friday night!" Thorn said. Now both Valley and Seven devolved into laughter before shushing each other through fits of laughter and tears.

"All right, the spell is a little complicated, so give me a second." Seven laughed nervously.

Valley rolled her eyes. "Oh boy."

Seven wiggled her arms and hands and rolled her head around like she was getting ready for a toad race. She was sweating in every conceivable place. Even her butt. It was one thing to find spells in books she had no business reading in the level-five section of the library; it was another to actually try those spells out. With only five days until they were toadified though, she was willing to try anything. Even this super-complicated aging spell.

It required a two-sided hand mirror, which Seven had brought along for just the occasion. She pulled it from the inside pocket of her red cloak and took turns switching it from one hand to the other as she wiped the sweat from her palms. The mirror was her mother's. It was bronze and heavy, with intricate carvings, and Seven was pretty sure it was at least two hundred years old. If she dropped it, she'd be dead.

They would be sneaking into the Hall of Elders tonight to sit in on the council meeting and hopefully narrow down their list of Nightbeast sidekicks. Seven took a deep breath.

"It's nearly nine o'clock, Seven. People will begin arriving soon," Thorn said.

"Right, right. Okay, who wants to go first?" Seven asked with a shaky laugh.

Valley shook her head. "Might as well be me."

"Perfect. Stand on the other side of the mirror. Closer, no, closer. Perfect. Now repeat the spell exactly as I say it and when you do, you take the mirror."

"What happens if she doesn't?" Thorn asked.

"I stay old forever. That or I turn into Beefy's new play-date," Valley said.

"Pretty much." Seven cringed.

"Then don't mess this up! I believe in you!" Thorn gave

her two thumbs-ups and said it so cheerfully, Seven knew she meant it sincerely.

Seven cleared her throat, holding the mirror up between her and Valley as she intoned the dangerous level-five spell. A spell that took witches years to perfect and that she, a Witchling and a Spare, was about to attempt. *Here goes nothing.*

"Bubble, bubble, boils and stubble, wrinkles triple, gray hairs double," Seven said and Valley repeated perfectly as Seven handed the mirror over to her. *"Spots and backaches, creaky bones, make this young witch into a crone."*

The moment Valley repeated the second part of the spell, she doubled over with the mirror in hand, her hood going over her head and covering her face and hair.

"Valley!" Thorn and Seven said, coming to either side of her.

Valley's body shook, and Seven felt horrible. What if she'd bungled the spell? What if Valley's face was covered in blisters or something? Valley seemed to be sobbing now and she made a high-pitched noise that sounded like wheezing, but when she straightened up and Seven saw her face, she was not crying. Valley was hysterically laughing.

"I look like my own grandmother," Valley said, tears running down her face. "I have hair coming out of my ears and nose!" She was in hysterics now, but more important, she was *old*. Ancient even! And Seven was filled with a new sense of confidence. Although Seven realized, deflating just a bit, that Valley still *sounded* like a kid. She guessed the spell hadn't worked that well after all.

"Your turn, Thorn," Seven said. They repeated the ritual, and Thorn turned into an adorable old lady, resembling Grandma Lilou down to the shiny silvery hair.

"I'll have to be careful if my maman is here tonight. She will think Grandma Lilou has taken a sudden interest in town politics." Thorn giggled.

"My turn," Seven said, holding up the mirror and facing the side of the building so the other Witchlings wouldn't get caught in the spell's cross fire and age even further. When Seven turned back around, she was a senior witch and her back *really* hurt. Excellent.

"Now for our cloaks," Thorn said. "They are enchanted to change color and shape if we need them to. I added that particular spell in case we needed to make a quick getaway and disguise ourselves, but this seems like a good occasion too. There are five buttons of various colors on the inner right side of the cloak that all do different things. Press the black one and say, 'Cambia,' and the look of your garment will change," Thorn said. "Don't press the gold one though, whatever you do. It will make you hover on the wind and people will think you're flying."

Seven's eyes opened wide; she'd have to remember that. She pressed the black button on the cloak, said, "Cambia," and her cloak changed from red to black. "Pretty cool.

The other two Witchlings followed suit, and soon Valley was in a magenta cloak and Thorn in a mustard yellow.

"We should enter separately, just in case," Valley said.

"Good thinking," Thorn said. "Such a smart young lady." Her hand flew to her mouth, and all three Witchlings cackled.

"We should avoid talking at all costs. The vocal transformation component of the spell must've gotten messed up somehow," said Seven sheepishly.

"Nobody is going to suspect us anyway. Don't worry," Valley said, patting Seven on the back. "This spell shouldn't even be possible for us, but somehow, you did it. You kicked toad butt."

Seven's old-lady heart fluttered, and they made their way to the lower level of the hall, shuffling along as other Ravenskillians began to arrive. By the time they'd reached the basement, Seven was out of breath and ready for a nap.

"Being old is tiring," she whispered to Thorn.

"I really want to knit something, with a warm cup of hot cocoa, and watch cozy witch murder mystery shows on the telecast," Thorn said.

"You always want to do that," Valley said as they found seats toward the back of the room.

The basement was big, paneled in dark wood, with a wine-red carpet and at least one hundred folding chairs. Seven and Poppy would often help Miss Dewey set up for meetings there . . . Funny that until that moment, Seven had not thought of the purple coven or Poppy in a long time. The chairs were arranged around a podium at the far end of the room. That's where residents stood up and gave their two cents about things like goose poop cleanup solutions and more funding for the Spegg. Nobody cared when Seven lingered at the corners of those meetings, but there were some meetings where Witchlings were absolutely never allowed, and tonight was one of them. It enraged Seven that even when a law or issue had to do with them, the simple fact of being young made them unqualified to have an opinion. Even in their own fates.

Ravenskillians filed into the warm basement. The room was filled with the smell of freshly baked goods, a cozy fireplace crackling, and the heavy perfume favored by some residents of the Hill. Thorn appeared with a plate full of chocolate chip cookies and balanced three orange fizzy drinks in her spindly arms before handing them to Seven and Valley.

"Thanks," Seven whispered.

The seats around them began to fill up, and Seven chuckled nervously as a real grown-up witch slid into the seat next to her. Talis and Fox arrived, with Beefy in tow. They had been too nervous to leave him alone or with Mrs. Villalobos again after the cuco attack, and they thought Seven was at Thorn's house. They mercifully sat on the other side of the room, but they were facing Seven, which made her squirm in her seat a little. Thorn's mother walked in moments later, wearing an all-black suit and pointy green heels and looking like someone out of a movie. Valley's dad had also arrived at some point and was busy talking to the Dimblewits near the podium. Valley's mom was nowhere to be found.

Valley leaned over and asked, "How long does this spell last anyway?"

"It *should* last for five to seven hours." Sweat trickled down Seven's forehead.

"It should? What if it doesn't?" Valley asked in a heated whisper.

"Then we run." Thorn smiled and looked out into the crowd. Trying to disguise her panic no doubt.

Valley slumped back in her chair, and Seven reached behind Thorn and poked her in the shoulder. "Sit like an old lady," she whispered.

Valley narrowed her eyes at her but sat up a little straighter, at least.

The Town Gran swept into the room, and everyone seemed to find their seats and stop talking at once. That was the power that she had. Without even uttering a word, her presence was enough. The Gran looked tired and maybe a bit angry but prepared. The look of determination on her face could leave no doubt she came to this meeting to fight. The Gran took her seat and the gavel pounded on the podium on its own, and the little old Witchlings perked up. The meeting was about to begin.

First up to speak was Mr. Dimblewit, a witch of medium height but enormous of mustache. He had beady eyes and thin eyebrows, and it wasn't until he smiled at Mrs. Dimblewit and it still looked like a frown that Seven realized his face was just always . . . *sour*. Not to mention smug.

"You remember what Mrs. Dimblewit said in your parents' bookshop the other day?" Seven whispered.

"Oh yeah! Didn't she say something about Mr. Dimblewit bringing up Spares not being allowed in businesses or something in the next town meeting?" Thorn opened her eyes wide.

"And then your mom said they'd been discussing 'terrible things' at the town meetings. I bet you anything *they* have something to do with all this," Seven said, narrowing her eyes at the memory of Pixel being dragged through the snow.

Mr. Dimblewit took the podium and shuffled papers in his hand, before clearing his throat and calling the meeting to order.

"As you all know, we have just been struck by monstruo attacks. A child was almost taken," he said, shaking his head.

Beefy, Seven thought angrily. As if he would care about the brother of a Spare.

"And one of our most cherished residents has been taken, not to mention, of course, the Town Uncle. The Gran"—Mr. Dimblewit gestured at Knox—"found herself in need of meeting with the Twelve Towns' council, which left Ravenskill completely vulnerable to attacks. And now we've learned the Uncles from Boggs Ferry and Stormville have been taken as well. These attacks are spreading throughout the Twelve Towns!"

As the crowd began to murmur, the Witchlings exchanged uncomfortable glances. What did any of this have to do with Amendment S?

Mr. Dimblewit cleared his throat. "It is no secret that the arrival of these monstruos coincides with the invocation of the impossible task, something our town has not witnessed since 1965. It is our understanding that the Town Gran is hoping to open up dialogue about Amendment S this evening." Mr. Dimblewit chuckled softly. "Well, I do not think that there is anything more irresponsible than that. We are focusing on the wrong thing. Giving our time, resources, and magic to witches who will never amount to much anyway, when our town is in grave danger. When our residents are being attacked and are not even safe to walk home on their own! I can think of no worse thing."

Again, the crowd began to talk; some were nodding in agreement, and others, most of the crowd in fact, were looking at Mr. Dimblewit wearily or even angrily. Seven could see her father holding her mother's hand and whispering to her calmly. He was probably trying to convince her not to hex him.

"It's got to be Mr. Dimblewit!" whispered Valley. Seven nodded. If anyone was trying to keep Spares down, it was this witch.

This was their moment. Seven nodded at Thorn, who was the best at long-range spells, especially this one. Thorn nodded back and murmured, "Descoser," ever so quietly as she pointed one old-lady finger at the buttons on Mr. Dimblewit's jacket. The spell whizzed right at the witch, and the thread holding one of his silver jacket buttons came undone. The jacket button tumbled onto the podium with a soft ping, and Mr. Dimblewit looked down, his cheeks turning red. He grabbed the button and stuffed it into his pocket.

"Rats," seethed Valley.

Mr. Dimblewit cleared his throat again and took off the ascot around his neck, putting it down on the chair beside the podium.

"There," Seven whispered. "We have to grab his little scarf. The moment the meeting is over, I'll go for it."

"So we suggest that instead of this . . . ill-timed amendment discussion, we instead talk about the proposition that my lovely wife and I, along with other members of the Hill Society, have put together. An amendment that would seek not to restore rights to Spares, but to restore law and order to our fair town. A law that would require Spares to be relocated and stripped of their magic in order to save Ravenskill from any further destruction. It is time we put Ravenskill *first*."

Now almost everyone—including the three old-lady Witchlings—stood up in their seats and began to protest.

"You can't possibly do this!"

"This is preposterous, barbaric!"

"You're all a bunch of butt-toads!"

That last one was Valley. Seven's wrinkly hands were shaking. Did they really want to send them away? To take all their magic away? Wasn't it punishment enough to live as Spares, with lesser magic, and now they had to be far from their families too? Far from the place she'd always called home but now felt more like a battlefield. How could her home not want her anymore? All for something she could not help. It was not Seven's fault she was a Spare. It was nobody's fault.

Mr. Dimblewit held his hands up, the smug smile spreading on his putty-like face as he tried to calm the audience down. But it was no use; all witches in attendance were arguing and yelling, and the room only grew louder and louder.

The Gran stood up and said, "That will be quite enough." The crowd simmered back down to soft whispers. "Mr. Dimblewit, please. Continue." The Gran sat.

One extremely large vein in Mr. Dimblewit's forehead looked like it was about to explode as he gave the Gran a tight smile. He went on. "Pollepel Island has more than enough room to house all of Ravenskill's Spares, or those of the entire Twelve Towns if they so choose. The beautiful land will be a wonderful home for the young and old Spares alike, and while they're there, we have devised a fruitful work schedule to keep them entertained! Why, everything from our cauldrons to our potions bottles can be manufactured there."

Several audience members shook their heads in disgust or spoke hotly among themselves. Pollepel Island was a few hours north of Ravenskill, in the middle of the Boggy Crone River. It housed an ancient castle as well as the Tombs—where Twelve Towns criminals went to receive punishment. It was rare for a witch to be jailed; only killings on a mass scale and usage of dangerous Forbidden Curses ever warranted it. And now some adults wanted to send Spares to live on the same island. With killer witches.

"I know what you're thinking!" Mr. Dimblewit said. "'But what of the Spares who are in the employ of the Hill?!' That is a simple enough solution! Any Spare with a work voucher will be permitted to stay in Ravenskill provided they are working for a Hill Society family and are of course not receiving compensation—"

The crowd began shouting once again.

Mr. Dimblewit's face went red as he yelled above the audience: "—COMPENSATION since they will not be manufacturing useful items on Pollepel Island and therefore costing us a pretty penny! Please, the sooner I finish, the sooner you can have your say!" he continued as the audience once again quieted down. "Lastly, as part of this new law, it should be noted that someone must pay for the havoc these

Spares and their little task have caused our town. Before the task, there were no attacks in Ravenskill. They likely not only brought this Nightbeast on us but are keeping any competent witches from stopping it since doing so would mean interfering with impossible task magic."

"That isn't true," Seven seethed under her breath. The Nightbeast was already there; everyone knew that. They hadn't brought it to Ravenskill. How could he lie so boldly?

Mr. Dimblewit smiled sadly, but Seven could see through it. He wasn't sad. He was enjoying every minute. "And I think it is clear who is responsible for it all. The Gran is tasked with keeping Ravenskill safe, and I know that most of us in this room have not felt safe in the past month. Am I wrong?"

Nobody spoke up.

"Right. Then I propose that along with our new law, which we have lovingly named the Spare Sanction"—Mr. Dimblewit took a deep breath, puffing his chest out as if to gather courage—"we swiftly vote to send the Gran to the Tombs."

Instead of screaming this time, the room fell completely silent. Seven was in shock, as she suspected everyone around her was as well. Thorn grabbed her hand, and on the other side, Valley grabbed Thorn's. They sat there in silence, old-lady hands clasped, and waited for whatever dreadful thing came next. Mr. Dimblewit looked very pleased indeed as he left the podium to sit back down with his foot bunion of a wife.

The room erupted then. Ravenskillians shouted over one another, at the Dimblewits; it was pure chaos.

"Now's our chance," Seven said.

The Witchlings got up and weaved through the crowd toward the front of the room. It had been less scary to fight a cuco, Seven thought. Her palms were sweaty, and she tried to keep an eye out to make sure nobody was watching her, without being obvious. The Dimblewits were on the other side of the room with Valley's dad. Thorn and Valley lingered near her, and Seven could almost feel the nervous energy coming from their direction. As naturally as she could, Seven grazed the top of the chair where Mr. Dimblewit's ascot was and balled the scarf into her fist before stuffing it into the pocket of her robe. Her heart was beating so hard she could feel it in her throat.

"Got it," Seven said, and in that very moment, her robes began to shift. She looked at Valley, and she was . . . shrinking.

"Oh no," Seven said.

"The spell! It's wearing off," Thorn whispered desperately.

"We have to get out of here—come on," Valley muttered, her face almost completely back to normal already.

Thankfully, the audience was still arguing heatedly among themselves, so nobody seemed to notice as they scrambled toward the door. They were going to get away with it. They were almost out—when Mr. Pepperhorn stepped in their path.

"And what is *this*, young lady?" Mr. Pepperhorn sneered at them and grabbed Valley roughly by the arm, shaking her until her hood slipped off.

"Stop it!" Seven yelled, and the crowd turned to look just as the Witchlings' crone disguises melted away completely and their true forms were revealed.

"Observe!" Mr. Pepperhorn said, dragging Valley to the front of the room.

"No, let her go!" Thorn ran after them and pulled on Mr. Pepperhorn's black blazer, but he did not even seem to notice her.

Talis and Fox met Seven's eyes before running to her. Fox put her hands on her shoulders. "Stay by us. You too, Thorn."

"Witchlings, mere Spares, using a dangerous level-five enchantment." Mr. Pepperhorn reached the front of the room and gestured at his own daughter and then at Thorn and Seven with disgust. "What better proof can there be for, at the very least, the temporary holding of the Gran on Pollepel Island until we get this town back under control? Something like this has *never* occurred in my lifetime. The Town Gran has been an adequate if flawed leader for many years but perhaps she is past her prime," he said. "This blatant use of high-level magic by incompetent Witchlings is basis for a sentence to the Tombs for these Spares. Either the Witchlings go, or the Gran does. There can be no other alternative."

Before the crowd could begin debating again, the Gran stood up. "There is no need for a fight over this. I will willingly go to Pollepel Island and await trial if that is what the council chooses, but please be aware, this will be decided by the Twelve Towns council, *not* the Hill Society. No matter how much you wish it would be." The Gran raised her chin up.

The gavel hit the podium three times, and Mr. Pepperhorn called for a vote.

"Everyone in favor of sending Knox Kosmos to the Tombs, say aye." Mr. Pepperhorn looked at the council members expectantly, and he along with Mr. Dimblewit and three other witches from the Hill voted to send her away.

"All opposed?" Seven's parents, Thorn's mother, and one other witch on the council voted against sending the Gran to the Tombs. Five votes in favor of arresting the Gran, four against. She was going to be taken away.

"Wait, aren't there supposed to be twelve members of the Ravenskill council?" Thorn asked.

"Yeah, guess which three are missing," Seven said.

Maddock Grimsbane, Apple Barlow, and Onyx Elvanfoot. The three witches whose families were attacked by cucos. They hadn't come tonight.

"He *planned* this!" Seven seethed.

Mr. Pepperhorn gestured to two of the Hill's private

security officers, who rushed over to put large iron cuffs on the Gran's wrists.

"You cannot do this!" Mrs. Laroux yelled. But it was too late.

"Mom, Dad, we have to stop them," Seven said, looking at her parents in desperation.

"Right now we can't. They watched the three of you break a high law in real time; it's technically the Gran's responsibility keep such things from happening. She does not have a choice but to go, at least for now," Fox said.

The Gran walked, head high, toward the exit. Mr. Pepperhorn's security grabbed her wrists tightly, but when they reached Seven and Thorn, the Gran stopped.

"This is not your fault. I promise you. They were going to find a way to do this no matter what."

"No talking. Let's go," said one of the guards.

"I can still make the bunions on your feet grow to the size of boulders," the Gran said, and the guard's eyes went wide with fear.

"Seven, it is up to the three of you now."

"We're only Witchlings. Spare Witchlings," Seven said.

The Gran struggled against the security until she was able to get closer to Seven and whispered, "Do you think they would be this scared if you were *only* anything? You are capable of so much more than you know. Stick together, remember!" The guards pulled the Gran up roughly, and the room descended into chaos once again. Shouts of indignation of "You can't do this to the Gran!" were met with dueling "It's for our own good!" or "It's what she deserves." Talis, Fox, Thimble, and Leaf all tried to calm them down, to reason with Dimblewit or his guards, but Seven had her eyes on one person: Valley.

Mr. Pepperhorn was dragging Valley down the aisle to the door, handling her as if . . . as if she were a rag doll. Valley's face was splotchy and red and streaked with tears as she struggled against her dad. Seven ran, standing directly in their path, fists clenched in anger. She would use a spell on him even if it meant she had to go to the Tombs as well.

"Stop being so awful to her, you warlock!" Seven yelled.

Mr. Pepperhorn only sneered. "I should never have let this go on as long as I did. Valley will not be seeing either you or that Thorn Witchling ever again. She is hereby withdrawn from the impossible task and will work in my employ instead. A marvelous loophole created by yours truly because, you see"—he leaned closer to Seven, a smug smile on his face— "when you control the magic, you control the town. The impossible task is only as binding and powerful as the witches enforcing it. That's something you didn't read in your little books, did you? When the Nightbeast devours you two, I will be sure to send only the most expensive of flowers to your graves." He yanked Valley roughly and stood up, but when he did there was someone standing behind Seven, and he came face-to-face with Talis Salazar.

"You let Valley go. *Now*."

Mr. Pepperhorn laughed. "Or what, you will report me to the magical insurance police? Useless, witch." He flicked his hand at Talis and sent a stream of fire at him. Seven's dad wasn't expecting it but defused the fire with his own stream of calming magic. Seven opened her eyes wide. She had never seen her father in actual combat before.

"That is your problem, Salazar. Unwilling to do what is necessary to win a fight!" Mr. Pepperhorn shoved Valley aside and threw his hands up at Seven's dad. "Veneno!"

Seven screamed as the magical poison snaked its way toward her father's chest. Quicker than lightning her mother appeared, her long red curls whipping around her as Fox grabbed Seven's cape off her with ease and precision and used it to block the spell. Her cape, Seven realized, her breath coming in fits and starts, was poison-proof thanks to Thorn. Beefy was safely on the other side of the room, sitting on Mrs. Villalobos's lap.

The few residents not too busy fighting to notice gasped or tried to apprehend Mr. Pepperhorn, but he already had his own security detail pushing them back. It was illegal to use that kind of magic against another witch, but there was nobody to report them to. The Hill Society always did what they wanted, but now it would truly be without consequences. Now everyone in Ravenskill was at their mercy.

"You have no right to do this. Any of it," Seven's mother said, her eyes narrowed at Mr. Pepperhorn.

"And who"—he paused, smiling wickedly—"is going to stop me?"

Seven felt the ascot in her pocket, wondering if maybe they had not suspected the wrong witch. Could Mr. Pepperhorn be evil enough to be using the cucos against the town? Everything was messed up, a bigger mess than before, and she felt all mixed up with fear and anger. Seven's heart shattered as she watched Mr. Pepperhorn grab Valley and storm out of the room.

Yes, she thought. He was.

"He's right," Thorn said through her tears. "There's nobody who can stop him now."

"Yeah. There is somebody." Seven turned to Thorn, fire in her gaze as she opened her hand to reveal the button she had taken from Mr. Pepperhorn's jacket while he was busy berating them. "Us."

CHAPTER TWENTY-TWO
A STOLEN MEMORY

THORN AND SEVEN RAN THROUGH THE NIGHT, the winter wind howling as it whipped their cloaks and threatened to send their witch's hats into the Boggy Crone River. The whole way, Seven felt Mr. Dimblewit's ascot and Mr. Pepperhorn's button burning a hole in her cloak pocket. They shimmied through a gap in the iron fence surrounding their school, just small enough for a Witchling.

"Desarmar," Seven said, throwing her hands up toward the giant lock at the front of the school. The lock shuddered and the cylinder popped out, hovering in the air, and then the springs and pins came out of the cylinder like they were being pulled apart by invisible hands. And the whole thing fell to the ground with a loud clank.

"I only know how to break locks, not open them," said Seven, cringing.

"Works just the same," said Thorn, and held her hand out to Seven. "It's creepy in there." Seven almost laughed. They had just run through a monstruo-infested town in the pitch darkness, but Thorn was scared of their school. Seven grabbed her friend's hand, and they ventured into the dark, drafty halls of the Goody Garlick Academy for Magic and hustled toward the potions room.

"Good, it's undisturbed," Seven said as they walked into the potions room and saw the cauldron still simmering with the lilac-colored roba recuerdos potion. Thorn and Seven looked into the cauldron and then at each other.

"Well, they're definitely both evil," Thorn said. "But which one of them do you think is working with the Nightbeast?"

"Let's do Mr. Pepperhorn first. After what he did today, I'm sure it's him," said Seven.

"Deal," said Thorn, and Seven took the shiny black button of Mr. Pepperhorn's coat and dropped it into the cauldron. They wouldn't be able to control what memories they saw, but they would be limited to recent ones unless the memory was particularly strong. If they were lucky, they might see something to connect one of the two witches with the Nightbeast.

The soft purple liquid rippled, what sounded like hundreds of voices whispered softly at once, and on the surface of the potion, an image formed. Seven could clearly see Valley. She was smiling on the night of the Black Moon Ceremony as her father chastised her.

Seven grimaced, and the vision changed. Mr. Pepperhorn was now on the phone with someone as he looked out the window. He was looking at Seven walking up the hill with Pixel. He had been watching her. Seven felt the heat of his anger rise from the cauldron, and she waved at the air in front of her.

"Wow, he really doesn't like me, huh?"

The potion rippled, and the next memory appeared. It was a Black Moon Ceremony. Mr. Pepperhorn was lifting up a pendant that hung from his neck and watching as it began to glow purple. House Hyacinth. This was Mr. Pepperhorn's memory of his own sorting ceremony.

"*He's* in the purple coven? Yuck," Seven said.

"There are terrible witches in every coven," said Thorn.

Seven knew she was right; covens were made up of a mix of all sorts of witches, but she couldn't imagine Mr. Pepperhorn being classified as virtuous. He was the opposite of that.

The vision rippled again, and Mr. Pepperhorn was speaking to a shadow of a witch, who the Witchlings could not see. Mr. Pepperhorn sounded angry. "I need the truth and I need it now," said Mr. Pepperhorn. "I found the book in *your* house, and this isn't what we agreed on. Those notes, this plan . . . why did you have it? Who is B. Birch?"

Birch. Seven took her dragon-scale notebook from her cloak and wrote the name down.

The vision fizzled, and a poof of smoke mushroomed

from its surface. "That's all this button will give," Seven said.

"Not much to go on," said Thorn.

"Yeah," said Seven, disappointed. "We still have one more suspect though."

Seven took the ascot from her pocket and dropped it into the cauldron. Like before, the potion rippled and a vision appeared. Mrs. Dimblewit, her face red, Pixel with her head down in the corner as Mrs. Dimblewit recounted the events of the Bruised Apple Bookshop.

"We will make them pay," said Mr. Dimblewit.

Seven and Thorn exchanged looks.

The vision rippled, and now Mr. Dimblewit was speaking to Apple Barlow, one of the town council members whose home had been attacked. Apple looked afraid, but Seven couldn't make out what they were saying. Rats.

The potion rippled once more, and Mr. Dimblewit was by the train tracks in the dead of night. A giant bag floated behind him, low to the ground. Mr. Dimblewit looked around and unzipped the bag. Seven leaned closer to the cauldron, her witch's hat nearly falling in before she grabbed it. The bag fell open. Inside were large pieces of meat.

"Oh my goats!" said Thorn.

Mr. Dimblewit loaded all the meat from the bag onto the train car, then hurried from the train station. Seven felt the fear from his memory before it fizzled like Mr. Pepperhorn's had, and the ascot had done all it could.

"That meat we saw . . . Mr. Dimblewit was leaving it there for the cucos . . . He was helping the cucos feed the Nightbeast!" Thorn said.

"That's why the cucos were there that day! They'd come to get the food," Seven responded. "It makes sense why the cucos haven't been attacking as often as they normally do. If Mr. Dimblewit was providing food at a set location, then there was no need for them to hunt." There was a small amount of potion left, and Seven scooped it into a vial and put it in her cloak.

"Remember Valley said she couldn't even find traces of cucos even though we knew they were walking around Ravenskill. If Mr. Dimblewit left them food in specific places, he knew where they'd leave traces. He could make it so nobody knew they were there."

"And he was talking to Apple. Probably intimidating her out of coming to the meeting," said Thorn.

It all fit. The Dimblewits hated Spares. They'd somehow teamed up with the Nightbeast to intimidate the town councils and make sure Amendment S didn't pass. They brought the monstruo to Boggs Ferry and Ravenskill, creating an environment of fear so that they could get the Spare Law through instead.

As for the impossible task being invoked—they'd gotten unlucky. They hadn't anticipated having three determined Witchlings on a mission to hunt their Nightbeast.

Seven knew they no longer had to simply defeat the Nightbeast. They had to take down the Dimblewits. And with the Uncle taken and the Gran imprisoned, they were on their own.

Like so many other times during the impossible task, Seven felt helpless. But at least there was one thing she could do to help.

Later that night, while Thorn snored on the extra mattress at the foot of her bed, Seven snuck to her parents' room as quietly as she could.

"Mom?" she asked, cracking the door open just a smidge.

Fox shot upright like a bolt of lightning, but she still seemed half-asleep.

"Huh, who, what happened, are you okay?" her mother asked, confusion and panic in her voice.

Seven stepped into the room. "We're okay. But I need to talk to you. It's about Valley."

CHAPTER TWENTY-THREE
THREE DAYS LEFT

SEVEN DOWNED A DOSE OF OPAL-HAWORTHIA potion and begged the Stars for good luck. It tasted like a foot, but soon, Seven's own feet, followed by her legs, torso, arms, and finally her head, disappeared into thin air. It had worked! She had finally made an invisibility potion.

Thorn opened her eyes wide in awe. "My turn."

Thorn drank from the potion and flickered like a dying image on the telecast before disappearing as well. Seven took the vial back from Thorn and put it into her rucksack, which was filled with jelly bean fish pods, just in case. Seven and Thorn were crouched behind a rosebush near the Dimblewits' estate—a large, garish house with green shutters and marble statues of the couple. They had been watching Mr. Dimblewit for the past two days.

They'd remembered Valley had said the Nightbeast had to

feed often, so they'd decided to stake out Mr. Dimblewit's house, waiting for him to go leave food for the cucos. If they caught him in the act, not only could they prove Mr. Dimblewit was responsible for the Nightbeast, but they could then—finally—follow the cucos back to the den. Two geese, one slice of bread.

"Do you think Valley is okay?" Thorn whispered.

Seven was quiet for a few moments, then shook her head. There was no sense in denying the truth or lying to Thorn or herself. She thought Valley was in a lot of danger. She might get out of being toadified somehow, even if Thorn and Seven didn't defeat the Nightbeast, but Seven thought that maybe her life at home would be even worse than that.

"I don't think she's okay. No, but we're gonna help her even if we're toads when we do it." Seven took a deep breath. "Valley might hate me for it, but I told my parents about her dad. He's done awful things to her in secret, and Valley shouldn't have to go through that alone."

Thorn reached out and squeezed Seven's hand. "Valley wouldn't hate you. You did the right thing."

Seven nodded and hoped Thorn was right. It was pretty overwhelming trying to solve their task and worrying about Valley, but at the very least, there were others helping the Gran. Seven reached into her pocket and gave Edgar a small pat. He had gotten into the habit of jumping into her cloak whenever she left the house, which was actually quite comforting. While the Witchlings were busy staking out Mr. Dimblewit, the older witches, led by the Salazars and the Laroux, were trying to break the Gran out of the Tombs. Their plan involved sending a legion of ghosts from the five covens to break her out. Big swarms of ghosts were almost impossible to stop and terribly powerful. The problem was they were tired from alive times. So, it was no easy feat convincing them all.

"There he goes!" Seven whispered as Mr. Dimblewit left his house.

He looked left and right, then walked out and toward the road leading down the Hill, the two Witchlings following in the shadows behind him. They weaved around bushes and through the alleyways, Mr. Dimblewit looking around nervously almost the entire way. He wasn't very good at sneaking. They reached Pavoroso Passage, and Mr. Dimblewit slinked into the alley beside Bloodworth's Meat Shop.

"This is it! Let's get closer," Seven whispered, and they crept over to the alley.

Strange smells wafted in the air around them as the Witchlings peered around the brick building and saw Mr. Dimblewit pulling something from a barrel.

"Ooof." Mr. Dimblewit struggled as he pulled out the bag and dropped it on the ground. It was filled with what looked like graying meat. He looked around, raised his hands, and whispered something in the direction of the meat. The bag shrunk to the size of Edgar Allan Toad, and Mr. Dimblewit picked it up and stuffed it in his pocket. So that's how he'd been transporting all that food. They followed him silently as he walked through Ravenskill's most hidden paths, luckily for them, since the invisibility potion was beginning to wear off. They'd passed the yellow brick road that led to the center of town and cut through the entrance to the Cursed Forest when Seven heard a low, rumbling growl.

"Seven, Seven, Seven, Seven," a voice repeated over and over.

"Who's there?" Seven asked, whipping around.

"What, what?" Thorn asked in a panic.

"Did you hear that?" Seven asked.

"No, what?"

"Someone was saying my name . . . I thought I heard . . ."

"I didn't hear anything." Thorn shook her head. "We're gonna lose him though—come on."

"Maybe it was my imagination." Seven shrugged and they kept walking, but she was afraid.

"Let us out!" the voices screamed. "Let us out, you evil witch!"

"Okay, you heard that, right?" Seven whispered, her voice shaky.

"You're scaring me now, Seven. Stop fooling around!" Thorn said.

"I'm not . . . Sorry, forget it. I'm just creeped out from being in the Cursed Forest."

"I can see you again," Thorn said. Seven nodded. The opal-haworthia potion had completely worn off now, and they would need to be extra careful.

Seven and Thorn hustled to catch up with Mr. Dimblewit, when a voice stopped them in their tracks.

"Seven, what are you doing here?" Seven turned and saw . . . the Gran.

"Oh my goats!" Seven said.

"Gran!" said Thorn.

How had she been let out this soon? It was a miracle, or perhaps she'd bested them with her magic like Seven knew she could. In any case, this was good news for them.

The Gran opened her arms wide, smiling and crouching down as Thorn ran to her. Seven's breath caught. Something wasn't right. As the Gran smiled, her mouth went wider, and wider, and wider until her teeth stretched over her skin, her eyes rolled to the back of her head, and Seven knew the truth of the illusion.

"Thorn, stop! It's a Shrouded!"

Seven ran, trying to grab the collar of Thorn's cape, but it was too late. The Shrouded had wrapped its now smokelike arms around Thorn and was pulling her into it. Soon Thorn would be devoured. Seven panicked. If she shot at it with magic, Thorn might die; if she did nothing, Thorn *would* die. She had to take a chance. Seven wished Valley, who would surely know how best to defeat this kind of monstruo, was here.

Seven raised her hands, prepared to use a blasting spell on the monstruo, when, from thin air, a man appeared and picked Thorn up from the waist and away from the Shrouded, putting her down next to Seven. He ran out of the Cursed Forest and toward the gazebo quick as lightning, a bluebird brooch glittering from his torn cloaks.

"Seven!" the Uncle yelled. "Run!"

For it really was the Town Uncle. He was back! He wasn't eaten! A rush of relief washed over Seven. They weren't out of the woods yet, but they weren't alone.

The Witchlings broke out of the Cursed Forest, and Seven led them toward the gazebo at the center of town, one of the safest, most protected areas of downtown Ravenskill. If they could make it there, they'd be safe. Another Shrouded, and then another, now in their true shadow form, rose from the cobblestone streets like fog and began to descend on the Uncle. The Shrouded never got this close to town, but maybe with the Gran gone, now they could. The Uncle pulled what looked like a sword encrusted with aquamarine gems from his side and began to fight off the monstruos. The Celestial Sword. He fought them off with grace and precision, dispatching monstruo after monstruo. The Uncle cleared the path for Thorn and Seven, dispatching monstruos as they ran to the center of town, where they would hopefully find protection and safety.

Residents opened their windows and doors and looked on with shock.

"Stay inside!" shouted the Uncle. "Close your doors, you fools—they'll get in!"

A few witches listened, while others ran out to help the Uncle fight. Meanwhile, Seven and Thorn ran into the protective magical safety of the Twilight Square gazebo and nearly collapsed onto the wooden floor.

"I'm sending my parents a message. Thank the Stars the Uncle returned when he did." Thorn typed fervently, not looking up from her portaphone.

"How is he using the Celestial Sword?" Seven asked.

Thorn stopped mid–portaphone message. "I—he shouldn't be able to, right?"

"Unless . . . he's the Gran now," Seven said. She didn't know everything there was to know about the Celestial Sword, but right now she was just glad the Uncle was back. Maybe now they'd stand a chance. "We should go help them fight," Seven said.

"Let's do this," Thorn said, but then she just stood there. "I can't move!"

Seven looked down. The wood of the gazebo floor had

turned to a quicksand-like mush. They weren't sinking, but they couldn't move either. The town square was filled with Ravenskillians, and Seven did the only thing she could think to do.

"Help!" she screamed. Thorn joined in and they were screaming their lungs off, but nobody came near them. As if they couldn't be seen or heard. What hex was this? The Uncle, sweaty and red-faced, slashed through the last monstruo and was met with a cheering crowd. He looked over to Seven and Thorn and ran toward them, when a loud whoosh sounded overhead.

Dozens of witches on brooms flew overhead and then landed as one like a flock of birds. All right in front of the Uncle.

"Is that the Gran's Guard?" asked Thorn.

"No, look at their uniforms."

The Hill's Guard was printed in large, elaborate gold lettering on the back of their witch's cloaks.

"Just what we needed. Now the Hill has its own guard?" Seven shook her head. "We have to get out of here. Help me with the unbinding spell, but be super careful you don't do it to your leg by accident."

Thorn gulped. "I'll do my best."

"Desastar," Seven began, and bit by bit, small splinters of wood began coming off the gazebo floor.

"This is preposterous! Let me through at once," the Uncle said, holding up the Celestial Sword. He was standing toe-to-toe with the Hill's Guard when Mr. Dimblewit strolled out in front of them.

"You know better than to brandish a weapon at a fellow Ravenskillian. Especially defending those two." Mr. Dimblewit turned and pointed at the Witchlings, who were still struggling to escape the gazebo. "We have discovered that they are responsible for bringing the Nightbeast to Ravenskill. Valley Pepperhorn has confessed *everything*."

Witches gasped, shook their heads, looked confused and angry, but the energy in the air was clear: They needed someone to blame for everything, and Mr. Dimblewit was giving that to them.

"No, it's not true!" Seven said. The whole world seemed to spin around her. Valley wouldn't have said that, would she? There was no way she'd betrayed them that way. There was just no way. The Nightbeast had come to Ravenskill before the impossible task had been invoked. Everyone had talked about it, and people were even warding their houses. Why was everyone just believing anything Mr. Dimblewit said?

"They were on their way to lure the Nightbeast to town as well. Just check their satchels—they are filled with jelly bean fish!"

Mrs. Dimblewit emerged from the crowd, climbed up the gazebo steps, and grabbed Seven's rucksack and dumped out the jelly bean fish pods and potion vials.

"It's true—look!" the witch shrieked, and unfortunately for the Witchlings, the crowd looked at first shocked but then angry.

"Stop it! That is not what we were doing!" Thorn tried.

"How much more proof do we need? From illegal magic usage to invoking an impossible task and putting us all in danger to luring dangerous monstruos to our town. Even the Shrouded are going beyond the Cursed Forest boundaries now! Something *must* be done. These Witchlings must be punished. *Quite severely.* With our beloved Gran gone, we held an emergency last-minute council meeting early this morning. In the absence of both the Gran and the Uncle, we decided that we should have an interim leader. To keep us all safe," Mr. Dimblewit said.

"They're just . . . getting away with everything." Thorn's voice cracked with desperation, and Seven could think of nothing to do but to continue chipping away at their wood prison and getting the hex out of there.

"I am honored to report that I was voted interim leader of Ravenskill, and as the current leader of this town, I will do what nobody else can—invoke an executive order to strip these Witchlings of their power. If they have no more power, they can cause no more mischief!"

"No!" the Witchlings screamed, as did much of the crowd, which had grown considerably. Witches murmured and yelled, angry and scandalized and confused all at once. Seven's face was hot; she tried to grab for her phone, to say something, to move, or to protest, but she was frozen in place, struck numb by fear and anger and a bit of a hex if her instincts were correct.

"Just one moment," the Uncle said, and the crowd quieted down. "In accordance with our law, I am second-in-command to the Gran and therefore will inherit any powers when she is no longer able to lead. Until a new Gran is chosen by the Stars, of course."

"That may be true, but since you have only just appeared, the council vote stands," said Mr. Dimblewit. "We will also have to investigate you, Rulean. Considering you disappeared and left us to fend for ourselves. Why, how can we be sure *you* are not involved?"

The crowd murmured again, but the Uncle looked undeterred. He held his hands up patiently.

"Very well. We will hold another meeting to undo the mess you have created. And when we do, we'll see who is really in charge," said the Uncle.

"Fine by us," said Mr. Dimblewit, gesturing at the Hill's Guard maliciously. "But so you are aware, I am recommending the most severe of punishments for anyone found to be a traitor to Ravenskill. Death by poison. Since we've already gotten a confession from Valley that the Gran has been enabling the three traitorous Witchlings, she must die first."

The crowd erupted, and everyone from shop owners to

warriors had their hands up, ready to fight. But for which side?

"It must be done before the waning moon or her powers will be too strong and she will be free to terrorize Ravenskill once more," said Mr. Dimblewit.

"You won't get away with this," Thorn whispered.

"Not if we have anything to do with it," said Seven.

Thorn cocked her head to the side. "Doesn't he look weird to you? His face is purply like an eggplant. Like he's been drowned or something."

Seven narrowed her eyes and inspected Mr. Dimblewit closely. His eyes were glassy, bloodshot. His skin covered in what looked like faint purple scales.

"Hex overload. It's what happens when someone uses too much evil magic. They start to look like an evil monstruo." The Witchlings had to get out of there and fast.

Seven spotted a sea of curly red hair running through the crowd. Her mother. Seven's eyes filled with tears, and she quieted the urge to call out for her mom, to scream for her parents to help her. Beside Fox stood Thimble, Leaf, and Talis. Thorn began to sob at spotting her parents there too.

"We're gonna get out of here, Thorn. Don't worry," Seven said. "This is going to take us all week though." On the floor around them were hundreds of wood chips, but they were still stuck up to their knees inside the gazebo. "Think, Seven. Think, think, think."

They were stuck because of magic. Not the warped wood on its own but a spell that made it so. If she undid the hex . . .

It will work, said a small voice inside her head. *You are capable and strong.*

Seven nodded, determined.

"I'm going to use the deshacer spell," Seven whispered at Thorn.

"What? But that's level—"

"Four, I know. But I'm capable and strong. And we have no other choice."

"They're going to see us though and come after us," Thorn said, gesturing toward Mr. Dimblewit and the Hill's Guard.

But there was something else happening in the crowd too. "No, they won't. Look," Seven whispered.

A big group of witches filtered into the crowd, led by Thorn's and Seven's parents. Thimble and Leaf and the rest of the witches they'd come with moved their fingers ever so slightly in the air on their way to Dimblewit and his witches. They were creating an illusion spell. Like a curtain to keep Seven and Thorn temporarily shielded from view. Fox turned and nodded at Seven.

This was their chance. Seven closed her eyes, opened her hands, and whispered, "Deshacer," and it was as if the entire earth beneath them shifted at once. Buildings around them began to rumble, witches looked around in confusion, but most important, the crackling energy of the gazebo fell. Seven and Thorn were spit out by the hexed wood and thrown backward onto the grass. And then they ran faster than a quickening spell, with Edgar Allan Toad, who Seven had completely forgotten about, croaking from her pocket the whole way.

CHAPTER TWENTY-FOUR
WHAT HAPPENED IN THE WOODS?

THIS TIME AROUND, Starlight Cottage looked a lot less magical. The world looked the same misty gray as the moment the Gran was sent off to the Tombs. The Uncle had broken from the crowd and caught up with the Witchlings, ushering them to the safety of the Gran's home.

"Hurry, hurry, inside," the Uncle instructed as Thorn and Seven made their way up the stairs and into the cottage. Once inside, he recounted his harrowing encounter with the cucos and the week he'd spent bloodied and on the brink of death in the Nightbeast's den. He had been using a powerful protection spell on himself so the Nightbeast couldn't eat him, and it had taken all his energy.

As the Uncle finished his tale, they sat quietly in the main room of the cottage. The Uncle wrapped thick knitted blankets around them and gave them hot tea, although of the three of them, he looked the frailest and in need of a rest. There were dark circles under his bloodshot eyes, his skin an almost grayish color. He was moving slowly, like every step hurt, and Seven's heart lurched with concern.

"Do you remember where it was? The Nightbeast's den?" Seven asked.

"I'm afraid that by the time I escaped, the Nightbeast had already moved on to a new location. I will try to perform some tracing magic, but I do not know how well it will work. That was . . . Knox's area of expertise." Rulean's voice cracked with grief. "We will get her out of there. I promise you."

"How *did* you escape?" Thorn asked.

"When the cucos brought me to the cave, I fought as hard as I could, but during the fight, I was knocked unconscious. I slept for . . . at least a few days. It's all quite hazy now. When I awoke, the den had been abandoned. Except for the bones of course . . ."

Thorn and Seven exchanged looks. That must've been when they'd tipped the Nightbeast off with their fighting. They were so close to the Uncle and didn't even know, but the argument with Valley might very well have saved his life.

"Unfortunately, I was still too weak to leave the den. I could barely stay awake for more than a few minutes at a time and ate nothing but berries. I waited until I was well enough to venture out, lest I run into the Nightbeast. When I was finally strong enough, I ran. When I reached Starlight

Cottage earlier today, the blue jays in the Gran's garden warned me you were in danger, so I ran to the Cursed Forest as fast as I could."

And not a moment too soon, thought Seven. With so many things going wrong, it was nice to finally have someone on their side and, most of all, to see the Uncle alive and sort of well. It was especially lucky that the Nightbeast had not eaten him right away. They knew because of Valley's lessons that they sometimes stored their meals for later, but if there were already bones in the den, someone else hadn't been as lucky. Seven shivered, and the Uncle poured her some more hot tea. He was pale and looked tired and skinnier than he had the last time they'd seen him. Seven hoped he really was okay and not faking for their sake.

"Uncle, we still need to find the Nightbeast, but we have a theory. We think someone is working with it," said Seven.

The Uncle's eyes went wide. "Who would—" But realization dawned on him almost immediately. "Drascal Dimblewit?"

Seven and Thorn nodded. "We found compelling evidence in his memories," Thorn said.

"Why that little—" The Uncle's face reddened with anger. "That is dastardly, even for him. I cannot interfere with the fight against the Nightbeast, as you know, but I can help you stop him at least. I will do my best to help, although I do need to get the Gran out and rest for a day or two. Oh, and repair my cloak! It was ruined when the cucos abducted me.

It was my favorite one. The Gran had it made specifically for me." The Uncle's eyes filled with tears. "And if I am to go toe-to-toe with witches using forbidden magic, I'm going to need it."

On the floor in a corner lay a bloody cloak. Thorn got up and ran to it, inspecting it. "I am certain my mother and I could mend this! It will only take us a few hours."

"Thank you, Thorn. That would be most helpful. Come, I will make sure you both get home safely."

"No, it's okay. You should sleep, you look . . . uh, a little . . ." Seven said, her face going hot.

The Uncle laughed. "I am in disarray, aren't I? Still, I insist. With the Dimblewits around and half the town out to crucify any Spare in sight, I would feel better if I escorted you home. I am still the Uncle. Don't you fear."

Seven and Thorn smiled, and as they walked home in the dark of night, Seven was grateful to feel safe. At least for one night, she was safe.

CHAPTER TWENTY-FIVE
THE FINAL NIGHT

SEVEN WAS GOING TO BREAK VALLEY out of Blood Rose Manor if it was the last thing she did. This was their last day before meeting their fate as toads, and she had to make sure Valley was okay. Standing behind a row of bushes that sat at the foot of the Hill, she took a teeny-tiny sip of a new batch of opal-haworthia potion from a glass vial and gagged as she went invisible.

She hustled out from behind the bushes and toward the Pepperhorns' home. Members of the Hill's Guard stood watch at the entrance to the Hill, but none so much as blinked as Seven passed undetected. Seven made it to Valley's front gate and hid behind a pillar as she texted her.

"I'm at your front gate."

A few moments passed, and the front door to Blood Rose Manor opened. Valley stood there in a thick black turtleneck sweater, her pink hair down in loose waves. She looked tired. "I don't see you?" she texted back.

"I'm invisible."

Valley let out a loud laugh, then reached her hand inside. The gate buzzed open, and Seven pushed it and slipped onto the front lawn. There were other guards beside the house, two of them, but from the Gran's Guard this time. The moment Seven walked through Valley's front door, the potion wore off.

"You finally made the potion, huh?" Valley crossed her arms and smirked.

"Yup, but it only lasts a few minutes."

"Still pretty neat."

Seven wiggled her arms and legs and made a weird face. "Feels totally bizarre though. What's up with the guards inside your gate?"

"Oh, someone tried to break into our house the other night. It's fine—we weren't hurt or anything. My mom nearly caught them in the act, but the witch was too fast for her and escaped. They did trash my dad's library though."

Seven cringed at the mention of Valley's dad, then took a deep breath. "Um, Valley . . . I have to tell you something."

Valley held her hand up. "I already know. You told your mom about my dad."

Seven prayed that a dragon would crash through the ceiling and take her away. She was embarrassed and scared and uncomfortable. She was worried she'd messed up, or that Valley would hate her forever, and she was terrified that she would lose her as a friend just as they were becoming closer.

"I'm not mad anymore. I was at first, but then I had a long talk with my mom. You did the right thing. You're a good friend." Valley looked down as she said it, her cheeks red.

Seven breathed out a sigh of relief. "Is your dad really mad?"

Valley shrugged. "I dunno. Your mom called my mom, and my mom freaked out and hexed my dad out of the house. She didn't know. I guess my dad was really good at keeping the things he did a secret and keeping me from talking about it too. Anyway, he's not here, so you don't have to feel weird. He's staying at the inn for now."

Seven nodded. "Can I . . . ask you a question? It's about your dad, so you don't have to answer."

"Shoot," said Valley.

"When we were sorted as Spares, I imagine, knowing how your dad feels about them now, that Mr. Pepperhorn was vexed. But you looked happy about it . . ."

"Yeah, I was. Because I wanted him to be upset. I know it's silly, but I didn't know how to . . . show how I was feeling. I thought I wasn't allowed to talk about it, so I let it out in anger."

"Like the candy dish at the Gran's," said Seven.

"Exactly like that. I'm gonna get better though. I want to

talk stuff out and not always just explode or run away when I don't wanna talk about stuff. My mom's gonna help me and so is Dr. Blackwood."

"Oh, he's real nice," said Seven of their local witch doctor.

"Now that everything is out in the open, I thought I would be embarrassed or something, and I guess part of me is, but I feel better too because at least I don't have to be sad in private and hide things."

Seven wanted to hug Valley, very much, but she wasn't sure if Valley would want that, so she gave her a small smile instead. "I'm glad you feel better."

Valley shrugged and smiled back, and then she changed the subject. "Where's Thorn?"

"You heard the Uncle's back?" Valley nodded. "She's mending the Uncle's cloak with her mom and then dropping it off at his place."

"Come upstairs. I need your help." Valley grabbed Seven's hand, and they ran upstairs to her room.

Valley's room was a giant mess. At least fifty books lay strewn across the room; a hundred small paper squares with writing on them lay all over the floor, so you could barely see the black hardwood underneath.

Valley tiptoed through the mess of papers and sat on the floor next to her notebook.

"What's all this?" Seven walked over to Valley carefully and sat down next to her.

"Research. I know it's probably too late since this is our last night before we're toadified. And I know I haven't been around, but I kept busy too. I wanted to keep trying," Valley said. "When my mom hexed my dad out of the house, he didn't have time to take anything with him . . ."

"His books!" Seven said.

"At first, I was focusing on the Nightbeast because there should've been traces of it when it first arrived in town. But if Mr. Dimblewit got rid of any traces of the Nightbeast and cucos, and made sure it didn't follow any of its normal conventions so nobody *could* find it, none of that mattered. Our only hope was figuring out the Dimblewits' plan." Valley held up a book.

"*The Nightbeast Archives*! How did you find it?" Seven asked.

Valley nodded. "You kept complaining about this book being checked out, and when you messaged me to tell me about the memory from my dad, the Birch one, I remembered that was the name of the person who checked out *The Nightbeast Archives*, and I went looking for it in my dad's library. I looked everywhere, for like ten hours, and it was hidden. Like, really hidden, in a special secret compartment. The problem is there isn't anything in the book we don't already know."

"That doesn't make any sense. Why would your dad go through all the trouble of hiding it if there's no new information?"

"He came here last night, trying to speak to my mom, begging her to let him back in." Valley's cheeks went red. "So I asked him. And do you know what he said?"

Seven quirked an eyebrow.

Valley put on a blank stare, looking far into the distance. "You know, I don't remember."

Seven's eyes went wide. "A forgetting hex."

It's what both Alaric and the Gran had said when Seven asked if they remembered the Cursed Toads' names. And if Mr. Pepperhorn had the book, and somebody knew, it would make sense why Valley's house had been broken into.

"Maybe the same person who put the hex on your father put some sort of enchantment on the book then. Maybe there is information we can't see," Seven said.

"That's my theory. It must've been Mr. Dimblewit who took out this book on the Nightbeast. He wanted to learn about it so he could control it. My dad didn't remember how he got it or wouldn't tell me, but I'm sure it's important. I tried to use the unveiling spell to reveal any hidden notes or writing, but whatever enchantment they used, it's too strong. That's why I need you."

"What am I supposed to do?"

"Didn't you notice how you've been able to do level-four and even level-five spells pretty much this whole time? It must've been all that studying or something, but of the three of us, you're the one who can pull off high-level magic," Valley said. She looked at Seven curiously, like she was trying to figure her out.

"The revelar spell is at least a five point five! I can't—"

"Just try it." Valley nudged the book toward Seven.

Seven sighed. "Fine."

She threw her hands up, looking at the book intently. "Revelar."

Light shot from the book, the cover opening on its own and the pages turning rapidly. It fell open on a diagram of the Nightbeast, and red ink began to bleed onto the page before transforming into notes.

"Told you." Valley crossed her arms and smiled smugly.

"Lucky shot," said Seven, but she felt shaky. That spell had been a powerful one, and her whole body was buzzing with magic.

Together they looked through the book. There had to be at least a hundred annotations, about the Nightbeast's diet, its preferred season for hibernation, even its favorite snack. Valley had been right about the jelly bean fish. Still, they weren't learning anything that would help them much, until they turned to the map of Ravenskill. There they found the thing they'd needed most all along.

"There are notes here about its hibernation period I didn't have before," Valley said. There was real excitement in her voice as she read the copious notes around the map.

"I was calculating the time all wrong before, but I should

be able to figure this out now. Do you have all our relevant dates in your notebook? I need to know when the Nightbeast was in Boggs Ferry. The night Petal died."

Seven took her notebook from her rucksack and opened it to the page where she'd written down their timeline. "First sighting was spring, tenth of this year. When Petal was taken."

Valley wrote it down in the book. "There were no other cuco attacks in spring, so the Nightbeast didn't stay in Boggs Ferry. It was just passing through, and Petal was unlucky enough to be in its path. They only travel at night, resting for days at a time when not at full strength, and it would've gone through the Cursed Forest to avoid detection in a weakened state."

The Cursed Forest was not a straight shot through the Twelve Towns; instead it made a sort of crescent shape. The Nightbeast had taken the long way around. Valley began to write numbers on the side of the map, her tongue sticking out slightly, her brow furrowed in a show of extreme concentration.

"It says a Nightbeast can normally make this trip in a day, but in a weakened state, it should've taken about a month to reach the outer caves of Ravenskill," Valley said.

"The notes say a Nightbeast emerges *exactly* six months from the beginning of its hibernation period, and it prefers to do so on the waning moon," said Valley.

"That's . . . tonight. The Nightbeast begins to hunt tonight."

CHAPTER TWENTY-SIX
SMELL THE ROSES

THE TWO WITCHLINGS SET OFF FOR the Uncle's home, which was down the lane from Starlight Cottage, to share what they had discovered.

"We have to get Thorn, tell the Uncle, and head toward the valley," said Seven as they took off toward downtown Ravenskill.

Despite the enchanted gloves that were part of her outfit, Seven's hands felt raw with cold. Tonight was the night. They were really going to fight the Nightbeast. She put her hands in one of her cloak pockets and felt something wriggling around inside.

"Rats!" she screamed, pulling her hand out.

"What is it?" Valley asked.

"I'm not sure, but there's something in my pocket—"

Seven said as she pulled the something out. It was in fact a someone.

"Edgar?" she asked.

"Croak," Edgar Allan Toad responded.

When had he gotten inside her cloak?

"That's weird. I thought he hated you," Valley said.

Seven held the toad up to her face and looked at him closely. "I thought so too. You made a big mistake coming here, buddy. Now you're gonna be Nightbeast food. I should let him go. He'd be happier in nature anyway." Seven crouched down and put Edgar on the grass. But no sooner had he touched the ground than he jumped back up onto Seven and into her cloak pocket. Seven sighed.

"Fine, it's your funeral."

The Uncle's cabin sat in a grove at the end of Hallow Lane. As they opened the iron fence and stepped into his garden, Seven let out a gasp. Every kind of flower she could imagine, birds of every color of the rainbow, and critters of all sorts, from blue tree toads to bunnybeavers, bloomed and flew and scampered about the garden. It must have been enchanted to be summer here, since there was no snow and it was pleasantly warm.

"It looks like a storybook," said Valley.

Together, the Witchlings walked past the brightly colored flowers and enormous willow trees and to the Uncle's door. Valley reached for the lion-head-shaped knocker, but before she could knock, the door creaked open on its own.

Valley shrugged. "Hmm, must've forgotten to lock it."

Inside, the Uncle's cabin was cool and smelled overwhelmingly of freshly cut roses.

"Wow, it smells like a perfume factory," said Seven, scrunching her nose.

"Thorn?" called out Valley.

They walked past the empty living room and into the hallway.

"Hello? Uncle?" Seven tried.

But nobody answered.

As they walked through the house, an eerie feeling began to come over Seven. Maybe it was the strong flower smell getting to her head, but something felt really off. Really wrong. They made their way into the kitchen.

"Look." Seven pointed at the floor of the kitchen. There was spilled rice all over the floor, along with a cracked ceramic container with delicate painted flowers on it.

"It looks like there was a fight . . ."

Valley and Seven noticed a trail of rice leading to a door in the kitchen at the same time and ran toward it. Seven opened the door, revealing stairs leading to a basement. They ran down the dark stairs, and when they finally found a light, they were met with a disaster of a room. And the most horrid smell ever.

"What the hex happened here?" asked Valley.

"And what is that smell?" Seven asked as she pulled her cloak over her nose.

There were broken chairs, vases of flowers knocked over, and water spilled everywhere. A huge broken mirror leaned against the wall.

As they inspected the room, the uneasy feeling in Seven's stomach began to grow. Where were Thorn and the Uncle? Were they okay? What had gotten in and done all this?

"Look," Valley gasped. There on the floor was the Uncle's bluebird brooch. The one he never ever took off and they had seen him with when he returned.

"Quick, I have a bit of roba recuerdos potion left. If we drop the brooch in, maybe we can see what happened and where he and Thorn went."

"Smart thinking." Valley pushed a cauldron from the other side of the room toward the small patch of light made by the overhead candelabra, and Seven poured the remaining roba recuerdos potion inside the cauldron. Valley dropped the bluebird brooch in the potion, and it began to ripple.

The first vision to appear was of the Uncle fighting the cucos and saving Thorn and Seven from the Shrouded. Although the Uncle dispatched the monstruo with ease, Seven could see it was quite powerful. Had it not been for him, they would've been toast.

The vision rippled again, and this time, there were hands

holding one of the poisoned trichotomous. The flowers the Cursed Toads had been meant to find for their impossible task. A soft laugh could be heard, but not the face of whoever was holding it. Then the vision shifted, and they saw a young boy with another one of the poison flowers, his eyes open wide at whoever he was seeing, before a flash of light hit the flower and destroyed it.

"What? Why would the Uncle have this memory?" Valley asked. Seven's stomach dropped as the next vision appeared. The door opening, Thorn and Thimble entering with a garment bag—and then leaving.

"So Thorn left. She's okay . . ." said Seven.

Valley held up a hand. "There's more."

Thorn was walking alone now, when the Uncle caught up to her and stopped her. They couldn't make out the words, but it was clear Thorn was surprised by something the Uncle said. She nodded and quickly followed him back to his cabin.

The vision rippled again. They were in the very basement they found themselves in now. Except this time, it was Thorn there and not them. Thorn opened a closet door and threw her hands over her mouth in shock, though they could not see what she was seeing. Instead, in the reflection of the now broken mirror, they saw the Uncle's face spread into a wide, disconcerting smile before he grabbed her shoulder.

"Holy goats, what is happening?" asked Valley.

A scream shrilled from the potion. Thorn's scream. The vision rippled, and Thorn's hands were up; she was fighting. Shooting at something they could not see. Something moving much, much too quickly. The figure swooped Thorn up and ran in the direction of a door leading out of the basement. As the vision fizzled and blurred, the last thing they saw was Thorn's hand, grabbing on to something made of gold and throwing it onto the floor. The pendant.

The memories stopped, and the air seemed to be sucked right from the room.

Seven looked around the basement and found the closet door from the memory. She flung it open, and she and Valley both threw their hands up, prepared for battle. But no sooner had they opened the door than they lowered their hands and covered their noses.

It was a closet filled with hundreds and hundreds of jelly bean fish. That explained the strong smell of roses. He was trying to mask their awful smell. The world around Seven began to spin, and she felt a heavy weight on her chest, making it hard to breathe or even move. Valley's face was drained of any color, and when they looked at each other, it was like an unspoken understanding: Something had gone terribly wrong. Seven and Valley ran to the basement door that Thorn had been taken through in the vision: It opened into the garden, and there was a path of muddy tracks going west, in the direction of the Cursed Forest.

The puzzle pieces began coming together then. The fires, the forgetting spells, the disappearances. They had gotten it all wrong.

"It was the Uncle," said Valley, clenching her fists.

And now he was on his way to see the Nightbeast. With Thorn.

CHAPTER TWENTY-SEVEN
BEHOLD THE NIGHTBEAST

JUST AS THE SUN BEGAN TO SET, the two Witchlings headed into the Cursed Forest. Their red capes shimmered in the orange light around them as they made their way toward their friend. Seven's heart lurched at the thought of Thorn fighting the Uncle alone. Of how scared she must be. Of her seeing the very beast that had taken Petal.

"How did he fool all of us?" Valley asked as they ran.

"He was careful and devious, and I bet you anything he used forbidden magic." Seven thought of Mr. Dimblewit's purplish face at the gazebo standoff and wondered if he hadn't been hexed.

The signs had been there from the start, she realized. It had all started with his hat.

"When Beefy took his hat, the Uncle must've sensed he

was powerful, and the perfect snack for the Nightbeast," said Seven.

"Why was he helping the Nightbeast though?"

"The same reason the Dimblewits want us sent off to the Tombs and the same reason they were all working together: They hate Spares. Think about it: The Uncle helped the Nightbeast hunt Beefy. He was the one who supposedly warded the upstairs of our house, but the cuco got in no problem," Seven said. "Because he didn't actually protect our house. He got all weird about the waning moon being the most beautiful that one time in the Gran's cottage. We should've known when Mr. Dimblewit said they had to kill the Gran before the waning moon because her powers would be stronger, but that's wrong. The *full* moon is when the Gran is most powerful. They knew the Nightbeast would be emerging on the waning moon tonight and wanted to get her out of the way before it did, in case she stopped the monstruo. And do you remember the vision we saw? The Uncle was watching one of the Cursed Toads. He had found the poison plant, but the Uncle stopped him. He probably stood in their way too."

"Which is why nobody can seem to remember them!" said Valley. "The Uncle was using forgetting hexes on the Gran and Alaric because he wanted them to forget that the Spares were going to solve the impossible task. Rulean just stopped them."

"And burned the Hall of Elders down in the process. The

memory hex causes fires if you do it wrong. So not only is he evil, he's rotten at magic too. And he also made your father forget the book, then tried to steal it, but didn't count on your mom stopping him," said Seven. "There is no B. Birch. He was using a phony name. Everything he did, he did to make us believe he was a victim instead of the butt-toad doing all the evil. Okay, let's stop here."

The Witchlings stood right at the entrance to the Cursed Forest, the one they'd first gone to together and where Beefy had been taken. Valley took jelly bean fish from her bag and looked at Seven.

"Ready?"

Seven scrunched her nose but nodded.

Valley stuffed rancid jelly bean fish from the Uncle's basement in Seven's pockets, in the hood of her cloak—she even put one in her shoe. Seven gagged; the smell was like a thousand Beefy farts at once, but that's just what they were counting on. And if they were right about the Nightbeast emerging tonight, the monstruo's appetite would be at its peak. Unlike the first time they'd tried to lure it, it wouldn't be able to resist its favorite snack.

"I think that should do it," said Valley. Seven nodded, and together they walked into the Cursed Forest and into a clearing where Seven would be completely exposed.

"I'll be just behind those trees and then behind you the whole way," said Valley. "Good luck, Seven."

"Thanks," Seven said.

Valley gave Seven a weird look, and then she hugged her.

Seven was frozen in place for just a moment, but she hugged Valley back. She hugged her friend back.

"Ugh, now I have jelly bean slime on me." Valley smirked, then slipped between the shadows and was gone.

Seven was alone. Her heart was beating so loudly that if the jelly bean fish didn't work, the thumping in her chest would. It was quiet all around her, but the skeleton birds watched her from their perches, the trees pulled close like they were feeding off her fear. Time passed in the way it does when you're waiting. One second stretched like putty into hours, and Seven was shaking with fear and anticipation. She tried to see if she could spot Valley, when something rustled in the trees.

Click, click, click came the sound of the cucos.

"They're coming," Seven said.

A cuco emerged from the woods, its snout up in the air, its beady eyes snapping to Seven. The cuco growled, then galloped at her. Seven stiffened, prepared for its claws to sink into her, or its teeth to grab the nape of her neck like she was a puppy. The cuco descended on her. Seven held her breath and closed her eyes. Then, using its large snout to lift her off the ground and into the air, it caught her, throwing her over its shoulder like a rag doll. Seven let out a scream. The cuco ran, one hand holding her in place. Its grip was so tight she could barely breathe, and the Cursed Forest passed before them in a blur of black and gray. Seven prayed Valley was keeping up with the cuco's fast pace, when suddenly they stopped. Had their plan worked? Had they reached the Nightbeast's den?

The cuco stopped suddenly. The monstruo grabbed Seven and held her in front of it like it was presenting her to someone. Like a sacrifice. It began to walk forward, and they were about to enter an unfamiliar place at the edge of the forest when the monstruo wailed and dropped Seven. She fell hard onto the ground and scrambled back. The cuco was sinking to the ground, eyes closed.

Valley emerged from the forest, a blow dart in her hands and a smirk on her face.

"I added a few extra doses of foxglove this time." Valley walked over and crouched over the unconscious cuco. "It'll wake up sometime next week."

Seven took a vial from her cloak. Opal-haworthia potion. Both she and Valley took a big gulp, then walked into the clearing. Suddenly Seven knew exactly where they were. Crow's Head Valley. Though it was not too far from their home, Seven had never ventured out this far in Ravenskill. Crow's Head Valley was not exactly a place for picnics. It was a place for perils. The mountains on either side were covered in forest, and there were large animals and monstruos living in those trees. Seven could almost imagine hundreds of blinking red eyes staring back at them from the darkness. A river, so quick and cold it would sweep you away in mere moments if you fell in, ran through the center of the valley. Seven looked at Valley and understood.

"Your name," she whispered. "This place is called Crow's Head Valley."

Valley's eyes welled with tears. When the Stars whispered a newborn Witchling's name to the Gran, it was always a prophecy. It could be something as small as someone being named River and being an excellent swimmer, or as significant as Valley's name being the key to their impossible task. Either way, discovering your name prophecy was a momentous occasion, even if it happened at the time of your death.

Valley wiped a tear from her cheek and smiled. It was a big, genuine smile, and it made Seven's heart feel full. Valley's name had been the answer all along. At least they could share this pocket of happiness before they met their fate.

They walked the grassy path on the right side of the river in silence. Seven's stomach churned with fear, and she practiced her combat skills and magical attacks in her head the whole way. She wished she could play some Kill Le Goose or something, to get her ready to fight. But more than anything, she hoped Thorn was okay.

The night around them was almost impossible to see in, the crescent moon covered with a blanket of gray clouds. The

Nightbeast could creep up to them, and they'd be none the wiser. Seven had checked her utility belt about twelve thousand times, trying to think of anything but the rows of sharp teeth in the Nightbeast's enormous mouth, when the clouds shifted in the sky and the moon appeared, full and bright. It lit up the valley around them, the rushing river gurgled and splashed, the giant trees swayed in the frigid breeze, the grass looked touched with silver. Climbing roses covered many of the trees, their prickly vines making the forest look like it was covered in armor.

First came the sound of leaves and ice being crushed underfoot. Then heavy breathing like the howl of the wind rushed toward them, and then a paw the size of a small car emerged from the foggy darkness of the valley. And then another.

"Get down." Valley threw her hands out, and they shuffled back and behind a cluster of tall oaks. The two Witchlings were quieter than rabbits avoiding a wolf.

On the other side of the river, the Nightbeast stalked into the light of the moon. The monstruo squinted its enormous eyes in the light, the moon probably the brightest thing it had seen in many months. Whatever other monstruos the Witchlings had fought, however scary they had seemed, was absolutely nothing compared with this.

Its head was high above the few trees scattered throughout the valley clearing. The Nightbeast's fur blended almost exactly with the color of the fog around them except for red markings along its face and mouth that looked a lot like blood. Its snout was long, like that of a rat, its eyes covered in a milky-white film. The Nightbeast's ears were long and pointy, pinned back, exposing the pink skin inside. It walked not on all fours but on its hind legs. As it snarled, its large teeth glimmered in the moonlight, spit hanging from its enormous mouth. Most noticeable of all was the stripe of white down the monstruo's left side, beginning at its ear and running all the way to its tail.

"That's it," Seven said softly. "The Nightbeast that took Petal."

A cuco appeared then, on their side of the river, with something draped in its arms. Thorn.

Seven moved to get on her feet, but Valley held her back. She looked at Seven and shook her head no. Not yet. Seven was desperate, every nerve in her body screaming at her to go save Thorn. But she knew Valley was right. They had to surprise the Nightbeast or they would have no chance.

The cuco laid Thorn on an elevated stone, like she was some sort of sacrifice. Seven looked for any sign of life, of breathing, but from this far away, she couldn't tell. Her insides felt like they were on fire. She was angry and sad and terrified. All thoughts of being turned into a toad, of missing out on the life she'd always hoped for, and of being a Spare felt small and insignificant right now. The only thing Seven cared about was saving Thorn.

Valley looked at Seven and put her hand between them. Seven stacked her hand on Valley's, and they stood there for just one more silent moment. It was as if their magic coursed through their hands, enveloping them in a warm glow. Seven had grown to trust both her and Thorn. To rely on them. But now, in what might be their final hour, she knew she had also learned to love them.

They took their final sips of opal-haworthia potion, threw their hands up, and stepped out from behind the trees, ready to fight.

"A touching display." A voice broke through the darkness, and the Witchlings turned toward the river.

There, standing beside the Nightbeast, was the Uncle. And he was not alone. There were two other men on either side of him, men Seven did not know but who looked oddly familiar to her. The Uncle flicked his hand, and Seven felt as if her skin were being ripped from her body. A bright blue light came off both her and Valley, and they were propelled forward a few toadstools, almost losing their balance. They were no longer invisible. The Uncle had simply ripped the magic off them. He took a deep breath as the blue light traveled in his direction, and he seemed to . . . to absorb it. A pendant around his throat flickered with light for a moment, and the Uncle smiled.

"I am impressed, I will admit, that you made it this far. But as you can see"—he gestured toward the Nightbeast—"you are no match for a Nightbeast. Or for me."

The Nightbeast made a low growl, and the Town Uncle smiled. "Yes, yes, I will let you eat them in good time. I want to relish this moment."

"Let Thorn go and fight us instead," Valley said to the three men.

The older witches exchanged amused expressions. "It is too late for you to be making any bargains," said one. "Will you not admit when you are defeated?"

Seven scoffed. "We're still standing here, butt-toad. We'll admit defeat when we're defeated."

"Yes, yes you will," said the third witch, and it suddenly all snapped into place.

Three witches, just like Seven, Valley, and Thorn. The fires that had happened not just in Ravenskill, but in Boggs Ferry and Stormville. The Uncle's memory of the Spare holding the cursed flower. These were the three Uncles who had gone missing from all three towns . . . but they weren't the Uncles at all.

"They're the Cursed Toads," Seven said. She eyed Thorn, trying to formulate a way to get her out of these terrible witches' path. "We got it all wrong. B. Birch wasn't a phony name—it was his real name. That's the real reason he made your father forget and wanted to make sure nobody saw the book or the records in the Hall of Elders. The reason nobody could remember the Cursed Toads' real names. They were hexing them."

The Ravenskill Uncle clapped. "Bravo, Seven! You were always a smart witch. Not smart enough to vanquish us, of course, but impressive for your age nonetheless. Please, meet my coven. The most powerful coven in all of Twelve Towns history."

The air around the three older witches rippled like water, and suddenly they looked like completely different witches. Younger, more hideous, and pocked by thousands of tiny cuts and large bruises and oozing welts all over their faces and hands. They looked almost green with infection, and Seven tried hard not to gag from the smell that had overtaken the valley as they transformed. These were all side effects of forbidden magic. As they transformed, three matching necklaces appeared around their necks, glowing red pendants hanging from each. Each of them held on to their necklace. A thought came to Seven's mind, of her mother holding her coven necklace for power.

"Aamon," said the witch on the fake Uncle's left, bowing.

"Gamigin," said the one on his right, who sounded like a horse that had suddenly learned to speak. He tipped his hat.

"And I, of course, am Barbatos Birch," said the witch they'd believed to be Rulean for all their lives.

"B. Birch . . ." said Seven.

"Yes, the very one. It was not easy to keep our glamours up for so many years, but it feels good to be free of them, at least for a little while." Barbatos smiled wickedly, his pointy teeth like those of a rat.

"Why are you doing this? We have nothing to do with your schemes," Valley said.

"You are mistaken. We cannot let you kill our Nightbeast or become a true coven. It just will not fit in with our plans," Aamon said.

"We worked hard, harder than anyone to get this far, and Spares today just want to be *handed* everything. GIVEN the power we worked to get! It won't do. And I will not be replaced," Barbatos said.

Replaced? Seven shot Valley a confused look, but she looked just as lost.

"For over fifty years now, we've used magic to not only cloak our true forms but to muddle the minds of our respective Grans. It was difficult to do, of course, but forbidden magic is much more powerful than the pitiful magic you are forced to endure."

"What did you do to the real Town Uncles?" Valley asked.

"They were toadified, of course," Gamigin said. "We hexed them to look like us and erased their memories so they would be like three little clueless lambs walking to their own doom. They took our place in the Twelve Towns Museum of Magical Artifacts, while we took theirs as Town Uncles."

Barbatos touched the shiny pendant at the end of his necklace. "I took Rulean's place first, absorbing some of his powers, before helping Aamon and then Gamigin infiltrate and replace the other two Uncles. It wasn't very hard at all."

And that was why Rulean, or rather Barbatos-as-Rulean, had been sick around the time of the Cursed Toads. He wasn't inconsolable; he was sick with forbidden magic and unable to perform all the Uncle's duties because he wasn't as strong as him. It had all been a cover.

"You couldn't even solve your own task," scoffed Valley.

"That is where you're wrong," Barbatos thundered. "We did solve our task, but by that point, we had decided to take the Uncles' identities, so we chose not to tell the Gran. Except the Gran found out somehow who we truly were, and we could not be sure who that old bat told. So we erased all of Ravenskill's memories of us with arcane magic. Beautiful, pure magic. The magic *we* are entitled to."

"You used the spell knowing that widespread use would create fires wherever it was cast if you weren't powerful enough," said Seven.

Because there was someone who had more than just memories. Someone who had records. Detailed, archived, copied, and not-easily-forgotten records.

"It was you who burned down the Hall of Elders. You erased Alaric's memory and created the fire that killed him," said Seven.

Alaric had even told them that Spares used to be assigned a Hall of Elders employee to follow them around and record everything they did. Alaric would've known everything.

Aamon clapped in delight. "She really is clever, Barbatos. May I take her powers, pretty please?"

"Don't be foolish!" Barbatos yelled. "That one belongs to me."

Seven clenched her fists in anger. Just then, Thorn turned her head ever so slightly. Enough so that Seven saw when she opened her eyes and winked. She was awake, and she was planning something. Relief flooded through Seven.

"The Gran had no right to name us Spares. We were deserving of more; Spares are *beneath* us. But we vowed on the night we took the Town Uncles' places that we would get our revenge on Knox, on all of Ravenskill. We vowed that we would rule the Twelve Towns.

"It has taken us many years to become powerful enough to carry out our plan. But now, with the help of our little pet, we can." Barbatos stroked the enormous Nightbeast, and the monstruo snapped at him. He leaned back in fear before regaining his composure. So the monstruo was not completely within their control, Seven thought. But how *was* he controlling it?

"After it appeared, after years of being dormant in the Twelve Towns and attacking that boy in Boggs Ferry, we knew we had to tame it. To make it ours," Barbatos said.

Even from this far away, Seven could see Thorn's face going white. Petal. They were talking about her brother. Seven felt a fury that she knew could never match her friend's, but one she was happy to use to help her defeat these butt-toads.

Barbatos seemed to whisper something to the Nightbeast, and it jumped over the river and to their side.

That's how he's controlling it, Seven realized. *The Uncle can speak to animals.*

He had used the power of the Uncles, of nature and animals and streams and flowers, a sacred power, for truly horrible things. To strike a deal with a beast.

"But the Dimblewits?" Valley asked. "And my . . ." Her face went red with shame, but Seven would want to know if her dad were involved too.

Barbatos smiled cruelly. "It was quite easy to fool the townspeople. All we had to do was keep them busy fighting one another so they wouldn't notice what we were up to," Barbatos bragged. "But your father was unfortunately not . . . receptive, so we moved on to better witches. The Dimblewits, well, manipulating them to do our bidding was a piece of cake. They are so hungry for power, even proximity to the Uncle was enough. We had a common enemy after all: you. Then all we had to do was stage a disappearance to keep the Gran from becoming even more suspicious of me and give me more time with our Nightbeast. And of course, that little fight you saw at the gazebo was also staged. Aided by a hex on Mr. Dimblewit, of course."

Aamon began to speak. "The Dimblewits simply wanted to keep their cheap labor. They had no idea of our true intentions. To take over not just Ravenskill but the Twelve Towns. To be the lords of all you witches, and to banish every Spare to the Tombs. Or to death. And now our plan has unfolded perfectly."

At every single step, they had been fooled. Seven wanted to scream, she was so mad at herself. The Cursed Toads—Spares whom she'd sympathized with, had tried to learn about, who she thought shared a common fate—had tricked and bested them. How could the Witchlings stop not only the Nightbeast but these powerful witches who manipulated even the Gran? It felt hopeless. Absolutely hopeless.

"There is just one final thing to attend to," Gamigin said. "Keeping our Nightbeast well fed is quite difficult. The meat of other monstruos will only go so far, but every so often, we are willing to accept a sacrifice. Namely, the three of you."

"Witchlings make for a succulent snack." Barbatos turned to the Nightbeast and smiled. "Eat them." He pointed at the Witchlings, and the Nightbeast, which was directly above Thorn now, tensed its hind legs as if it were about to pounce.

"GO!" Valley said, and the Witchlings sprung into fight mode.

Right in that moment, Thorn turned over quicker than a chipmunk and shot her hands straight up at the Nightbeast.

"Incendio!"

A stream of fire shot from Thorn's hands and got the monstruo directly on the snout. It recoiled, howling in pain, its enormous paws landing indiscriminately. The Cursed Toads scampered back in shock. Thorn got up and ran toward Seven and Valley.

"Thorn!" Seven threw her arms around her.

"No time for hugging—we gotta fight these absolute geese!" said Valley, her hands up in fighting stance. "But I'm glad you're okay, Thorn."

Thorn smiled. "I played dead."

Seven, Valley, and Thorn nodded at one another. It was Witchling time.

The Nightbeast had recovered from Thorn's exceptional attack and ran toward them, a patch of burnt fur on its face and its red eyes aflame with rage. Seven ran to the left. She pulled poison dart after dart and blew it in the Nightbeast's direction. At least three landed on the creature, but it did not have any effect. At least not for now. Thorn ran and slid under the Nightbeast and slashed its neck to its belly with her spiked gloves, coming out on the other side and throwing a stream of incendio fire at its tail. The monstruo howled, and the

Cursed Toads still on the other side of the river clapped and laughed.

"Incredible!" they said.

"Outstanding!"

"They will do quite nicely for feeding our pet, yes, indeed."

The Nightbeast whipped its head in the Cursed Toads' direction and let out an angry breath. It was annoyed with them.

If they were impressed by Seven and Thorn, Valley's skill would truly astound them. She threw her hands up and hurled spell after spell at the Nightbeast. Fire, and magical daggers, and blows to the head and chest. The Nightbeast howled, and a pang of sorrow hit Seven. Unexpectedly, she felt guilt, and sadness for it. She shook her head angrily. This was probably yet another of its tricks. *Focus, Seven*, she chastised herself.

"Hit it with everything we've got!" Valley said.

Seven and Thorn did as she said, surrounding the Nightbeast as best they could and barraging it with combat spells as fast as they could go. But it simply was not working. The Nightbeast barely slowed down, snapping and swiping at the Witchlings, only the force of their magic keeping it far enough away not to get them. But they would tire soon; they could only keep up the fight, use magic, for so long. The Nightbeast seemed like it could fight all night long.

"This isn't working!" Seven said.

"What do we do?" asked Thorn between spells.

"Follow my lead!" Seven said. She began to run around the Nightbeast, throwing the viento wind spell at the monstruo and creating a small cyclone around it. Valley and Thorn joined, and soon, the Nightbeast was picked up by a Witchling-made tornado.

"Keep going! Throw it out into the forest!" Valley yelled.

The Witchlings yelled, "VIENTO!" in unison, stopping and picking their hands up and over the river, sending the Nightbeast hurtling into the mountains.

"AHHHH!" Barbatos screamed, waving his hands wildly. The Witchlings were all dragged toward the roaring river. But Valley and Seven were able to find purchase and avoid being thrown in. Thorn wasn't as lucky.

Seven ran to the edge of the river. "Thorn, grab on to my hand!" Seven screamed as Thorn scrambled for purchase on a slippery rock.

"I can't!" Thorn said. "My needle gloves!"

"I don't care. Just grab on," Seven said.

"They're poisoned!" Thorn said.

"You can't die, Thorn! I won't let you die!"

"AHH!" Thorn screamed as the river swelled and shot her downstream.

"THORN!" Seven ran along the side of the river, looking back quickly to see Valley holding off the Cursed Toads alone. Seven briefly debated what to do, but she knew Valley had a few minutes at least; Thorn had almost no time before she would be taken away forever.

Thorn was able to grab on to a root on the other side of the river, buying a few moments.

"Help me, Stars," Seven said as she attempted to jump across, using the way-too-slippery rocks to land on.

With one enormous push, she made it to the other side and ran to Thorn, who was quickly losing her grip on the root. Seven grabbed her friend by the cloak and pulled her onto the grass. Thorn spluttered, her whole body shaking from the ice-cold water. "Valley," she said. "Get to Valley."

Seven gathered all the strength she had left and jumped back across the river to Valley's side. Thorn followed after, gracefully floating across the water and landing gently on the ground. Seven had nearly forgotten the gold button on their cloaks that allowed them to float on the wind. Just then, the Nightbeast ripped through the forest and came straight at them.

The Witchlings were pinned: the Cursed Toads and the Nightbeast in front of them, the raging water behind them growing wilder as Barbatos waved his hands in the air and mumbled an incantation. If they fell in now, they'd be done for. They backed up, dangerously close to the river.

"It's no use!" said Barbatos. "Surrender to us and your death will be quick."

They launched spell after spell, trying desperately to

push the monstruo back, but it did not so much as flinch. The Nightbeast's fur was on fire, its sides dripping blood, but it came at them, ferocious and hungry. They were about to die. The Nightbeast lunged and Seven lost her footing at the edge of the river.

Seven felt cold envelop her. A cold so frigid her body instantly went numb. Confusion overtook her. Had the Nightbeast eaten her? Had one of the Cursed Toads cast a freezing spell? But then she coughed, water coming out of her mouth as her body rushed downstream. She had fallen in the river. She came to enough to look to her sides, where red fabric bobbed and thrashed—Valley and Thorn had fallen in too. The Nightbeast was running alongside the water, snapping and growling viciously, trying to grab them from the clutches of the freezing river and into its own. But not even the Nightbeast could save them from a drowning death now. Perhaps it was better this way, to die by water instead of being eaten or toadified. Maybe this was the most Seven could ask for.

No, a voice in her head said. She was Seven Nightshade Salazar, and the one thing she wouldn't do was give up. She knew what she had to do. She didn't want to die; she had so many dreams, so much she wanted to say to her friends, to her family. She wanted to talk to Poppy at least one last time . . . to write something that made someone happy. She wanted to become someone important, but if she couldn't do that, if there was no hope for Seven living the life she'd always hoped to live, she would make sure her two best friends in the world got that chance. She would give up her life for theirs.

With the final ounce of strength she had, her mind already muddled from the cold, her fingers numb, Seven pulled the ceramic bird from her cloak pocket, brought it to her mouth, and blew.

CHAPTER TWENTY-EIGHT
VALLEY, SEVEN, THORN

BIRDS, HUNDREDS OF BIRDS, erupted from the trees the moment the note on Seven's ceramic bird resounded. It filled her with warmth and magic. Seven waited to pass out, to lose all her strength and just drown. But she didn't. She was still awake and alive. Maybe the bird hadn't worked.

"Your button!" yelled Thorn. "Press the second button on your cloaks!" Thorn was flailing beside Seven in the water, but where was Valley? Seven swallowed her panic and did as Thorn said. She tried to press the button on her cloak and floated up, just a bit. The water pulled her back down as she pressed again.

All at once, Valley bobbed up and floated just above the water. Then all three Witchlings hovered up and landed with hard thumps against the ground on the other side of the river. They had floated far enough away from the Nightbeast and the Cursed Toads that they had a moment to hide and regroup. They were shaking, their teeth chattering as they found a dark part of the forest behind a large tree and a row of rosebushes and hunkered down. They used the drying spell exprimir to dry themselves off, but it did little to stop the cold.

"Do you think they think we're dead?" Thorn asked.

"Maybe, but we can't just hide. Either way, when the sun rises, we'll be toads if we don't fight back," Seven said.

"What was that thing you did?" Valley asked.

"A signal, to call for help. I don't know if it will work, but the magic was enough to warm me up so I was able to think straight. That water was froggin' cold," Seven said.

"You're telling me. I think my butt has icicles," Valley said.

"We have to get back out there. We don't have much time left," Thorn said.

The Witchlings got up, but before they stepped out into the woods, they hugged one another.

"No matter what happens," Seven said, "I am proud of us and happy we got to be best friends."

"Me too," cried Thorn.

"Same here," Valley said. When they pulled away, they all smiled.

Seven furrowed her brow. "Now let's kick some monstruo butt!"

They ran along the forest, quiet as they could, and when they saw the Nightbeast again, they attacked, catching it by surprise. But then a sound like a large flock of birds came from above them, and Seven nearly collapsed. Fox and Talis were there, each of them on a broom. Even Beefy was there, in a baby sling on Talis's chest.

"MOM! DAD!" Seven cried, and the Nightbeast looked up.

"NO!" she heard a voice say. A low voice that echoed through the valley, a voice like she had never heard before. Seven's eyes opened wide.

The Nightbeast lowered its head and looked at her, its eyes narrowed. Seven was frozen in place. This couldn't be . . . She couldn't be . . .

"You are," the voice said. "I should not eat one with powers like yours. I did not want to hurt the others, but it was out of my control and now . . . I am so hungry!"

The Nightbeast launched itself at Seven, and she could not move. She had heard it speak.

"SEVEN!" a million voices erupted from the woods, the sky, and the water. The world around her spun. Had the others heard the monstruo too? Just as the Nightbeast was about to open its mouth and chomp down, Seven took a chance.

"If you eat me, they will just kill you. Let me help you!"

The Nightbeast stopped in its tracks. The large wolf monster cocked its head.

"How?" it asked in its rumbling echo of a voice.

"We can get you food, not witches, but delicious food all the same, and you won't need to hurt us."

"That is what those witches promised, but they lied. They kept me hungry; they hurt my cucos so they could not help me," snarled the Nightbeast.

"I won't do that. I'm not a butt-toad. If I break my promise—"

"You'll let me eat the fat baby." The Nightbeast . . . it almost smiled as it said this.

In the distance, Seven could hear spells being hurled. She chanced a glance and saw her family and coven engaged in battle with the Cursed Toads.

"ALTO!" Barbatos intoned, shooting at Fox, and in his hand he had the Gran's wand. How had he managed that?

Her mother countered with "Paliza!" and Barbatos began thrashing around as if someone was punching him from all sides. The other two Cursed Toads joined in, and Seven noticed something.

"Not Beefy," said Seven, turning back to the Nightbeast, "but you have my word that you can have me if I don't keep my promise."

The Nightbeast seemed to consider this. Seven noticed faint purple scales sprouting on the Nightbeast's body. That and the fact that she was having a calm conversation with the Nightbeast when moments before it was trying to eat her told her that maybe the Cursed Toads hadn't just hexed Mr. Dimblewit to do their bidding; maybe forbidden magic was how they were controlling the Nightbeast too. Speaking to it was how they gave it instructions, but that did not mean the Nightbeast had to listen.

"You see my family over there? They are fighting the witches that did this to you. That made you do things you didn't want to do."

The Nightbeast looked across the river at the battle unfolding and snarled.

"Let me help you. I can undo the hex they put on you if you want me to."

The Nightbeast looked at Seven intensely, like it was trying to figure out if she was lying, and then it nodded.

"If you are lying, I will eat you," it said.

"Fair enough." Seven cringed, then raised her hands. "Deshacer!" she intoned, and a bright light enveloped the Nightbeast. It roared so loudly, the entire valley shook around them. The Nightbeast collapsed, and Seven ran over to her coven.

The Uncles were being held off by her parents, but they weren't losing steam and they were still holding those red necklaces around their throats. Seven had a plan.

"Goats," she said to Valley and Thorn as they backed up her parents and, surprisingly, Beefy, who was adding strength to each spell with his little fists.

"Is there a spell for breaking a magical item, like those necklaces the Cursed Toads keep holding?" she asked.

"I think estallar would work," Valley said. "But I'm not super sure."

"It's worth a shot, if you think it will help," Thorn said.

"We need them to fall over, trip, or something so they let go of the necklaces. Then we break them," Seven said.

"Got it," Valley said.

"Viento," Thorn said, and together she and Valley churned the wind around them and sent it in the direction of the Cursed Toads. The three of them landed on their butts.

"NOW!" screamed Seven, and the three Witchlings pointed at the Cursed Toads' necklaces.

"Estallar!" Their magic flowed directly at their marks.

"NO!" screamed Barbatos, but it was too late.

Their necklaces shattered, sending shards of red flying in all directions. A flash of bright light made everyone shield their eyes momentarily, and when Seven could see again, the Gran was standing there in her cloak made of stars.

"I believe that belongs to me." She threw her hands out, and her wand came flying from Barbatos's hand into hers.

"You cannot stop us!" screamed Barbatos as the Gran held her wand up in their direction. "We aren't the only ones who want to end the Spares."

"Sweetheart, you are the Spares. No amount of convincing will change that truth."

"Even so, we bested you! We kept you imprisoned and hexed." Barbatos coughed. With their necklaces gone, something had changed. The Cursed Toads seemed weaker, like they were fading.

"Spares or not, you were capable. You always had been. The only thing that stopped you was your own greed. You were not wrong to be angry about your fate. You went wrong when you let your anger corrupt your heart. You will do no more mischief though. Now you will meet the destiny that had always been yours."

The Gran made a circle with her wand, and green light shone around her, but just then, Barbatos threw one hand up and in the direction of the Nightbeast, the other clutching the remnants of his necklace.

"MATANZA!"

The Nightbeast roared, struggling to its feet before charging at the Witchlings and Seven's family.

"No, not again!" Thorn said, and she threw her hands up on both sides. The climbing roses unraveled from the trees like snakes and slithered quicker than a lightning strike toward the Nightbeast.

"Don't kill him!" Seven screamed, but she feared it was too late.

Thorn's eyes were alight with fury.

"Viento!" she said, moving her hands across the air like she was weaving an intricate design and manipulating the wind so it interlaced and made . . . a cage of thorns.

The Nightbeast howled helplessly, but it was imprisoned, surrounded by a sphere of spiky vines that Thorn had weaved together.

Thorn collapsed to the ground, tears falling down her face as Valley and Seven held on tight to her, crying as well.

They had defeated the Nightbeast.

The Gran finished what she had begun, intoning, "Sapo!" and issuing one final devastating blow to the three imposter Uncles. Suddenly they became the squat green toads they were always meant to be. The moment they transformed, the Nightbeast lay down in the cage Thorn had made, looking at Seven.

Seven nodded. "I won't break my promise."

The Nightbeast had spoken to her, and her heart swelled with a million conflicting emotions at once. Now she understood why the Uncle had been so insistent on killing Beefy. He had touched Barbatos's hat, but so had she. They thought they were tracing Beefy's magic; they never imagined it could be Seven's because she was a Spare. From her pocket, something wriggled out and hung over the edge, turning up to look at her.

"I knew you could do it. You might be a terrible racer, but you are a masterful fighter," said Edgar Allan Toad.

CHAPTER TWENTY-NINE
THE LONG AND TWISTY PATH

THE WITCHLINGS, Seven's family, and the Town Gran rode back to town on brooms. Seven had never thought she'd get to see Ravenskill from way up in the air. It looked even more beautiful than her dreams. The twinkling lights glittered against the fresh white snow, and Seven took in a deep breath of the crisp, cold night, trying to absorb every feeling, every smell.

On their way home, the Gran explained that the legion of ghosts their parents had sent to break her out of the Tombs had succeeded, but the Cursed Toads' necklaces were creating a sort of force field against the Gran. They had been the key to most of their plans, Seven learned. The power they absorbed from the Uncles was stored in them, and with it they were able to control the Nightbeast. She had been hovering above their fight, trying to help, and when the necklaces had shattered, she had swooped in.

"They knew they would've been no match for Knox Kosmos," the Gran said, throwing her head back and cackling in the light of the moon.

Seven could not remember falling asleep that night or changing out of her cloak and fighting gear, but somehow, she awoke the next day to sunlight streaming into her room.

"Seven," her mom whispered as she wiggled one of her toes to wake her up. "There's someone here to see you."

Seven rubbed her eyes, put on her house slippers, and ran downstairs. She was sure it was Valley and Thorn, and they had so much to talk about. They had done it! They were going to be a real coven! They were going to be legends! But when Seven opened the door, it wasn't Valley or Thorn. It was Poppy.

"Oh," Seven said, suddenly embarrassed to be in her pajamas while Poppy was in her beautiful House Hyacinth colors.

"Hey, Seven, I wanted to make sure you were okay after last night," Poppy said. She looked shy, embarrassed even.

Seven crossed her arms in front of her chest and leaned against the door, Valley-style. "Oh yeah? I didn't know you still cared what happened to me."

"Seven, I'm sorry. I was a butt-toad, I know. But I was just figuring out how to still be friends with you when I felt like maybe you hated me for getting the thing you wanted."

"What?" Seven's mouth fell open. "Was I jealous? Sure, but I never hated you, Poppy. I never ever blamed you either. I was happy for you. No matter what, I thought we'd always be friends."

Poppy's face turned red. "Really?"

"Yep. And I'm okay now. Believe it or not, I'm glad to be a Spare."

Poppy raised an eyebrow. "Even with Valley?"

Seven took a deep breath. "You know, we were wrong about her. One day I'll tell you everything, but . . . let's just say I'm a big believer in second chances now."

Poppy beamed, and Seven hoped her old friend knew she didn't just mean a second chance for Valley. Seven hoped Poppy knew that she would always have a very special place in her heart.

"I'm glad to hear that. I want you to be happy," Poppy said. "I have to get back to my coven house, but I'll see you around?"

"Yeah, Poppy." Seven smiled. "See you around."

That night, the Witchlings celebrated their victory, and their name prophecies: Valley, for the place they found the Nightbeast; Thorn, for the way they trapped the monstruo; and Seven, for the number of witches who defeated it. As Seven had pineapple-jam cake with Valley and Thorn, the setting sun turned the sky the color of poppy flowers. Seven smiled, thinking of her old friend, of how much losing her had hurt, and how that hurt had turned into something new. She looked at Valley and Thorn at her sides and knew she'd never be alone; even if one day they lost one another, the friends you make always stick around somehow. She looked up at the fluffy clouds lit up pink against the orange sunset— even if it's in the colors of the sky.

CHAPTER THIRTY
THE FESTIVAL OF
THE HOLLY KING

"DAD, do you need to take two hundred pictures?"

"It's not every day your town throws a parade for your only daughter and her two best friends." Talis smiled and snapped another picture of Seven, Valley, and Thorn as they got off their parade float, which had been shaped like an enormous Nightbeast. Seven tried to scowl at her dad as he kept taking pictures, but she started laughing instead. Thorn posed dramatically as she walked, and Valley covered her face, nearly tripping on a tree root. Together they walked into a tent to await the Gran.

It seemed all of Ravenskill was decorated in twinkling lights and gold tinsel for the Festival of the Holly King: a yearly event on the longest night of the year that celebrated the return of the sun and the changes in nature to come with it. That night, they would exchange gifts in honor of the winter solstice, and the next morning, they would ice-skate on the Boggy Crone River, dress their toads in warm fuzzy sweaters, have chocolate ponche, and tell old stories around fires. It was Seven's favorite holiday, and she couldn't believe that the Gran had asked them to be the honored witches during the traditional yearly parade. There had been confetti and balloons and a band and everything! Almost their whole town, and even witches from other towns, had come to see the famous, stupendous Spares. Not everyone was present at the celebration. Some members of the Hill were noticeably absent, including Valley's father and the Dimblewits. But that was just as well.

Fox picked confetti out of Seven's curls and flitted around the tent behind the stage they had erected for the Gran's speech.

"Do you think it's starting soon? Why am I so nervous?" Fox asked.

"It is normal." Thimble smiled, squeezing Fox's shoulder.

The Gran had a big announcement to make, and if Seven were being honest, she was pretty nervous too.

They had learned a lot in the past few weeks. The Dimblewits had in fact been working with the Cursed Toads, but not exactly how the Witchlings had thought. They were very much trying to suppress a vote to give Spares more rights and believed that was the extent of the fake Uncles' agenda. They had known about the Nightbeast and helped the Uncle bring food to the cucos, but they didn't know that their final plan included taking over all the Twelve Towns. Once they had found out, they had been hexed with forbidden magic in order to go along with the Uncles' schemes when they did not want to.

"Preposterous!" Mr. Dimblewit had shouted when the Gran leveled the accusations against them just a few days after the final showdown with the Nightbeast.

Seven, Valley, and Thorn had made sure to make a bit of extra opal-haworthia potion in order to have a front-row seat to him being dragged off and interrogated. The Witchlings had giggled as they watched a crying Mrs. Dimblewit, her face the color of an eggplant, scream, "Don't you know who I am?!" at anyone who would listen.

Their crimes had been bad enough to send them both to the Tombs. They had been sentenced to years on the island for criminal witches. But despite all that, Valley had overheard her mother saying the Dimblewits had pulled some strings and used some of their considerable wealth to shorten their sentence. Typical. With the Dimblewits gone and Valley's dad halting his opposition to Amendment S, they would have a short rest from fighting for Spare equality. But Seven wasn't planning on giving up that battle.

They also learned that the Cursed Toads hadn't just hexed the Dimblewits. The Gran had discovered that she, along with the Stormville and Boggs Ferry Grans, had been hexed to do the Cursed Toads' bidding in dire circumstances. Like the Nightbeast attacks in Boggs Ferry, which they wanted to keep under wraps until the monstruo was stronger, so that the Gran would be no match for it. They'd tried to make the Ravenskill and Stormville Grans put a shush order on their respective towns too, like they had the Boggs Ferry Gran, but it hadn't worked, which explained why they were able to learn about the cuco attacks via telecast. They had been using those freaky necklaces they'd worn during the battle in the valley to not only absorb power from other witches but to influence the Grans through powerful and corrupted magic.

"Archaic relics," the Gran had explained, with the power to absorb magic from other witches and control them. It was why the Uncle could use the Gran's weapons, why the Gran was unable to join the fight against the Cursed Toads until their necklaces were broken. In a way, she was being held captive in plain sight. "I do not know who they got them from, or who taught them to use such treacherous items, but we will find out."

Seven shivered at the thought of another evil witch being out there somewhere, but she couldn't worry about that now. Right now, she had to worry about how all of Ravenskill would react to the Gran's news in just moments. It was enough to turn her insides into fairy floss.

"These capes must be worth at least ten million gold

coins. Maybe more," said Valley as she admired the Laroux' matching capes.

Their clothing line, Oh La La, Laroux, had become the most popular brand in all of Ravenskill, and they could not keep their signature stupendous Spare ensemble in stock. Beefy walked over to Seven and held his arms up. He was walking already, which was scary since he could now pick Seven up. He had also learned a new word: *cheese*. Seven patted her lap, and the big baby climbed up her legs and leaned his head on her chest. Seven rested her chin on her baby brother's head and smiled. Everything felt right and good, and she couldn't wait till that night. She and Thorn had finally finished the new Witches of Heartbreak Cove, and they were going to her house to eat pineapple-jam cake and talk about the book. It had come as a big twist that a dragon entered the cave just as the Wicked One awoke, and he had helped save the sisters. Even though Bianca forgave him, they went their separate ways and she chose to go back with her coven.

"Witchlings." Miss Dewey stuck her head in the tent and smiled. "It's time."

Seven, Valley, and Thorn walked out onto the stage, and they exchanged shocked looks as their whole town erupted in cheers, screaming their names. The Gran signaled to the Witchlings, and they walked over to her podium. The stage was decorated with colorful streamers and hundreds of twinkle lights, and it lit up the Gran's special winter solstice cape beautifully. She smiled at them and then raised her hands at the crowd. Their loud cheers simmered to excited whispers.

"Ravenskillians, it has been a trying time in our fair home. I commend you all for your patience, your resilience, and your commitment to your community."

Everyone clapped happily as the Gran continued.

"And nowhere have those traits been more apparent than in our three young witches, and newly minted Spare coven." Again the crowd cheered, and Seven, Valley, and Thorn smiled at one another.

They were, in fact, a full coven now. They had not killed the Nightbeast, but they had stopped it, which was enough to satisfy the impossible task. Their coven had been sealed shortly after the battle had ended. Seven's heart lurched thinking of the Nightbeast. It was living in a protected sector of woods that was sealed and enchanted by all the Twelve Towns' Grans to keep the creature safe and stop it from being used for nefarious reasons ever again. Together, the Gran and Seven had read the monstruos' memories and confirmed what Seven had suspected. The Nightbeast was being controlled, much like the Dimblewits had been, and the first attack on Thorn's brother, Petal, and indeed every attack after, had not been of its own free will. They knew the Cursed Toads' magic was involved in controlling it after Petal's death, but that first attack had been someone else's magic entirely.

Much like the mystery of the archaic relics though, they had not been able to identify whose. Seven hadn't been able to find where the Nightbeast was being kept, but when she did, she vowed to herself she would go visit it. She would keep her promise to keep it safe.

"Today, on the Festival of the Holly King, I present to the three witches here before us a token of the town's gratitude." The Gran signaled to Valley, Seven, and Thorn to step forward.

"To Valley Pepperhorn, I present twin crystal blades! Forged from the tears of a star and made once every five hundred years, in honor of her exceptional fighting and monstruo-tracking skills." The Gran passed a box lined in black velvet material with two shimmering blades to Valley.

"Holy goats," Valley said, mouth agape as she stared at the blades.

"To Thorn Laroux, I present the needle of never-ending mending! For overcoming your fears, and incredible bravery, in the face of terrible loss." The Gran passed a bright blue box with golden needles inside.

"These sew anything. Even appendages," said Thorn in awe.

"I really hope we don't need them," Seven said, loosening her collar. She was next, and she was going to barf. If a dragon could come pick her up right now, that would be great. Perfect timing.

"Finally, to Seven Nightshade Salazar, I present your very own pendant of the woods!"

The crowd gasped, many of them looking confused and shocked. Seven could see her parents smiling and crying happy tears from the side of the stage. Thorn's parents and Valley's mom were standing by their sides and smiling big.

The Gran conjured a pendant of a toad with a mustache, and it attached itself to Seven's cloak. Of course her pendant would be Edgar.

"It's because I was the first animal to speak to you," Edgar Allan Toad said, hanging from her pocket.

"Technically it was the Nightbeast," Seven said.

"It is a monstruo, *I* am an animal," said Edgar smugly.

"I know, I know, be quiet, the entire town is watching," she whispered.

"All they hear are croaks, my dear Witchling!"

"This pendant honors not only Seven's incredible bravery and selflessness, but also symbolizes something that has not been seen in the history of the Twelve Towns. Seven Salazar, a Spare, is our next Town Uncle!"

If Seven thought the crowd was loud before, now it was as if an earthquake shook their entire town. Seven had thought it impossible to believe that she could ever be the second-most-powerful witch in her town, since a Spare had never ever been an Uncle before. But now Seven knew that impossible things were not always what they seemed.

That friendship, and love, and trust made anything possible.

"I might use that as the last line of my piece," she said as she smiled at the crowd.

"Huh?" Valley asked.

"I'm gonna write a piece about the impossible task for the *Squawking Crow*. Or try to anyway," Seven said. "And I think I just figured out the last line."

"You're gonna be famous," said Thorn.

"Uh, I think she already is. Look at all the people who came to see us," Valley said.

"We kind of changed history, you know," Seven said. "We're a big froggin' deal."

"*That* should be the last line of your piece," Valley said.

The Witchlings laughed, and Seven looked at Valley and Thorn and felt so much warmth and happiness, she wanted to shout. They had done it. They had beat every odd, they had stuck by one another, and most important of all, they had become friends. Real friends. She never thought in a billion years that she would call Valley Pepperhorn a friend, or that she would meet someone like Thorn and feel so very close to her. Just then, Seven knew how she would end the piece about the impossible task.

Any witch can be a friend, if you just give them a chance.

EPILOGUE

SPRING WAS IN FULL BLOOM IN RAVENSKILL, and Seven was on her way to Valley's new home with a plant and Edgar Allan Toad in her black wagon. Dogwood trees with bright pink flowers and rosebushes of every color lined the brick road that led to Division Street. Maybe it was her new, more powerful magic talking, but Seven had never remembered a more beautiful spring in Ravenskill.

"Oh, can't you make them do something about that smoke! Who uses their chimney in spring, honestly?" a squirrel complained to Seven.

"Sorry, I can't intervene just yet." Seven smiled.

The squirrel scowled at her, and Seven cringed.

Although Seven *was* technically the Town Uncle, she needed a lot of training before she could assume her duties and be the intermediary for animal affairs and complaints.

That didn't stop the animals from complaining to her though. Other Twelve Towns Uncles had been doing rotations since the Cursed Toads were discovered, but it was a lot of work.

"A small glimpse into your future." The Gran had winked at Seven when she explained all the duties of the Uncle.

Well, that may very well be, but Seven wasn't ready to give up on her oldest, dearest dream just yet. In fact, she was on her way to Valley's for just that reason. She reached the brick building that housed an art gallery below and an apartment above, and Valley stuck her head out the window of her apartment.

"Heya, weirdo! Leave your wagon downstairs and send that stuff up in this!" Valley threw a bucket from her window, which very nearly hit Seven and broke the glass of the art gallery in one fell swoop.

"Don't you dare," said Edgar, but Seven put his little mushroom tank in the bucket anyway. She wanted to hand the plant, a housewarming gift, to Valley and Mrs. Pepperhorn . . . the soon to be ex–Mrs. Pepperhorn, that is, personally.

Valley pulled a complaining Edgar up gently, and Seven bolted up the stairs to Valley's place. The front door opened, and a woman, pale and thin, gave Seven a small smile. Mrs. Pepperhorn.

"Hi, Mrs. . . . uh," Seven said shyly.

"You can call me Quill. Come in," Valley's mom said.

Seven handed her the plant, a fully grown opal-haworthia, which she was now an expert in growing.

"Oh . . . thank you! These are impossible to come by."

"You're welcome, and yeah, I grew that thing myself. Was a real pain in the buns to learn how."

They walked into the apartment in awkward silence. Quill put the plant down and wrung her hands nervously. She kept opening and closing her mouth as if she was going to say something but then fell silent. Seven smiled and looked around. She walked around with her hands behind her back like she was inspecting the place.

"Your house is real nice," she said.

Mrs. Pepperhorn laughed. "I like it a lot better than Blood Rose Manor."

Seven looked at a glass display case that held several awards the town and various witch organizations had awarded to Valley for her monster-hunting prowess. At the very bottom of the case were a whole slew of awards bunched together and pushed to the back. Seven squinted. And then her mouth fell open. She stood up and spun around.

"V. V. Avenmora. Why are her awards here?" she asked.

"Because V. V. Avenmora is my mom, you butt-toad." Valley walked into the living room with Edgar, a smug smile on her face. "I was feeding Edgar some flies."

"Valley, please be kind to your friends," Quill—no,

V. V. AVENMORA, the author of Witches of Heartbreak Cove—said.

"Not to completely go bananas here, but OH MY GOSH!" Seven screamed. "I am your biggest fan. Your books are incredible. Valley, how come you never told me? I am calling Thorn right now!"

"How did you think I had the advance copy of her book so early? There are no other advance copies in the Twelve Towns except ours."

"Why did you use a pen name? I mean, Quill is a perfect writer name," Seven said, still in awe.

Quill gave a small laugh. "I thought V. V. Avenmora had a nice ring to it. Avenmora is my first name, and the V. V. is for Valley—Valley Valerian."

"Quill is her middle name, and she goes by that instead because witches get all weird and starstruck if they figure out who she is," Valley said.

"Valley, that is not true." Quill shook her head.

Seven shot Valley an indignant look. "I can't believe you've held out on us this long."

Valley smirked. "I really thought you knew."

Seven shook her head, and then, remembering why she had come to visit Valley, her face fell. Oh no. Her hand flew inadvertently to her mouth. She had sent her article, the one about the impossible task, to Valley, and Valley had insisted her mom could help make it better. V. V. Avenmora had read *her* writing. If a witch-eating plant would just suddenly materialize and make Seven its lunch, she would've been very much appreciative.

"I'll make some tea," Valley said, disappearing into the kitchen.

"Come, Seven. Sit." Quill patted the old floral sofa as she sat down herself.

All their new furniture was nothing like the stuff in Blood Rose Manor. That place had felt like a museum except for Valley's room. But this new apartment felt homey and welcoming. Sure, a lot of the stuff looked older, but so was pretty much everything in Seven's house. This place felt nicer, even if Seven was on the verge of passing out from embarrassment. She sat down and chuckled awkwardly.

"So, how bad was my piece?"

Quill opened her eyes wide. "It wasn't bad at all! I made a few edits, but I think it was solid. A great first effort for a future reporter. I have it here and we can go over it, but"— Quill looked toward the kitchen, where Valley was loudly, and quite badly, singing a Kill Le Goose song as she made tea—"before Valley comes back, I wanted to talk to you about something first."

Seven shifted in her seat. She always feared that one day she'd get in trouble for ratting out Mr. Pepperhorn, and now it was actually happening.

Quill took a deep breath. "I wanted to thank you."

". . . You what?"

"You had the courage to do something really hard. Something I wish I had had the courage to do myself, but . . . I was too afraid."

"It's not your fault. My mom explained all about how people who get abused feel they can't get help."

Quill nodded. "You're right, but I want you to know I'm glad you told someone when you saw something happening. It gave me the strength to leave and to start a better life for me and Valley. You're a good friend, Seven. A real Seraphina."

Seven's mouth flew open at the mention of her favorite Witches of Heartbreak Cove character.

"You really mean that?" she asked.

Quill laughed. "Doing the right thing in the face of danger and fear? I would say so, yes. Now, let's go over this article. You need to make sure it's in the best shape possible before sending it to Tiordan. They are tough."

Seven nearly passed out again. "One hero at a time. I can't think about Tiordan right now or I'll faint!"

Quill laughed as Valley brought their tea into the room, and together, the three of them went over the story of the impossible task from Seven's perspective, the sun setting a brilliant red behind Oso Mountain.

ACKNOWLEDGMENTS

I want to start with a big thank-you to all the readers who continue to support me, especially through my debut with *Ghost Squad*. *Witchlings* wouldn't be here without you, so thank you from the bottom of my heart. If you are a kid reading this and you've made it this far, please know that Edgar Allan Toad loves *you* specifically. He told me so.

To my incredible editor, Emily Seife, who pushed me to become a better writer with each draft and is the fastest reader I know (seriously, how?): a giant thanks for believing in me and my story so much. Your excitement for this book kept me excited, and during the year we've just had, I really needed it. I am so grateful I get to work with you!

To the rest of my Scholastic team, including Taylan Salvati, Lizette Serrano, Emily Heddleson, Rachel Feld, Janell Harris, Chris Stengel, Becky Benett, and everyone who supported me and *Witchlings*, thank you so, so much for believing in this story. It's an honor to be part of the Scholastic family.

To my team at New Leaf, especially Suzie Townsend, my amazing agent, and her incredible assistants Dani Segelbaum and Miranda Stinson, as well as Kate Sullivan, and Pouya Shahbazian—I would not survive without you all. Thank you for the countless hours of hard work you do for me and my books. I love you all. 🖤

A big thank-you to the *Witchlings* cover artist, Lissy Marlin, for illustrating what's one of the most beautiful middle grade book covers I've ever seen!

To my family, and all my friends who constantly share my posts, buy my books, and check in on me to see if I'm still alive during deadlines, thank you for your constant love and encouragement.

And to the members of the book community, bloggers, booksellers, readers, reviewers, librarians, teachers, and online pals who have supported me and my writing (especially the ones who have been here since day one!), thank you for being there, for believing in me, and for putting up with my bad jokes online. I am grateful that you have not blocked me yet.

ABOUT THE AUTHOR

Claribel A. Ortega, author of *Ghost Squad*, is a former reporter who writes middle grade and young adult fantasy inspired by her Dominican heritage. When she's not busy turning her obsession with eighties pop culture, magic, and video games into books, she's cohosting her podcasts *Write or Die* and *Bad Author Book Club* and helping authors navigate publishing with her consulting business, GIFGRRL. Claribel has been featured on BuzzFeed, NPR, *Good Morning America*, and *Deadline*.

You can find her on Twitter, Instagram, and TikTok at @Claribel_Ortega and on her website at claribelortega.com.